TRUTH OR DARE

SHADOWS OF LONDON #4

ARIANA NASH

Truth or Dare, Shadows of London #4

Ariana Nash ~ *Dark Fantasy Author*

Subscribe to Ariana's mailing list & get the exclusive story 'Sealed with a Kiss' free.

Join the Ariana Nash Facebook group for all the news, as it happens.

Copyright © 2022 Ariana Nash.

Edited by No Stone Unturned Editing.

Proofread by Marked and Read.

Cover design by Natasha Snow.

Warning: The unauthorized reproduction or distribution of this copyrighted work is illegal. Criminal copyright infringement, including infringement without monetary gain, is investigated by the FBI and is punishable by up to five years in federal prison and a fine of $250,000.

Please note: Crazy Ace Publishing monitors popular international pirate sites for infringing material. If infringement is found (illegal downloading or uploading of works) legal action will be taken.

US Edition. All rights reserved.

No part of this book may be reproduced in any form or by any electronic or mechanical means, including information storage and retrieval systems, without written permission from the author, except for the use of brief quotations in a book review.

All characters and events in this publication, other than those clearly

The bell above Cecil Court's front door tinkled, signaling Dom's arrival. He stomped into the shop, trailing clumps of slushy snow.

"Boots!" Gina scolded from somewhere behind me in Cecil Court's new-look lounge.

He grumbled, turned, and spent the next five minutes picking off wet gloves and trying to pry off his boots without leaving more puddles on the old shop's freshly stripped and varnished floorboards. "Sorry I'm late. I don't know why the tube doesn't bloody run when it snows. It's not like it's snowing *underground*."

"You posh West Enders are shit in the snow," Cassie, the newest member of the team, said in her cockney twang. A moment later, a coin plunked into the swear jar.

Most of the time she pre-paid at the beginning of the day by slotting five pounds through the jar's lid and proceeded to bring a whole array of animated and colorful words into Cecil Court. The jar had been her idea.

"I resent being called a West Ender, thanks, *Pink*." Dom smiled and my heart flip-flopped in my chest. I'd tried to ignore the general furor and focus on the business accounts Gina had printed off for me, but as with anything John Domenici related, the moment he appeared, I could think of little else.

Dom shrugged off his coat and sauntered toward the Victorian fireplace we'd recently discovered while redecorating the shop into something more like a home—a home with a lot of shelves. And books. After warming his hands over the fire, he sensed my gaze and glanced up. His smile thawed, growing.

"Hey." He dropped into the sofa beside me, thigh touching mine. He smelled of the cold air and road salt. Color had nipped at his cheeks and his dark-lashed eyes shone. It had been almost a month since Wordsworth and Montgomery, since I'd died and Dom had dragged me back by sheer stubbornness, and whatever this was between us burned brighter and hotter than any fire.

"What yah doin'?" He peeked at the documents on the coffee table.

"Trying to concentrate."

"Oh." His hand slid up my thigh. "Really?" Fingers dug in, reminding me of exactly how he'd dug them in last night, and the night before that. He reclined, hand shifting to my back, and a little of his trick spilled in, tingling, familiar, and warm.

"How was our lovely IRL friend, Doris Worthington?" I asked. He'd been summoned there for the typical monthly competency tests.

"I passed, ruining her day."

I smirked at that. "Good for you."

"Fuck, yeah," Cassie blurted. A moment later: *clink*.

"Or you could just ease up on the swearing," Gina suggested.

"Not bloody likely."

I leaned back and spread my arm along the back of the sofa, behind Dom, at the same time as glancing at Gina. She had her head bent close to Cassie's as they went over some marketing initiative that Gina had thought up. A way to advertise our endeavor as latent-friendly, and less like the other agencies, which only wanted to throw latents in prison, or worse. Cassie had been with us a week and was still finding her place. My instinct said she was right for us, but a niggling tickle at the back of my mind warned me that there was more to her being here than wanting to help latents and get paid, while getting out of the East End.

"She'll be all right," Dom said softly. He liked her. Even if she did shock him as much as the rest of us.

"Yes, I think so."

The shining sparkle in his eyes lost some of its luster. "Listen... I need to tell you something."

"The reason you wanted to meet me here?"

He'd called on his way to the IRL processing center

and left a message to make sure I waited for him at the shop. He'd be back for ten a.m., and we needed to talk.

"Detective Diaz called for you, Dom," Gina said. "He sent an email? Said he was waiting on your go. I guess you know what he means?"

"Yeah, thanks." Dom caught my eye, then shifted forward on the sofa and rubbed his hands together. He was on his feet next and drifting back toward the fire. Restless. Anxious. Why? "Okay, so... Cas, this probably won't mean much to you, but you're here so... you need to know."

His gaze clipped me, moving quickly on. "A few weeks back... I dropped by Kage's place." He stared at Gina, skipping me altogether.

Ah.

A few weeks ago. When he hadn't called me, when he'd vanished... He'd gone to see Kage. "And what did the American have to say?"

"Wait, who's Kage?" Cassie asked.

"The guy who shot the girl to save you and Dom," Gina offered, as a quick explanation.

"Oh, *him*," she purred. "The badass supermodel American, that one."

Dom found the ceiling fascinating, Gina gulped, and I discovered I'd quite like a whiskey.

There was a lot more to it than Kage having saved Dom when I couldn't. Such as how he'd drugged Dom, stalked him, reported on him to his superiors, and how he'd cuffed him, hellbent on kidnapping him for the Latent Observation Agency, the American version of our IRL, but with guns, and teeth. He had also slept with Dom, and for a while, they'd been... close. So close, I'd saved Kage's life for Dom, a decision that continued to circle back around and bite me on the arse.

I got to my feet.

"Wait—where are you going?" Dom asked.

"Getting a drink." I climbed the stairs, all the way to the top, anger building with every step. It wasn't a lot to ask that Kage Mitchell not feature in our lives, was it? I disliked the man, mostly because he was in love with Dom, but also because he shot latents for a living. I should have shoved him out of a window long ago.

I retrieved a bottle of whiskey and three glasses—all I could fit in my fingers—and carried them back downstairs to find the three of them seated on the sofas, heads bent together, muttering in hushed tones, no doubt bringing Cassie up to speed on Kage and Dom's history.

If I had nothing to worry about, why wouldn't Dom meet my gaze? What had happened in that week? He said he'd gone home to his mother's. Perhaps he had. For a day. Perhaps he spent the rest of the time with Kage?

I poured three drinks, grabbed a mug, and poured mine. Jealousy was an ugly emotion. Hideously unfair and irrational. I'd never thought of myself as the jealous type. Until now.

"Well? What did you talk about during the week you vanished and visited Kage?" The weather? How Kage wanted me dead? And how, now that Montgomery was out of the way, I was probably next on his hit list?

My tone was barbed and Dom narrowed his eyes, disliking it, and me. "He wasn't there. But this was." He tossed a slip of creased, stained paper onto the coffee table.

"Oh God. Is that blood?" Gina picked it up, turned ashen, and passed it to Cassie.

Maybe it was a suicide note? One could hope. *Good Lord, I'm a horrible person.*

"The apartment was trashed. He'd been taken—by force. I found bullet holes, and Detective Diaz found casings. There was enough there for the Met to open a MISPER file."

So dramatic, so American, so Kage.

"Jesus, Alex," Dom growled, reading my unguarded face. "I know you don't like him, but he could be dead."

"How terrible."

Now all three of them stared. I pinched my lips together. This was why I struggled to keep friends or maintain relationships.

Cassie handed me the note.

Don't come for me.

Don't do the right thing.

It's what I deserve.

~ K

Telling them the note was meant for Dom to go chasing after Kage, because that was exactly what Kage Mitchell, an FBI-trained psychoanalyst, would do, would not endear me to any of them. So I kept my thoughts to myself and dropped the note. "The Met will find him."

"But they haven't. It's been weeks. Diaz's email... He says there's chatter among the LOA that one of their agents has been kidnapped on UK soil." Dom hesitated.

"They're looking at you, Kempthorne, because Kage had orders to procure you. You were his last target."

"*Procure* me?" And I was the one in the wrong? "Excuse me." I couldn't participate in this conversation without digging myself a hole to climb into. I took my mug of whiskey back upstairs.

"Alex?" Dom called up.

"Carry on... I have nothing to add."

He jogged up the stairs, and by the time I'd made it to my loft, he breezed in a step behind me and slammed the door. "Don't be a dick about this."

He didn't see my flinch because I kept it inside and hid it by sipping whiskey. "What do you want me to say?" I thunked the mug down, spilling whiskey on the table, and sneered at it instead of Dom. "The man works for the LOA. We aren't the only people he's crossed. He likely has many enemies. He made his thoughts regarding you and I very clear. This is not our problem." I turned and found Dom standing very still, his jaw locked and his hand clenched at his side. Did he care that much for Kage? "The Met will deal with this."

"You just don't want to help."

"No, frankly, I don't."

His brow furrowed. "I don't know what I thought... Maybe that you'd help me? Something has happened to him. He was one of us."

"He *betrayed* us."

"He had to."

I didn't understand why we were arguing about Kage Mitchell. I had enough to battle with without pulling the American back in. Or maybe it was because Dom couldn't let him go? I leaned against the table and clamped my hands around its edges, holding myself rigid. Dom had that look on his face, the soft expression, the one I couldn't guard against or say no to. I'd do anything for him and the more I held his gaze, the more the hardness around my heart melted away. "What do you want?"

"Your help."

"Do you want me to find him?"

"Yes... You have connections. I just... Look." He gestured at the air, grasping for an explanation. "It's not what you think. Okay? I don't... There's nothing between us. I just can't let this go. It's not right."

"Can't let *him* go."

He stilled, frowned, then snorted a laugh and sauntered up to me. I didn't move but, slouched as I was, I had to lift my chin to meet his smoldering eyes. He knew he'd won. "I didn't think you'd be the jealous type," he purred.

"Neither did I." I didn't want to be *that* kind of man. Hadn't expected to feel helpless in all of this. If he knew how much I cared for him, wanted him to be mine, nobody else's, he wouldn't tease. This—him—us—it was all new. Like walking on thin ice. One crack, one wrong step, and I'd shatter everything.

Dom's firm, warm hands eased around my waist. "Would you just trust me?"

I straightened, parting my knees, slotting him between my thighs, where I'd discovered he felt so right.

I did trust him, more than anyone. So much it was terrifying. Because he had no idea how he held my heart in his rough hands, where it could so easily be crushed. His mouth teased mine, breaths mingling. "I barely know who I am around you," I told him, and meant it. This was all new. My whole world had crumbled around us. *I* was new.

"Is that a yes?" He nuzzled my neck, breaths fluttering warm against my skin, each one a tease that soared through me, gradually breaking me down and filling me. Well, parts of me. How could I say no?

"I'll pull some strings."

2

D^{om}

I knew I was asking a lot and it didn't take much to figure out why Kempthorne had run to his attic. I should have told him I'd gone looking for Kage, but there never seemed to be the right time, until Diaz had emailed, wanting to know how far we could go. The Met could only do so much, and with no leads, just some mirky CCTV footage of three apparently drunk guys who may or may not have had Kage propped up between them, we had to go further.

Kempthorne could do that.

"I suppose we should go down…" I started to ease back, out from between Kempthorne's legs. His thighs clamped closed, and now that he was sitting on the edge of the table, he was able to lock his ankles behind me. I was trapped. A new, boyish thrill shortened my breath. Raw need burned in his eyes, so bloody irresistible. "If we don't go down soon, they'll know what's going on."

"We're having a discussion."

His hands slid up my back, fingers spreading, then digging into my shoulder blades. I stifled a groan. "That's what this is?"

His mouth skimmed my cheek. He whispered, "I would like—" His hands dove downward and cupped my arse, grinding me close. "—to thoroughly discuss your *position*."

Before he'd bent me over his desk in the basement some weeks ago, I'd made the mistake of thinking him inexperienced. But there was another side to Kempthorne, multiple sides. This Kempthorne, the one who looked as though he wanted to devour all of me in one bite, was a very close second place on my list of Top Kempthorne Personalities. In first place was the morning-after Kempthorne, who fumbled his words and carried a sheet around his waist and invited me to a dinner we still hadn't had—Christ, that man killed me every time I woke up next to him, which had been most mornings. This man looked as though he wanted to kill me, preferably with me on my back and his cock buried—

His kiss severed all thought. His tongue plunged and roamed, and I gave back as good as I got, rocking with him, breathing him in, shuddering as his chest heaved against mine. He was stronger than he appeared—all corded muscle inside an athletic frame. Once he was fired up, like this, I couldn't think around him. He became everything. My world. To touch and taste and bite and make him moan.

My phone rang, vibrating in my back pocket. Probably nothing. Although it could have been Diaz. I turned my head, still tangled in the kiss. "I just—"

Kempthorne's quick hands plucked the phone from my pocket. He glanced at the screen and arched an eyebrow. Then showed me.

Sawyer.

What. The. Fuck.

I hadn't heard from that prick since he'd gotten me kicked out of the military and killed my career. I grabbed the phone and hit end, silencing it.

"That's a blast from the past," he said.

No, wasn't thinking about Sawyer. I dropped the phone onto the table, bracketed Kempthorne's mildly shocked face, and kissed him hard, pushing out all thoughts of Sawyer. He turned to molten flame in my grip, rocking and writhing, hips rolling, rubbing the both of us, igniting delicious friction. Christ, yes. I didn't care it was the middle of the morning, didn't care Gina and Cas were downstairs. "Want you," I mumbled around the kiss, trying to unbutton his shirt and get to his chest. He made some kind of grumbling, moaning sound that was definitely a good noise. The heat between us was crazy—maddening, rough, and desperate. We'd fallen into a routine of fucking each other mindless first, and then later, after the initial rabid lust was sated, we fell into his bed, tangled between kisses and lazy stroking and moments of pure fucking bliss when we didn't speak, just lay together, fingers and limbs entwined. I mean, Jesus... I didn't do this. One-night stands, a quick blow job behind a Soho bar. Sawyer had been... different. Kage was... Kage. Nothing was like Kempthorne. Like he burned me up every time we touched.

The lust I could handle. Most days it was all I could think about. But the quiet, soft, hand holding, fluttering kisses, and gentle stroking... that filled my heart full of fear and doubt and stupid ideas about keeping him. About there being a Me and Him. An Alex and John.

But it was all good, because he still hadn't taken me to dinner, and if he didn't, then none of this meant anything. Or so I told myself at night, when I lay staring at the ceiling, my heart racing a hundred miles an hour while he snored softly against my arm.

My phone rang again—right as I was about to bruise my knees and bury my head between his legs.

"Bloody hell." Kempthorne grabbed it. "Answer it or turn it off."

I couldn't answer it while I had my hand around Kempthorne's dick, could I? I mean, this was Sawyer. The dickhead who had ruined my career because he was too afraid to be gay.

I lifted the phone to my ear in my right hand and kept my left encircled around Kempthorne's firm erection. "Hello?"

Kempthorne's eyes widened in the perfect look of sudden shock and devastating lust. His hips jerked a little, his cock sliding.

"John?" Sawyer barked in my ear.

"Hm?"

Kempthorne tilted his hips, just enough to urge me

on, and I couldn't think of anything I wanted to do more than make my man come while the twat on the other end of the line thought he was the special one. Kempthorne braced his arms either side of him. His shirt had bunched around his middle, and with his sleeves rolled up, his pupils blown, and mouth parted in silent moans, I figured I'd made the right call. Jesus, he was hot for this. Really hot for it. His scrunched abs shuddered with every stroke, the flat plane of his belly twitching, and his cock… I stroked it, sliding the soft head over my palm and between my fingers and thumb.

"John, are you there!?" Sawyer's deep, commanding voice had been one of the things I'd loved about him. Thought I'd loved…

"Fuck, yes. What?"

"I know we didn't part on the best of terms—"

"The best of terms? You prick. You screwed me every way you could."

Kempthorne's eyes rolled and I almost went down on him, but I'd have a hard time bitching to Sawyer with a mouthful, and Kempthorne was *really* enjoying my hand. Damn, he was slick. He shuddered and his moan had a direct link to my cock, making it ache for attention.

"I… Never mind, that's not why I'm calling."

"Hurry up," I snapped. Kempthorne's eyes shot open. "Not you. Him."

"What?" Sawyer demanded.

"Jesus, what do you want, Sawyer, I'm busy here."

Kempthorne's hips jerked. My own dick twitched with an echo of need. I almost dropped the phone but bared my teeth instead, and the next words I growled into the phone came out in a breathless rush. "You bastard... You lying, cocksucking bastard. You lied about me, about us. You're a fucking coward—" I pumped, almost moaned. Kempthorne's breathing tightened, coming faster. Christ, he was going to come. "Don't ever call me again."

"John, wait—"

No, hell no. I dropped the phone—wasn't even sure I'd turned it off—and Kempthorne came with a strangled bark. I slumped over him, coaxing the aftershocks out of him. We kissed, messily and hard.

"*Ughlord*," he garbled, panting.

"You liked that, huh?"

He grunted, then slurred, "You'd be surprised what I like."

Oh... hell, yes. My eyebrows lifted. "Do you think the boss will mind if we call in sick?"

He laughed, the sound rich and deep and sex-thick. "I need a shower."

I let him up and enjoyed the view of him clutching his trousers and stumbling his way toward the bathroom. Morning-after Kempthorne. So good.

He stopped and tossed me a serious expression, one made for boardrooms or fancy dinners with high-society friends. The polished effect was dampened a bit by the fact he looked as though I'd fucked him against a wall. "It's far more economical for two people to shower together."

Something warm and bright bloomed around my heart, something now a part of my veins, like the trick. But just between us.

3

A lexander

We emerged too late in the day to be productive. Dom spent much of the evening going through Detective Diaz's report on the general disarray found in Kage Mitchell's apartment and I made some calls, setting the gears in motion to discover anything in Kage's background that might point us in the direction of the trouble he was in now.

The next day, Dom and I visited Kage's apartment—already cleaned by the Met's professionals. The apartment itself was sparse, yielding no new evidence. Kage had lived neatly, never intending to stay. There was something in that, some comment about his commitment to Dom having always been shallow, but I kept it to myself.

Dom had fallen quiet during our visit. He'd seen the crime scene intact. I hadn't. He was concerned. Because he was a good person and cared for his friend. There was plenty I could say about that, too, but kept my lips sealed.

"We should go to dinner," I said. We'd left the Docklands twenty minutes ago but the traffic near Westminster had snarled to a stop and the early January nightfall had closed in. Now the minutes dragged, the Aston purred, and Dom stewed in more silence.

He didn't reply. He had rested his chin on a loose fist and stared out his passenger window. I only saw his face in profile, lit by the red taillights from the stationary cars around us. His hair had grown, and small hints of a curl began to show near the nape of his neck. I liked to tease that curl through my fingers when we lay together. I liked to do a lot of things.

"Huh?" He shifted, eyes refocusing. Gina had been the first to comment on Dom's beautiful eyes. When she'd thought him available. I found myself thinking about those words now—words like sultry, smoldering, his Italian blood—and quickly steered my thoughts back to my earlier comment.

"Dinner?" I said, with a smile. The traffic moved and I eased the Aston forward. "I did ask, but with everything... it's managed to slip down the list."

"Oh right, yeah. Dinner. Okay."

He didn't sound enthused by the idea. He was probably just distracted. My life wasn't the only one to have turned upside down in the past few weeks. We'd all been through a lot. The wounds were still raw.

"There's a lovely restaurant at the Shard—"

"Is that the one without any prices on the menu? Because the last time I tried to dress up and play at being one of your people an artifact nearly blew us all to pieces." He flashed his typical smile, and in the soft light from the Aston's dash, his eyes sparkled with humor.

I tried to laugh it off and faced ahead, pretending to focus on driving while untangling the feelings his words had sparked. My people? I didn't have a people. So, did he not want to go to dinner somewhere nice? "Not there then."

He shrugged. "Wherever. Doesn't matter."

If it didn't matter, then why bother at all? I tightened my grip on the steering wheel. I wanted to take him out, wanted to have him beside me, to enjoy something normal, something good, for the both of us. Perhaps he didn't want to be seen with the newly revealed latent Alexander Kempthorne, who wasn't anything like everyone believed him to be.

"It's weird that Kage goes missing now," he said. "Why now? What's changed?"

I sighed and shouldn't have, because what had been a curious expression on his face hardened into disdain. "I don't know." Perhaps I could still salvage something of this conversation? "The LOA grew tired of waiting for him to serve my head on a platter?"

"Never mind." He went back to looking out of the window.

We stewed in more silence all the way back to Cecil Court. Dom hopped out at the end of the pedestrian street and I parked the Aston, then walked through the bitter evening air back toward the shop.

Two men, both well-built, in dark jackets, and heavy boots, took an interest in my passing through Trafalgar Square and fell into my slipstream through the winter tourists some distance behind me. Since coming out as a latent, most people went out of their way to avoid me. My face was well-known, which made an easy target. I'd had more than a few insults thrown at me from passing cars. This was the first time I'd been followed.

I stopped outside 16a Cecil Court as though to admire the shop window. The interior was now hidden behind closed blinds. The two men veered into the street, neither talking. They weren't the typical chatty tourists who dawdled down Cecil Court as though they had all the time in the world. The men were professionals and had me in their sights.

I opened the door and stepped inside. The bell tinkled.

Warmth wrapped around me. The fire was already lit and doing a grand job of heating the open space. Gina had a radio on and hummed along to the music behind her desk. Dom wasn't in the lounge, but his coat hung on the hook. He was here somewhere.

Two sharp knocks rapped on the door.

Gina looked up and saw my face. "Want me to—"

I cut her off with a shake of my head, turned on my heel, and opened the door. "Gentlemen?"

The biggest of the pair, a man who was probably twice my weight, with the majority of that being muscle, held up an ID card in a wallet. RMP. Royal *Military* Police. "I'm Lance Corporal James Branson—"

"Yes, I can read."

He narrowed his eyes. "This is Lance Corporal Adams. Can we come in?"

Making their lives difficult would no doubt make mine difficult too. But I suspected they weren't here for me. "What's this about?"

"It won't take long," Adams said, playing the softer, more approachable one. "We'd just like to ask John Domenici a few questions. Is he here?"

"Yeah…?" Dom said, entering the room, ruining any chance I had of lying to keep him hidden. "What's up, fellas?" He joined me at the door, half-smiling, relaxed, although I knew him well enough to know his mind would be working multiple angles. He thrust out a hand and the three of them shook like old friends.

"We have a few questions, Mister Domenici, about some of your old squad mates."

"Come in," he said. When he should have slammed the door in their faces.

I tried to catch Dom's eye, but he'd turned away and hollered for Gina to put the kettle on. "Wanna cuppa tea?"

"Yeah, thanks," Adams said.

The corporals eyed me as they clomped inside. They'd probably read or heard about some of my recent revelations. At the very least, they'd researched my name.

"What's going on?" Dom asked, leading them to the sofas and the fireplace.

I shrugged off my coat and hung it on the hook, keeping our guests in the corner of my eye. I'd long suspected the military would one day realize they'd made a mistake in letting Dom go, and they'd want him back. These men being here could easily be a prelude to having him leave me.

"What's your relationship with Lieutenant Sean Sawyer?" Adams asked.

Dom snorted. "Do you want the nice version or the truth?"

"The truth."

"He's a dickhead."

"When did you last see Lieutenant Sawyer?" Branson asked.

I maneuvered my way around the back of the sofa the men had made themselves comfortable in and leaned an arm against the fireplace mantle. Nothing about this felt right. The military police didn't question civilians.

"Over two years ago," Dom said.

"You haven't heard from him recently?"

Dom's eyes narrowed, then his gaze flicked to me for a second. Branson turned, looking over his shoulder, checking my whereabouts. I smiled, said nothing. And the big man straightened but kept me in his peripheral vision.

"Yeah, I did... He called. Why?"

"What did he say to you in that call?" Branson continued.

"What's going on, guys?"

"Just answer the question please, Mister Domenici."

"Has something happened to Sawyer?"

"What did you discuss during the phone call?"

"Nothing. We…" Dom's glance found me again.

"He called you and you said nothing?" Branson asked, accusing Dom of lying.

"I mean, we didn't talk, I er… I said some things."

"Such as?"

Dom's jaw worked.

Gina chose that moment to appear with four mugs of steaming tea. "I didn't know if you guys liked sugar or not, so there's a bowl and…" She laughed nervously and backed away. "Anyway, I'll just leave you to it."

Adams reached for the tea, dumped in three heaped spoonfuls, and stirred, clanking his spoon against the side of the mug.

"You were saying, Lieutenant Sawyer called you," Branson recapped, "out of the blue, and you had nothing to say to him."

"Dom had a great deal to say to him," I said.

Branson's big shoulders locked. "We'll get to you, Mister Kempthorne."

"Should we have a solicitor present?" I asked.

"Not yet. This is informal, for now."

"Then we are not obliged to answer anything."

"No… you're not. But if you don't help us now, we might ask ourselves why that is, and perhaps proceedings will be taken further. Is that what you want, Mister Kempthorne?"

I was beginning to think Lance Corporal Branson didn't like me. He glowered, raised an eyebrow, and when I stayed quiet, he faced Dom again. "What did you discuss during this phone call?"

"Not much. Like I said. I called him a few things."

Dom looked at me again and I couldn't decide if he was asking for my help or wanted me to remain quiet.

"We need the details, Mister Domenici," Adams said, sounding sympathetic.

"I don't know. I was distracted."

Adams sipped his tea. "By what?"

Dom's face crinkled into a muddle of expressions. If it was just him, he'd have told them already, but he was likely trying to keep our relationship out of this, if only so it didn't complicate things. But it was already complicating matters. Better to rip off the bandage than pick around its edges. "Sean Sawyer called while Dom was performing some manual labor on me."

Both of the corporals turned and fixed me with their stares.

Gina coughed somewhere at the back of the store. Thankfully, Cassie was out, or there would have been more coins plinking into the swear jar.

"Right," Branson said, cheeks reddening.

"What?" Adams glanced at this partner.

"Never mind," Branson replied.

"Like I said, I was *busy*." Dom cleared his throat. "I told Sawyer to hurry up, and er... I think I hung up on him." Dom swallowed. "I didn't let him talk. He said nothing. Now can you tell me why you're here?"

"Where were you yesterday morning, around midday?"

He huffed. "Here, upstairs."

In the shower with me. And I didn't like the tone of this conversation.

"You have witnesses?"

"Yeah. Now fucking tell me or I'm not saying another word."

"Sean Sawyer was found dead yesterday, Mister Domenici."

Dom's mouth fell open. He shut it and slumped back on the sofa. "Shit."

"Yours was the last number he called."

"How? How did he die?"

"Suspected suicide," Adams said.

Dom frowned. He didn't believe it. From what I knew of Sean Sawyer, he was the type to blame everyone else, never himself. He wouldn't take his own life.

"You don't believe that?" Branson asked.

"I dunno... I haven't seen him in ages. We didn't get along."

"You were medically discharged from the military, Mister Domenici?"

"I was."

"And your CO signed off on that?"

"Yeah."

"Some people we've spoken to have said you were pretty vocal at the time... about not liking that decision? There are rumors you had a personal relationship with your commanding officer?"

I saw where this was going. "Dom, don't say another word." I straightened and stepped in front of the fireplace, blocking the heat. "It's time you left."

"We're trying to ascertain the facts—"

"No, you're hoping your shoddy case can be wrapped up by blaming an ex-lover—"

"Mister Kempthorne, don't you find it interesting that

a number of John's known associates have either been killed or disappeared lately?"

My mind worked, coming at this from his angle. Charles Renick, found dead in the Thames. Kage Mitchell, missing. And now Sean Sawyer? "It's easy to find patterns in sand, Corporal. John has alibis. I have two other staff members who can confirm we didn't leave my upstairs apartment all afternoon. John isn't a cold-blooded killer. Look elsewhere for a suspect."

"Like at you, Mister Kempthorne?" Branson asked.

I could hardly deny being a killer. I'd thought myself one for half my life. And while it hadn't turned out to be true, what difference did it make? I *had* killed. So I smiled, because it was what he wanted to see and because I had no power, no trick, no weapons, just my tattered name and reputation.

Dom shot to his feet. "You need to leave, right now."

"Thank you for your time." Adams rushed one last sip of tea. "And for the tea."

Branson glowered. "If you think of anything that might be useful, please call the base and ask for me," he told Dom.

Dom nodded, and the pair left to the sound of the tinkling bell.

"Wow," came Gina's remark. She reappeared from the back of the shop, behind the shelves. "You okay, Dom?"

"Yeah..." His shoulders sloped. He wasn't even close to okay. None of us were. "I'm just going to er..." He grabbed his coat off the hook, threw it on, and headed for the door. "I'll be back later."

The bell tinkled and he was gone too. I stared at the

door, wanting to go after him, but froze in place, having no idea what to say or do to fix this.

"I've got him," Gina said. "I know where he's going."

I swallowed, nodded, watched her go, too, and stood alone in Cecil Court, wishing everything were different.

4

D^{om}

"Line 'm up, Rick."

Big Rick, all five-foot-something of him, with his glinting earring and bartender smile, did as I'd asked, pouring a shot for me and one for Gina, after she'd stumbled through the crowd to catch up with me. Her huge purple puffer coat gleamed under the bar's lights. She could fall out of bed and look ready for a night in Soho.

I downed a shot, Rick poured another, raised a judgmental eyebrow but said nothing, then glided off to tend his other customers. The second shot went down as easy as the first. "Don't tell me to slow down," I wheezed. "Or to go back. I need this."

She snorted. "I'm not Robin." And she threw back her drink, wincing. "Sometimes wish I was." She plonked her elbow on the bar and her head on her hand, making her tightly curled hair bounce, and frowned.

I side-eyed her. "What's that mean?"

"I dunno, like maybe out of the two of us, she was more useful and I'm just... the sidekick."

"That's bollocks." I waved Rick over. "Robin was awesome with numbers and getting shit done, but you... people love you. You're fuckin' funny. Kempthorne & Co would be dull as dirt without you there. Kempthorne said so."

She grunted a dirty laugh. "He did *not* say that."

"He kinda did, in his own way."

"Whatever." She giggled, and more shots went down.

I was on my sixth when the lights began to shine and blur at their edges. "It's not about Sawyer..." I said, needing her to know that dick didn't get to camp in my head. "It's everything else. It's... Wordsworth, and Annie, seeing Kempthorne dying on that desk, and Robin." We talked about Robin some more, about the way she used to glare over the rim of her glasses, and how she could order Kempthorne to do almost anything. Kempthorne & Co was a very different place with her. *Cas* was different. She brought a whole new level of weirdness into the mix, a good weirdness, but she wasn't Robin.

By the time we were done discussing Robin, the mood was so damn low Rick would have to scrape us both off the floor. "So how's it goin'?" Gina asked, brightening. Her words slurred. "With you an' dah boss?" She saw my glare and laughed. "C'mon, I live vicariously through you."

"You need a boyfriend. Or a girlfriend."

She chuckled and flung a hand. "Men are way too much trouble. Girls are hot."

I arched an eyebrow. "It's good… Kempthorne and me. I think."

"Uh oh. What's up? It can't be the sex. Bloody hell, the two of you are always throwing eyes at each other. We're gonna need a sex jar." She shuddered. "Ew, no. Terrible thought."

She could always wrench a smile from me. "It's definitely not the sex." I swirled my glass—we'd moved on to beer, but I was too drunk to taste it. "Sometimes it feels like we're further apart than before, right?"

"What. How?"

I shrugged. "Since Wordsworth." Something caught in my voice and I washed it back with a swig of drink. That bloody place was going to haunt me for years.

"He lost his trick…" she said carefully.

"Yeah." Kempthorne had been through the ringer. *He'd died.* He'd given up on Montgomery's desk. He said it was so Montgomery absorbed everything, inciting the shadows, but there was a lot more to it than that. He'd wanted to give up. He'd been tired of fighting and losing. I knew that feeling.

A big guy made a meal of moving through the crowd toward us. "*Fuuuck*," I said, recognizing Lance Corporal Branson. His eyes darted and when he brushed up against someone, his quick smile appeared like a snap of static. He was as straight as an arrow and looking for trouble in a gay bar.

He stumbled next to Gina, bumping into her arm. Her drink sloshed.

"Hey, watch it, mate…" Gina's gaze flicked questioningly to me. I shook my head. He wasn't worth the argument.

Branson ordered a drink and leered at Gina. "What's a girl like you doin' with a fag?"

A prickle of anger skittered under my skin. I laughed it off. And before I could suggest he leave, Gina said, "Maybe I'm here for a date?"

"What are *you* doing here?" I asked him. I could have asked him if he was cruising for a date, but I wasn't drunk enough to be stupid. Not yet.

Rick dumped Branson's drink in front of him and glided off, catching my eye on the way. *No trouble,* that glance said.

"It's a free country." He planted himself on the barstool, glancing around and grimacing as though he might catch the gay if he stayed too long. "You cut up about Sawyer?"

Okay. I was too drunk for this shit. "Fuck off."

Gina—trapped between us—shrank, wanting to be anywhere else. She slipped off the stool. "I'll just leave you two—"

Branson grabbed her arm. Her drink sloshed over her fingers a second time. There was one thing you didn't do, and that was grab someone when they'd made it clear they want nothing to do with you. Gina whirled and shoved him in the chest, but he was a big guy and he clung on. "Get your thick mitts off me."

"C'mon, darling. You're not going to find a real man in here."

Her lip curled.

My trick sizzled at the end of my fingers.

No trouble.

The doormen carved their way through the crowd, like sharks through a school of minnows, heading toward Branson, who still had his paw around Gina's arm. She could handle herself. But Branson was bloody big. And they were slow, and I was right there.

"How about we go around the back—"

Her hand swung and slapped him across the face. Branson jerked, more stunned than hurt. I saw it happening, saw his eyes change from light humor to bloodlust. He didn't understand no.

I lunged around Gina, knocking her back because I was off-my-arse drunk, and slammed a hand against his chest, sending a small pulse of trick into him. Just enough to rattle his teeth. He gulped a yelp and fell backward off his stool, landing like a bag of bricks on the floor. Half the crowd fell silent, waiting to see what happened next. Someone cheered. "Whey hey!"

The floor tilted, and I grabbed the bar.

Definitely too drunk for this shit.

"C'mon, big guy." One of the doormen grabbed for Branson's arm, but he shook him off. "Outside, eh?" they urged. Branson snarled and snapped like an angry pit bull, shot Gina and me a warning glare, and left swearing up a storm.

"Nice slap," I told Gina as we returned to our stools.

She grinned and shook her hand. "Stings like a bitch, though."

We laughed, the crowd fizzled away, and after a few more drinks when the room had started to spin on its

own, a niggling voice told me Kempthorne would disap-
prove of my being shitfaced, but then I remembered what
had happened when he'd polished off half a bottle of
whiskey. He'd hammered me into his desk, so maybe he
might crack open another bottle and we'd visit the basement again. My dick warmed just thinking it.

"Oh my god, would you stop." Gina laughed as we
stumbled from the bar into the frigid night air. She
fought with her purple coat, trying to get her arms in the
holes that wouldn't stop moving.

"*Shtopwhat*?" I snickered.

"You're all gooey-eyed and flushed. You get that look
—" Coat on, she hiccupped and almost tripped over her
own feet. "—when you're thinking about all the nasty
things you get up to with Kempthorne."

I grabbed her, pivoting her upright so she didn't fall
off the pavement, and laughed. "This is my shitfaced
look." It came out more like *thishishmahshitfacedlook*.

She grinned, stumbling into my arms, then her eyes
widened, and she tensed. "Look out!"

The back of my neck tingled too late. Something hard
struck, ringing my head like a bell. For a blink, everything
was black, I was moving, falling forward, and would have
toppled over if the wall hadn't caught my stagger. Pain
throbbed down my neck, into my shoulders, hot, like
water. Gina cried my name.

I turned my head. Branson had her. His bulk was
twice her size. There were others on the street, people
backing up, none moving in to help. The old military
switch inside flicked on. I shoved off the wall, took a card
from my pocket, lit it up with trick.

Branson threw Gina into the crowd, as though she was nothing. I lifted my chin, jerking an invite for him to fucking try it and come at me. His brutish face screwed up. Gina shouted something. Branson swung. I flicked the card. With the small amount of trick I'd fed the card it should have popped by his head, enough to startle him, but it overshot and flew over the crowd. Branson's fist kept coming. I tried to duck, managed to whip my head back, but his knuckles still skimmed my cheek hard. Blood burst across my tongue.

Christ, he hit like a truck.

Thick fingers locked around my neck. Branson dragged me off my feet and leered into my face. "This is for Sawyer, you fuckin' fag." His forehead smacked into mine. Blackness and sparks swirled. Instinct curled my hand into a fist and planted it into his thick side, and it was like hitting a bloody tree. Even with trick, Branson just grunted. He slammed me against the wall, and my head and back snapped against brick. Then the bitch landed a punch to my gut that ended my fight right there. My whole body spasmed. I bent over, grabbed for him, and went down when he stepped away. Slushy snow cushioned some of the fall. But not the glob of spit he spat into my face.

A doorman appeared—too bloody late. Branson was done by then, his point made.

I rolled onto my back and concentrated on making my lungs work again. Gina's worried face hovered in front of me.

"You all right, mate?" some unhelpful prick asked. Did I bloody look all right?

Gina and one of the other doormen scooped me onto my feet. "Can you get back to Cecil Court?" the doorman asked, recognizing us.

I leaned on Gina and nodded, feeling like an idiot, my pride dented more than anything else. Gina swore, staggered, and propped me up the ten-minute walk back from Soho.

We stumbled into the shop. It was late, all the lights were off. If we could tiptoe upstairs, nobody had to know. "Don't tell Kempthorne," I whispered.

Gina frowned.

"Don't tell me what?"

Fuck. He was sitting on the sofa in the dark, lit by the dying fireplace like some moody mafia king.

"Dom got his arse kicked," Gina blurted.

My pride slithered into a hole and hid there as Kempthorne rose to his feet. He frowned down at me. I smiled. A dribble of blood chose that moment to trickle down my cheek.

"You should see the other guy," I mumbled.

Kempthorne sighed and hooked an arm under mine. Then he and Gina tried to manhandle me up the stairs into my room. I flopped onto the bed, heard mumbling, then the bed springs groaned and Kempthorne's dark eyes shimmered in the gloom. "I'm all right," I grouched.

"I'm sure you are, but you have a split lip and you're clutching your side like something might fall out if you let go." He didn't sound pissed off. His voice was tinged with amusement. "Take off your shirt."

"I'm fine." I didn't know what I was saying and was already taking off my shirt anyway. I flopped back again and Kempthorne's warm fingers probed my bruised side, sending tingles through me. Not trick-tingles, the other kind. "Where's Gina?"

"Throwing up."

I groaned, flopped a hand over my eyes, and wondered if that might be me by morning.

"I can't heal you," he said. "But it doesn't look bad. The best thing you can do is sleep it off."

"Yes, boss," I grumbled, eyes still firmly shut. He thought I was an idiot. This was awful. I *was* an idiot.

He stroked my bangs back and his lips fluttered a soft kiss on my bruised forehead. I opened my eyes to find him so close I could reach up and drag him into a kiss, but my damn lip throbbed and I doubted he'd want to taste beer and vodka.

"Get some rest." Then the bed springs creaked and I was out like a light before he'd even left the room.

5

A lexander

"It's not a great night out unless someone starts a fight," Cassie said. She grinned, bright-eyed and on the cusp of laughing at Dom and Gina, who both sat on the sofas, nursing hangovers.

The pair had emerged after lunch, Gina in fluffy slippers and a thick dressing gown, brighter than Dom, who sported a bruise over his right eye and a cut on his lip. But he looked better than last night. When he'd stumbled in, leaning on Gina, I'd assumed he'd had too much to drink, but the second I'd learned he was hurt, it was a good thing my trick had gone quiet, or I might have hunted the perpetrators down.

Cassie hung up her coat and clomped to the sofas, then dropped next to Gina and kicked her boots up onto the coffee table. Gina tapped her leg before I had a chance to comment, and her boots thumped back to the floor. "Sorry."

"I've discovered some information about Sawyer's death," I said. "We can talk about it now, or later, when you've both recovered."

Dom rubbed his hands down his face, trying to scrub off a headache, and winced when he snagged his scabbed lip. "Now," he growled, his voice full of gravel. After he'd settled last night, and without any power to pursue Branson, I'd worked through the night, making calls, pulling up old files on Robin's computer, and chased a few threads that led back to the military base, and to Sawyer, whom I'd already had a line of communication with since he'd routinely sold me information regarding the military's interest in Dom. Unfortunately, that line was now severed. But I'd salvaged some interesting information.

"Mister Sawyer was about to have his career brought to an end under misconduct charges," I explained, moving to sit on the edge of the sofa next to Dom. Dom snorted and reclined on the sofa beside me, stretching an arm along the back cushion. "He was found with a Glock Seventeen in his hand and a precise hole in his head, but forensic evidence makes it clear the scene was staged. The blood splatter pattern is all wrong for the angle of his body. Which is why the two lance corporals were here trying to accuse Dom of breaking into the base and murdering his ex-lover."

"I wish I'd been here yesterday. Sounds like it was pretty tense," Cassie said.

"When Branson couldn't pin it on Dom, he accused Kempthorne," Gina said, reaching for her glass of water.

"Clutching at straws, much?"

"Not really," I said. "He had a point. Sawyer's death is suspicious, and so is Kage Mitchell's disappearance."

"And Renick?" Gina asked, sounding innocent but being far from it.

She wasn't a fool; she suspected I was involved in that man's untimely death. I'd never confirmed or denied my involvement. But Dom had known almost immediately. Cassie seemed to be sure too.

Cassie leaned forward, her green eyes very keen. She'd been one of Renick's latents. A tool for the East End mob boss to get what he wanted. I hadn't yet learned how deep her allegiance went, just that she was pleased the King of Hearts was no longer around.

"An unfortunate accident."

"You think Sawyer's death and Kage Mitchell's disappearance are connected?" Dom asked.

"Yes, I do. Because of this..." I pulled up a picture on my phone and set it down on the coffee table for them all to see. The image showed a city map of New York, with a building ringed in red. "It was found in Sawyer's belongings."

"What's that address?" Dom asked.

"Kage Mitchell's apartment."

Dom's eyes widened. He snatched up the phone. "He has a place in New York?"

"There's a lot about Mister Mitchell we don't know."

Dom's eyebrows lifted. He heard the implications. That he hadn't known Kage at all.

"Is Kage there?" Gina asked.

"No, I've hired a PI to check. No activity for months. Not since he started working here."

"So why had this Sawyer bloke circled that address?" Cassie asked. "Do they know each other?"

"Not as far as we were aware. But clearly there must be a connection. Sawyer was about to be dismissed. His position was tenuous. I suspect he knew something that got him killed. He may have suspected he was on thin ice. He tried to call Dom during his last moments alive—"

Dom groaned and dropped his head back. "I should have listened to him."

"You weren't to know."

"He calls out of the blue after years—of course it was important. And I..." His throat moved and for a few moments the only sound was the crackling fire.

"Do you think Kage was after this Sawyer, or do you think Sawyer was after Kage?" Cassie asked. The question was an excellent one.

"I think Kage Mitchell had a knack for digging up information people wanted to keep buried."

"*Has* a knack," Dom said. "He's not dead."

"Of course."

More silence hung thick in the air.

"Unless you know something more about Kage's disappearance that you'd like to share with the class?" Dom asked, his tone close to an accusation.

"I don't."

"You don't know any more or you just want to keep it a secret?"

"Dom," Gina scolded. "Even I don't think Kempthorne did this."

"It's all right," I told her. He had good reason to suspect me, but I'd thought we'd moved past the stage of thinking me a murderer. "Let's all be clear about something. I don't like Mister Mitchell, but I'm not going to kill a man because I don't like him."

Gina coughed, spluttered two words: "Charles Renick," then coughed again.

Cassie laughed, then choked off when she noticed our faces. "Oh shit, you're all serious. And I thought you were all cutesy book shop owners or something."

Dom finally chuckled and the tension eased.

I couldn't pretend his words hadn't hurt, although I made sure to keep it from my face. He didn't trust me. Which hurt in a way I struggled to put words to. "Cassie has asked a pertinent question. Who was hunting whom? Sawyer or Kage? And why?"

"I hate to say it, but..." Gina sighed. "Dom's at the middle of this, isn't he?"

Dom groaned again.

"I'm not sure this is about Dom, but rather he's tangled within it somehow. The MOD, Ministry of Defense, has been experimenting on latents for as long as Montgomery had been plotting his rise. They are fully aware of a latent's potential in combat. Dom may work with us, but he's still very much on their radar. I suspect this has more to do with latents and the military in general, and less likely to do with Dom, personally."

"Despite me screwing both men," Dom drawled, taking a shot at himself.

Cassie snickered. "You get around, mate."

He smiled ironically. "It's a skill."

Their joking helped soften the atmosphere, which was clearly needed, but solved little.

Gina had fallen quiet for the last few minutes. She had my phone and studied the picture, her hangover frown sharpening. Dom and Cassie continued to joke, sounding dangerously close to flirting. Thankfully, I knew Dom well enough to know flirting was his default setting. "Your thoughts?" I asked Gina.

"You should go to America."

"Why?" I shifted from my place beside Dom and squeezed in beside Gina, forcing her to scuttle over, into Cassie, who continued to joke with Dom.

"Kage didn't want to go home. We all knew it. He liked it here, and even though he was a lying dirtbag, he did try and do the right thing by us. The agency he worked for made it clear they wanted you and Dom. He delayed for ages... For too long maybe?"

"You think the LOA grew tired of his stalling?"

"I do. You saved his life. He knew he owed you. So he put the LOA off. Maybe in the end he refused to give you up. So they took him."

I sighed. "If that's the case, it puts a very different slant on things." If she told Dom her theory he'd be on the next plane to New York. "Keep this between us for a little while. I want to do some checks. America is not a safe place for latents. If we're going to go, then we need to be sure it'll be worth the risk."

She nodded and handed me back the phone. "You'll do the right thing."

Would I? She was more confident in that than I was.

Snow flurried against the attic's window. The thin glass had fogged up, misting the street outside. Some sad song played from Robin's laptop—her playlist, that I'd left on repeat.

I'd discovered some things, buried in Robin's file she'd put together on Kage Mitchell prior to his joining us. Things I had to tell Dom. The only problem was, he'd leap on a plane and be gone, with no thought for the danger he was walking into. He didn't know the extent to which the military kept watch on him. He didn't know how the military was selling assets to the US, assets like him. Renick had sold latents, trafficked them across borders. When it came to latents, the UK government was no different. And someone high up wanted John Domenici. Sawyer had called to warn him. Kage was missing. The signs were ominous.

The door creaked. "Brooding in the dark?"

Dom wandered in, hands in his pockets. He'd showered but hadn't fixed his hair all day. He probably didn't know it flicked out, the ends trying to curl. He ran a hand through it now. "About last night—"

"You don't need to explain."

He stopped at the window beside me and wiped the condensation away. The quirky, narrow street sparkled below. "I heard you and Gina talking. America, huh?"

"You heard that?"

He propped himself against the windowsill, back to

the window. "You thought I wasn't listening. That's the best time to listen."

Clever.

"When do we leave?" he asked.

"It's not that simple."

"Then I'll go—"

"No."

His eyes widened but then a small smile lifted the corner of his mouth in a smirk.

"That is—" Clearing my throat, I went on, "Kage's life in America is riddled with authorities that don't like latents. I'm not letting you go alone."

"Letting me?" His eyebrows lifted and his smirk grew. He straightened and closed the distance between us in a single step. "I'm torn between telling you where to shove your order and the fact this new possessiveness *really* turns me on."

His smile, the smooth timbre of his voice, the fact he stood so close, radiating heat—I hadn't known a man, or anyone, could so easily ignite desires I'd so long pushed aside, not neglected, just didn't need.

However, he was distracting.

"We need to discuss a course of action."

"Yes, we do," he agreed, prying open my shirt's top button. His knuckles brushed my jaw, then my collarbone. Whether they were deliberate or careless touches, didn't matter. Each one shorted my breaths and made my heart race. "But you mentioned something about being surprised by what you liked, and that's worth further investigation." His eyes flicked up. "Christ, that raised eyebrow and look on your face. You have no idea how hot you are."

I caught his wrist, trying to stop him, stop this. We did need to talk. But now he'd stopped and his eyes asked questions like why stop, when this was both what we wanted. He was insatiable, so was I, but I couldn't help but feel the sex was masking everything we weren't saying. If only I knew what those things were.

He spread his hand on my chest, his touch like a firebrand through my shirt, and I let his wrist go. His lips skimmed mine. "I need this right now. Need you."

"I'd never tell you no."

"You just did. Literally minutes ago." He eased back, stealing the almost-kiss away, amused, not angry.

"America is different for people like us." I chased his mouth, him, as he stepped back, leading me along with him. "My name and money can shield us from some of—"

He pressed a finger to my lips. "Tell me about these things that will *surprise me*."

Glass shattered behind me. A blast of cold air rolled in. I spun. Flames licked across the polished floorboards, fueled by spilled alcohol. Some already climbed the side of the sofa. "Water!"

Dom filled a jug from the kitchen sink. He sloshed it at the flames, quenching some, but more had spread, catching the corner of the rug. I yanked the rug away and stamped the fire out. Dom threw more water, but the dry floorboards had caught. Fire crawled up the drapes.

"Shit!" He grabbed a dishtowel, soaked it, and beat the flames; it was a losing battle.

Panic raced through my veins. Gina. The books. "Fire!" I yelled down the stairs. "Gina, get out!" Smoke rolled down from the eaves and out of the door. Fumes burned my eyes, my throat.

Dom was still trying to beat the flames, but there were too many.

I grabbed him, hauling him back. "*Go.*" Smoke filled my lungs. I coughed, couldn't stop coughing. Fire leaped up the sloped walls. There was no saving it now. It was lost. I thought perhaps I heard sirens beneath a horrible thudding in my head. Couldn't breathe. Dom stumbled down the stairs and dashed out of sight. I fumbled with my phone, dialing 999.

The rest happened like a fever dream. Smoke and noise, flashing lights, and hollering. The fire crew arrived. I tried to breathe around the ache in my chest.

When the chaos passed, I was sitting on the step on the back of an ambulance, watching water from the fire-hoses pour out of 16a Cecil Court's door, and that was when I saw it:

LOCK UP LATENTS

The red spray paint had dripped down the shop window, but the words were clear.

Dom and Gina stood nearby. They'd seen it too.

It was, perhaps, time for a change of scenery.

6

D^{om}

You know you've pissed off the wrong people when you get a Molotov cocktail thrown through the window. Cecil Court had been saved by the swift arrival of the fire service, for the most part. The smoke had done more damage than the flames. But the graffiti on the window had been the worst of it.

Kempthorne made an easy target. The British public had fallen in love with him. The golden boy of London's elite. Tragic backstory. Handsome. Suave. Sophisticated. He could do no wrong. Until the so-called truth had been revealed. And Brits liked nothing more than pulling a celebrity off their pedestal and trampling them into the dirt.

Events moved quickly after the fire. Less than twenty-four hours later, I was sprawled in the supple leather chair of a private jet, breathing in the new car smell of money, listening and watching Kempthorne talk tersely into his phone.

Cas and Gina had stayed behind, to help with the cleanup and keep their finger on the UK pulse for all things Kage Mitchell.

This wasn't Kage's fault, or mine, but the guilt squirming in my gut still pointed the finger at me. I was in the middle of it. Sawyer, Kage, the military. But we didn't know why. Not yet. Finding Kage would solve that.

Kempthorne ended his call and dropped into the large, comfortable seat opposite mine. The private jet had been kitted out like a small apartment, with a small sleeping area at the rear for longer journeys, a bar, and the seating area. Kage's riverboat had been smaller.

We were several hours into a seven-hour flight. I'd examined the minibar, flicked through the selection of movies, and was now thoroughly bored. Kempthorne had spent the flight so far on calls, trying to smooth our way through US immigration. He'd been polite, apart from the one person who'd learned where to creatively place their phone. He'd paced, muttered, growled a few times, and had barely said a word to me, except to offer me a bag of KP Nuts.

He was tired, strung out, and didn't want to be here. He was here *for me*. Not for Kage. Because I'd asked. And I was getting the impression his silence was punishment.

Sighing, he loosened the top button on his striped shirt. His hand fluttered to his forehead.

"We good?" I asked.

"Yes, they'll let us in. But we have a dozen forms to complete, and they'll take our biometrics when we land. We don't have a choice."

"Okay, but… are *we* good?"

He looked up. "What?"

"You and me?"

He blinked. "Why wouldn't we be?"

"I don't know. I've spent three hours rattling around this tin can, and two hours in the airport before that, and you haven't said more than six words to me."

His lips twisted. "There's a lot to organize."

I'd told Gina how it felt as though Kempthorne and me were growing further apart, not closer together. I'd hoped the flight would help thrash some things out. It hadn't.

I leaned forward. "Are you okay?"

"Yes, of course."

I wasn't buying that. There was no fucking way he was okay. Cecil Court was his second home. Someone had set it on fire and spray-painted the window. He liked to pretend nothing touched him like water off a duck's back, but I knew him well enough now to know it went straight to his heart. "You see, I have a problem with that answer—"

He shot from the chair, crossed the cabin to the mini-bar, and poured himself a drink. He did it all so quickly, he'd clearly been thinking about it for a while.

"You think this whole trip is a dangerous waste of time," I said.

"It's reckless, yes." He threw back the whiskey too fast for a man who was okay and sloshed more into a glass. I moved fast, got my hand over the top of the glass before he could down that one too. He stilled, eyes momentarily wild, then sighed through his nose. "No... I'm not all right. I don't understand why we're doing this and I... I can't control what will be waiting for us when we land."

I plucked the drink from his hand and slotted myself between him and the bar, making him see me. "I get it."

"I don't think you do." He tried to extract himself.

I caught him by the hips, fighting back the thrill I got every time I was allowed to touch him. Our trick didn't dance like it used to, but it didn't matter, I still got a kick out of pulling Alexander Kempthorne against me. He stiffened, then melted, resistance crumbling. His dark hair had flopped over his forehead and he looked all serious and Kempthorne-like. "Alex," I said, liking how his name sounded and how he lifted his eyes, fighting his way out of whatever dark thoughts had a hold of him. "Talk to me."

All the resistance fell away and he shifted, leaning into me. The backs of his fingers brushed my face and then his thumb ran across my lips, skirting the cut. "If you must know, I'm afraid of what we'll find. Afraid of a lot more than I used to be. Afraid my trick won't return. Afraid I'll... lose you."

I collected his hand and planted a kiss on the knuckles. He wasn't the only one afraid of all this. Everything was terrifying. I'd gone into war zones less afraid. Getting involved with him might have been right at the top of that list of things I knew fuck all how to do. "I'm not going anywhere. You know that, right?"

The thin line of his lips curved. He planted a hand on

the bar top, fencing me in. "I'm not entirely sure I deserve you."

"We've been through this."

"Do you believe I'd hurt Kage?"

I laughed. That was an easy answer. "Yeah, you would. But he's not special. You'll do things most people wouldn't dream of. I know who you are, remember? You can't frighten me off."

Something complicated crossed his face, then he was kissing me, hard and brutal. He struck like a tidal wave, rolling in and over me.

"America is going to be difficult," he mumbled, sliding a kiss down my neck. I leaned back, relishing the feel of his tongue sweeping over my collarbone. His fingers clamped loose around my throat, making sure I was paying attention. "It's going to test us."

I saw the fear in his eyes now, thinly masked as desperate lust. I wanted to tell him we'd already been through everything the world could throw at us, but just because we'd survived, didn't mean we hadn't been hurt. The thought of more of the same made me want to tell him to turn the plane around and have us elope some-where far away where nobody would find us. Switzer-land, maybe. Where latents were just people.

I dropped my hand between us, found the hard ridge through his trousers, and nudged his parted lips with mine. His lust-filled eyes shone. "You and me? We'll survive anything they can throw at us." I breathed into him, taking his breaths into me. Having him this close was always hot. Keeping my hands off him was the diffi-cult part. "Because it's who they fucking made us to be." I caught him by the back of the neck and kissed him with everything I had, giving back the wave he'd washed over me. He moaned and pulled me into his arms. We didn't need trick to light us up. Whatever the connection we had did that. And the shitty world we lived in couldn't ever take that away.

***

The plane set down on asphalt during the night, its blinking lights reflecting on dirty snow piled high along the edges of the airport runway.

"The man is the son of an old family friend." Kempthorne threw on his heavy, one-third-length coat and flicked the collar up. "He's helped alleviate some of the latent issues we would have encountered."

I tried not to openly wince. My experience of the Kempthornes' family friends had taught me they were all homicidal rich gits.

The jet's door thunked and yawned open, revealing glistening metal steps, the landing crew, and a guy, maybe my age, with a shock of blond hair, freckles, and a neat, toothy grin to rival Hollywood's. He thrust out a hand. "Alex, it's been years!"

Kempthorne smiled his polite society smile, shook his hand, then did that not-quite-hug thing of squeezing his shoulder. "Trent, this is my associate, John Domenici, who I told you about over the phone. Dom, meet Trent Anderson."

I was the associate. Not a boyfriend. At least I knew where I stood.

Trent grabbed my hand and tried to shake it free of my wrist. "Hi there," he beamed. "Any friend of Alex's yaddah yaddah."

"Hi." *Alex has told me* nothing *about you.*

They both looked at me as though I should say something more, but I had no idea what and grinned like a clueless idiot.

"Let's get inside, where it's warmer." Trent ushered us down the steps while the ground crew dealt with our bags.

Immigration was the typical paper exercise, including scanning thumbs and irises just in case we got any funny ideas about freedom and rights. We were given Latent ID cards that we were supposed to keep on us at all times. If we stepped out of line, we got an *infraction*. Three of those, and it was an automatic trip to the copshop. The message was clear. Behave.

I signed a form that said I agreed not to use my trick in public, at the risk of arrest. A nice warm welcome then. Trent escorted us through and outside the airport in an hour, then left us briefly standing like lemons with our bags in the pick-up zone. Huge cars and busses trundled by. Some parked up to load bags and people. A *No Latents* sign caught my eye in the door of one of those busses. Thumbprints were scanned as people climbed aboard. Okay, this was how it was going to be, huh.

"Trent seems nice."

Kempthorne's smile warmed. "He does, doesn't he. Honestly, I wasn't sure of our reception. The last time I saw him, he wasn't aware of my... situation."

Being gay or being a latent? The question was on the

tip of my tongue when Trent leaped from an SUV like a happy Labrador and grabbed our bags. "Let's get you boys out of here. The Hudson Yard penthouse is all made up. Heating's on. You're going to love it."

I almost preferred Hollywood's lazy American accent to Trent's chipper American. A slight twang in Trent's smooth voice and his surfer's tan suggested west coast, but I didn't know enough about Americans to guess with any more accuracy.

At least Hudson Yard didn't sound like too fancy a place; I might actually be able to relax there.

I climbed into the back of the SUV, Kempthorne climbed into the front, and Trent got behind the wheel. Which meant I was relegated to listening to them swap stories about pushy relatives and what they'd gotten up to at weddings. Trent made an effort to have me included, but the conversation soon flipped back to the pair of them with me on the fringes. What the fuck did I know about posh weddings and charity dinners?

My cheeks began to ache from all the fake smiles. It had been a long flight, coupled with lack of sleep and the frosty reception for latents, and I was not in the mood for bubbly Trent and his family fortune stories.

Hudson Yard was not what I'd been expecting, although I should have guessed. The gated complex was all shining glass high-rises and manicured lawns. Trent guided us to a penthouse, a split-level apartment the size of most houses back in the UK. Huge, shiny, modern glass and steel, looking out over the Hudson. The price tag had to be in the multi-millions.

Kempthorne and Trent breezed in, as though the

floor-to-ceiling glass framing a sparkling view of New York was nothing worth mentioning, and I tagged behind, trying to keep my eyes inside my head.

"Daddy says to make yourselves at home. Get some rest, and I'll be back tomorrow to help familiarize you with things. Ciao." Trent bounded back out of the door.

I leaned against the glitzy granite kitchen unit, so shiny I could see my face in the surface. "He doesn't mean 'daddy' like I'd mean daddy, does he?"

Kempthorne's sharp gaze cut to me but softened quickly. "You said he was nice."

"That was before I had to listen to him talk about how cousin Chad had embarrassed the family by buying the wrong Rembrandt or something. Christ, is he for real?"

Kempthorne's glare sharpened again. He tugged off his coat and hung it in a closet the size of my Cecil Court bedroom. "He's going out of his way to be kind, which we should be grateful for. Getting a hotel as a latent in New York is almost impossible."

And now I felt like a dick. "I'm gonna take a shower." I kicked off my boots and climbed the polished death-trap stairs, wondering if the windows went all the way to the bathroom so half of New York could see my arse.

Alexander

Trent: *Come to dinner tonight. Reservation made at Per Se...*

The text message blinked on my phone. Jet-lagged and disorientated, I swiped it away and rolled over in bed, searching for Dom beside me. He wasn't there. He hadn't joined me last night, which didn't mean anything. We hadn't talked about him always being welcome in my bed. He'd just so often fallen into it at Cecil Court, I'd assumed the same would continue.

I showered, dressed, and padded downstairs to find him freshly shaved and hunched over the kitchen worktop with multiple maps of the city spread in front of him. He'd found and circled Kage's address on one.

"When you're ready, we'll go take a look," he said without looking up.

I poured a coffee from the pot. "Good morning."

"Couldn't sleep." He flashed a smile.

The warmth it sparked in my chest chased away any niggling worry that I'd done something wrong and upset him without realizing it.

"Thought I might as well get the lay of the land before Trippy-Trent makes an appearance," he added.

"You *should* sleep, it makes the jet lag easier."

He grunted a noncommittal noise and went back to studying the street maps. Mention of Trent reminded me of the text. I lifted my phone from my pocket but a knock at the door interrupted. Dom answered it and Trent breezed in, like a whirlwind in a mauve coat and multi-colored scarf. He opened a box of croissants at the kitchen island. "Voila. I brought breakfast! How did you sleep? Isn't the view just divine?" He glided toward the windows. "Like you're on top of the world. This is my favorite apartment of Daddy's."

Dom rolled his eyes and tried to smile it off when I frowned. Trent didn't deserve Dom's contempt. He'd been more than helpful. And we needed him, if we were to stay out of trouble.

Trent grabbed a croissant and poured himself a coffee. "Fill your tanks and let's go. Any sights you'd like to see first? The Highline? Empire State Building?"

"Yeah." Dom grabbed a map and shoved it across the island counter so Trent couldn't miss it. "There." He tapped Kage's apartment address. "Ready when you are."

"There?" Trent turned the map and eyed it curiously. "Nice area. Someone you know live there?"

"Yes," I replied, before Dom said too much. "We'll just see if he's in."

We left after devouring the croissants, and Trent ferried us across Manhattan, through Brooklyn, to Kage's neighborhood. Kage's building was an old brownstone, split into apartments. At the door, I slipped a set of keys from my pocket and tried one.

"Where did you get those?" Dom asked, peering over my shoulder. Trent had started up a conversation with a woman walking her tiny dog.

"Kage's Docklands' apartment."

"You stole his keys?"

"I borrowed them." The first key didn't work. I tried another.

"And you didn't tell me?"

"They may not work—" The lock clunked and the door opened. Dom's dry glare wasn't all disapproval, there was some heat in it too. He knew my methods were sometimes morally questionable. If I told him everything I had planned, we'd never get anything done.

We climbed the stairs to Kage's apartment. And as Trent hurried to catch up, I knocked on Kage's door.

"He's not home?" Trent asked, stating the obvious.

Discreetly, I pulled my sleeve down to use as a glove and tried the handle. Locked. A few more tries with the keys and the door popped open. A dark, narrow corridor greeted us. The apartment blinds were closed, muffling the space. Small, but efficient. Dom flicked on the lights. "Don't touch anything," I said, wiping the light switch after him.

"Isn't this trespassing?" Trent asked.

"No," Dom said. "We have his keys."

"Oh, okay." Trent hung back.

"Why don't you wait outside?" Dom suggested.

Trent swallowed and retreated outside.

Dom brushed by me, putting himself ahead. He lowered his right hand to his side, close to his pocket where his deck of cards waited. "Stay back, just in case..."

He checked the right door first. "Bedroom, clear." Then moved on down the short corridor. A slight glow emanated from his fingers as we approached the gloom of the living area. He wasn't the only one expecting the worst. Kage had been missing for weeks. There was a chance we'd find his remains.

Dom flicked on the light.

Nobody was home, no *body* either. I might not have liked the man but I didn't want Dom to find him dead. His apartment, however, had been turned over. Drawers pulled from the sideboard, sofa cushions tossed and torn at the seams, suggesting whoever had been here had been searching for something.

"Should we call nine-one-one?" Trent asked, making me jump. He'd snuck back in, surprisingly quiet on his feet.

"After we're gone," I replied. And when we were a few blocks away. Two latents arrested at a crime scene was not how I planned to begin our US trip.

"Look for anything that might suggest where he is," I said, maneuvering around a fallen side table. "Notes, reading material..." Despite the mess, the apartment was sparse, just like his life at Docklands. I'd assumed he lived without clutter because he hadn't planned on staying, but now I wondered if he was one of those people who liked everything neatly in its place.

"He's missing, your friend?" Trent whispered.

"Wait outside," Dom said, harsher than before.

"Yeah…"

Trent left and Dom's gaze snagged mine. "Can we trust him?"

"I think so. He's harmless enough." I'd run a few preliminary checks before arriving, and there was nothing in Trent's background to suggest he'd be trouble. Quite the opposite. He towed the Anderson family line, never rocking the boat.

Dom made his way between the sofas to me by the window and handed over a slip of paper. I recognized Kage's handwriting from the unconvincing note he'd left for Dom to find. The date on it was from a few weeks ago. It triggered a memory—the CCTV. The same day we'd seen footage of him being bundled out of his Docklands apartment. "Interesting."

"Yeah," Dom agreed. "His deadline for taking you in?"

"Possibly."

"All right, let's check the rest of the place and get out of here before Twitchy Trent calls the cops on us."

Outside, Trent did do the right thing and called in, citing *"something suspicious"* at Kage's building. With that formality out of the way, he suggested a quick tour of Manhattan. I agreed. It was necessary to keep up the ruse we were here on business and not investigating a missing LOA agent. Dom soon fell quiet in the back of Trent's car as Trent twittered on.

Someone had turned over Kage's apartment,

searching for something. Or perhaps it wasn't that at all; it could just as easily be a jilted lover, or something more personal. Kage could have left the apartment in that state himself, although I doubted it. The man was too particular to go abroad knowing his apartment looked like a crime scene.

Trent dropped us off outside the Hudson Yard building and leaned out of the SUV's window. "I'll see you at eight tonight, Alex?"

The invite to dinner. I'd forgotten all about it. "I er... well. It's... very kind—"

"What's this?" Dom asked. He'd stopped halfway up the building's steps, his smile wooden.

"I asked Alex to join me for dinner," Trent said.

"It was hardly—" I began.

"Oh?" Dom's smile grew, and not in a good way.

"Er, you can come," Trent said. "Both of you, I mean. My treat. It'll be fun."

"It'll be fun, Alex," Dom said, smirking. He'd shoved his hands into his pockets, appearing at ease, but the tone of his voice suggested Trent was grating on his last nerve.

"Of course," I said. "We'll be there."

"Great! It's a double date." He pulled away and moments later the security gates closed behind him. The sounds of distant traffic honked and hummed. I stood on the steps, wondering if I should somehow explain something, but having no idea what I was explaining. So I started up the steps toward the building and John joined me.

"A date, huh?" He smirked. "Were you going to tell me?"

"It wasn't a date. He was being kind. I wasn't going to go. It had slipped my mind."

"Uh huh." We entered the building and summoned the elevator. Dom smirked some more. "A threesome," he said. "It'll be fun all right."

Fun was not the word that sprang to mind after seeing the sparkle of mischief in his eyes.

8

D^{om}

The restaurant Trent had chosen for his dinner with Alex that I was tagging along to was formal wear. I managed to rustle up a pair of black trousers and dug out the one expensive shirt I'd owned—bought by Gina because I had no fucking clue what shirt brand was good. I borrowed a jacket from Kempthorne. It was too long in the arms and bloody tight around the shoulders, but when I emerged from the bedroom and he stared as though wanting to shove me back into the bedroom and keep me there, I figured it'd do. We might have delayed for a quick hand job in the kitchen, but the Uber driver pinged to say he was waiting.

Kempthorne's distracted glances gave me a rush I hadn't expected. In the back of the Uber, he twined his fingers with mine and leaned in. "You look breathtaking in my jacket. Please wear it tonight, after this..."

Fuck. Heat rushed to all the right places and I turned my head, having him close enough to kiss.

"We'll talk about Kage later," he added, gaze dropping to my lips. Then he sat back and smiled his wicked Kempthorne smile, knowing how much he turned me on and making sure he kept himself just out of reach. The anticipation was sweeter that way. "Why don't we try and enjoy ourselves?"

"Like the dinner date you promised?"

"Well, no. That will be just the two of us. This is a date plus one."

"Hm." Fucking Trent. Maybe we could ditch him?

The restaurant was like something off James Cameron's *Titanic*. Swish and shiny. I could only hope I wasn't about to sink anything by being grossly out of place.

Trent waved us over. We sat in the latent section—something he apologized for, sparking a debate about the difference between policing latents in the UK and America.

"Artifacts!" Trent blurted, halfway through dinner, his blue eyes fixed on me. "So strange. We don't have many here. Why is that?" He directed the question at Kempthorne, assuming *my boss* knew more. I was, after all, just the associate.

"There's no official evidence as to why America has less artifacts, but it's likely the same reason this country also has less latents," Kempthorne said in his official agency voice. "London is considered the heart of latent activity. The further one is from London, the weaker the source."

Trent's gazed puppy-dog eyes at Kempthorne like a five-year-old gazes at their teacher during story time. "Fascinating. What makes London so special?" He propped his chin on his hand and fluttered his golden lashes.

"A shit load of murder and war," I butted in, startling Trent out of his dreamy state. "Give or take a few thousand years. Boudicca burned London to ash around sixty AD, pissing off a bunch of Romans. She went on to torture and kill sixty thousand people. Then the plague. There goes another hundred thousand. The Great Fire killed hundreds of thousands. Most were poor, so nobody cared. Then there's the Blitz. And that's on top of the everyday murders, knife crime, rapes, and suicides. London's built on blood."

They both blinked.

"What?" I said, grinning behind my glass. "I know shit too." I'd been reading some of Cecil Court's books on the sly. Robin would have been proud.

Trent didn't sneer, he was too polite for that, but he did straighten in his chair. "I can tell Alex's accent is English," Trent said. "But what accent is yours, Dom?"

"Gutter."

Kempthorne—sitting opposite me at the circular table—jabbed his shoe against my shin. "Dom is joking. He's from the East End of London."

Trent's face lit up. "Oh, a cockney? *Aw-right me govner,* like that?"

I didn't know whether to laugh or hit him. "Nah mate, not *Oliver Twist*."

He chuckled but clearly had no clue who Oliver Twist was. Kempthorne's honeyed laugh rumbled, then the polished oxford shoe that had struck my leg so rudely stroked up my shin. "The East End was historically where London's iron heart beat," Kempthorne said to Trent. "The area was industrial, mostly factories, docks. Also slums, in Victorian times."

"Now it's industrial chic," I added, distracted by Kempthorne's meandering foot.

We talked some more; Trent loudly and animatedly had an opinion on everything. I began to warm to him. He was harmless, and helpful. We did need him on our side and there were worse people out there than Trent Anderson.

After we'd eaten dessert, and we'd all downed more than a few glasses of posh wine, he excused himself to go to the bathroom. I watched him leave and saw him bump into someone and somehow manage to have them smiling and laughing in seconds.

Chuckling, I said, "He's so gay."

Kempthorne spluttered, almost spilling his drink. He laughed and leaned a little closer, keeping his voice low. "He's not gay."

I leaned a bit closer too. Our heads now bowed together. The restaurant's lights glittered in his eyes. "Why else would he agree to help you and your *associate* sightsee?"

Kempthorne's lips did that strange, thin twitch thing they did when he was hiding a smile. "Jealousy doesn't suit you." His foot, which had been stroking me on and off for most of the meal, started up again, shifting higher, finding my knees and prying them apart.

"I'm not jealous. He's all teeth, tits, and tan, but I like him."

"Is that an expression?"

"It is where I come from. Means all his flouncing is for show. He wants you thinking he's free, sexy, and single. Has he ever had a girlfriend?"

"I believe so, but there's no point discussing it." He leaned back and raised his glass but still tried to fight off his smile. "Because he's not gay."

His foot eased between my thighs. I leaned back, too, and didn't put up much resistance. "He keeps touching your hand."

"He's always been that way. He's being friendly." Kempthorne's right eyebrow twitched. I couldn't decide if he was deliberately stringing me along, and knew Trent was gay, or if he was just horny and teasing me because of it.

"Which one of us is more experienced in flirting?" I asked.

Something illicit and dangerous flashed in his eyes. "He's not gay, his father wouldn't approve."

I laughed aloud, catching the eye of the people across the room who believed latents shouldn't enjoy themselves, and if they were going to have fun, they should do it somewhere else. "Oh... okay, Daddy won't approve, so he's definitely *not* gay." Kempthorne's leg had to be horizontal under the table now, his heel rested firmly between my thighs while the flat of his foot was poised over my hard cock. If he'd just inch it a bit higher... "You know what I think?" I said. "He read about you coming out—celebrity gossip travels across the pond, right? He's had a crush on you since Chad's wedding or whatever—believe me, I know what that feels like. He thinks this is his chance. He's thoughtful, considerate, kind." I leaned back some, resting my case, then added, "And he bought you croissants."

"He bought *us* croissants. Buying croissants doesn't make a man gay." Kempthorne raised his glass to his lips, the picture of gentlemanly poise, while under the table, his shoe pushed in, rubbing against my erection. I shifted on the chair, my dick too hard to be comfortable. Maybe I could get a bonus rub before Trent came back?

Kempthorne sipped his drink, eyeing me over the glass. What if we visited the men's room? He could fuck me in one of those posh stalls?

Christ... I fought to keep the lust from my face, but his smirk said he saw it. "He looks at you like you've featured in his dreams, like he's rubbed a few off to old photos of you."

Kempthorne's eyebrows lifted. "Go on," he growled.

"He wants a piece of your tight British arse—"

Trent pulled out his chair. "What did I miss?"

Kempthorne choked and his foot jerked, hitting me in the fucking balls. I jumped, my knee hitting the table, sending my glass and dessert bowl flying.

"Oh! You boys all right?" Trent laughed. "Jumpy much?"

Kempthorne flicked wine from his hand. Some had stained his shirt. Trent grabbed a napkin and helped dab at the mess, almost climbing into Kempthorne's lap. How very helpful of him.

I grinned behind Trent's back and Kempthorne's quick, knowing smile just about branded his name on my heart right there. *Bloody hell, let me drag him somewhere soon and suck him off, until he holds my head and moans my name and comes down my throat.* I dropped my hand to my lap while Trent fussed over Kempthorne and gave myself a few alleviating tugs. My elbow clipped my fork, sending it clattering to the floor.

Trent leaned down. "You dropped—"

Shit, he'd see my hard-on. "I've got it." I bent down.

Glass shattered, shards peppering the back of my neck.

"Get down!" Kempthorne yelled.

Trent or Kempthorne flew into me, toppling me out of my chair to the floor. High-caliber shots *plinked*—I'd heard similar in Syria. Sniper rounds.

Keeping low, I looked left, at Kempthorne, saw blood on his cheek. "You hurt?"

"No," he gasped, then dabbed his face. "It was the glass. Just a cut."

Trent was sprawled between us, white as a sheet and breathing like a terrified rabbit. He'd been the one to grab me, though, and drag me to the floor. He might have just saved my life.

Another shot *plinked*, coming from our left. Someone screamed, the rest of the crowd joined in, and the entire restaurant of people surged toward the doors.

"Fuck." I kicked the table over for cover. "Stay low," I

hissed at Trent and shoved him toward the fleeing people.

Kempthorne scooted to my side. "Sniper," he said, his breath hot on my cheek.

"Yeah."

My trick boiled to the tips of my fingers. My cards sang, wanting to be freed. Kempthorne grabbed both my hands, pushed them to the floor, and shook his head. "Not here. Not in public."

"Bloody hell." I'd forgotten where we were. I shook out the trick before anyone saw. "Who is the target?" I hadn't seen whose glass had been hit, but it had been fucking close.

"You, I think," he said. "Your glass was hit."

The crowd still surged, which was good for us. There was no way the sniper could get a clean shot in now.

"We need to move."

We dashed into the crowd and let it carry us along until spilling outside into the cold night air. A row of body-armored, gun-carrying cops poured in, manhandling members of the crowd to one side. By the time I'd realized those being singled out were latents, one of the cops swooped in.

"Dom, don't do any—" Kempthorne's voice cut off.

Hands grabbed me from behind, jerking me around. "Get against the wall," a voice muffled by a helmet barked.

I looked up at the neighboring buildings. Several had open flat roofs where a sniper could sit and wait. Was he or she still up there?

"I said, get against the fucking wall!" The cop shoved.

I shoved back. "What the fuck, mate—"

Three rushed me at once. One kicked my legs out, and I toppled backward, slamming onto the sidewalk—jarring my teeth and skull. A forearm locked under my chin and a knee slammed into my chest. *Shit*—couldn't breathe. Kempthorne shouted something, his British accent like an alarm bell.

"Get his ID."

Fuck, can't move.

"Stay the fuck down or you get another infraction on your card."

Trick simmered, desperate to spill free and blast them back. Darkness throbbed at the edges of my vision, spots floating. I couldn't draw breath to tell them to ease off.

Kempthorne loomed, he said something, probably thought it was reasonable, but the police didn't think so. One of the cops cracked a rifle across Kempthorne's jaw, whipping his head back. He staggered out of my line of sight.

Fuck this.

Trick burst from my hands. The cop on my chest flew backward. Trick sizzled over his body armor. I had a second to grin. And all hell broke loose. Cops surged, boots flew in, cattle prods sparked—and I didn't stand a chance. The blows kept coming, only easing after I'd curled into a bruised ball, trying to protect my ribs and head. The blows rained in, and then stopped abruptly.

Hands hauled me up and threw me face-first against the wall.

"Two infractions." The cop threw my card at my back—taken from my wallet sometime when they'd been laying into me. "You're lucky we're not locking you up."

I wiped blood from my lip and stood in line, like a good fucking latent, and wondered if the sniper had seen it all.

9

A lexander

"He shouldn't have goaded them. They don't react well to taunts. This isn't England you know, where the police ride bicycles and rescue puppies from trees."

I rubbed my face, wincing as my fingers skimmed the bruise on my jaw. "Thank you. We are aware." There was little point in enlightening Trent on British policing. All I really wanted to do was get my hands on Dom to check he was all right.

Trent drove us toward Hudson Yard, twittering about laws and infractions and all the things we couldn't do, while Dom sat in the back seat and bled in silence. The sight of him being beaten played over and over in my head. Every blow, every kick, every jab with a cattle prod. And he hadn't done a bloody thing wrong.

I focused on my fists, unlocking my fingers and *breathing*, then poked at my jaw and worked my tongue into the sore lump inside my cheek.

Coming to America had been a terrible idea.

"Here we are," Trent announced, pulling the SUV into Hudson Yard's parking area. "You boys want to tell me what's really going on?" he asked, losing his smile for the first time since we'd arrived. He leaned an arm on the steering wheel and looked at me sternly. "Alex?"

I slid my gaze out of the window. "What's the security like here?"

"Good. Nobody can get in or out without being registered. Guests need to be buzzed up by a resident. Thumbprint keys make sure of that."

I opened the door and slid out, then opened Dom's door. The fire in his eyes said he was furious. Blood had caked in his hair. His lip had split open for a second time in a few days and he hugged his middle, his old bruises from the Soho beating flaring up.

"Are you going to be all right?" Trent asked, coming around the front of the car to check on us.

"Yes. Fine. Thank you."

Dom climbed gingerly from his seat. He had to be hurting for him to lean into me. We climbed the steps. Trent said something about tomorrow. I ignored him and let the building's door close between him and us, then led Dom into the elevator, hitting the button for the penthouse. My thumbprint acted as a key and the elevator rumbled upward.

Dom slumped against the wall. "So much for a nice dinner."

Under the harsh lights, the cuts on his face were so fresh, they almost glowed. I didn't know what to say, and stayed quiet, clenching and unclenching my fists as we arrived at the apartment. The penthouse glittered, all its shiny surfaces sparkling under modern lighting. I closed the blinds, sealing New York outside, making the space smaller.

"Take off your shirt," I ordered.

"You say the sexiest things." His tone joked, but his eyes burned.

"Let's take a look at your ribs."

"One feels broken." He peeled off the jacket and undid his shirt buttons, frowning at the droplets of blood, then eased his bruised body onto a breakfast bar stool and leaned most of his weight on an elbow. His torso's middle section was a patchwork of angry bruising, and it would get worse.

"I'm going to touch you." I stepped in and pressed both hands on his skin.

He jumped and chuckled. "Cold hands."

"Sorry." It took a moment to slide my thoughts aside and reach for the tiny embers of trick glowing inside me. My power had sizzled back to life as the police had held me back and I'd watched them beat Dom, unable to lift a finger to help. There was no use in both of us being arrested on our first night in New York.

Dom gasped. His eyes fluttered closed. "Okay... hm... got your power back?"

"Some." I concentrated on the flow, giving and taking back, like threading a needle, but threading trick through his bruises, using it to massage muscle, flesh, and bone.

Finished with his chest, I cupped his jaw and tingled some trick through my fingers, smoothing away the bruises there. His gaze roamed my face. Some of his fury had faded, but not all.

"There." I stepped back and sighed. "Better?"

He stretched and rolled his shoulders, making his abdominal muscles flex. Well-built, from head to toe, he wore muscle well. Although, that muscle was hidden most of the time, until he removed his shirt, like now. "Yeah, good. You're amazing. You know that, right?"

I flicked out my fingers. "And spent. That took all I've got."

"It'll come back." He dropped onto his feet, still stretching and shifting, testing his body.

I could think of a much more enjoyable way of testing his body. Adrenaline and fear mixed in my veins, turning into something sharp and dangerous. But he was bruised on the inside, too, in a way I couldn't heal with trick. He needed time, not me shoving him against the kitchen island and fucking him raw.

He plucked his ID card from his wallet and dropped it onto the counter. Two black strikes marked the infractions box. "If I get three, I win a prize." His smile collapsed into a snarl. "Kage is beginning to look like a fucking saint compared to the New York cops."

Kage... I'd almost forgotten we were here for him. What mess had he dragged us into?

I leaned against the counter next to him. "Why does someone want you dead?"

"Or you. That was a professional hit. Military or government."

It had been close. I might have lost him—gone, in a blink. He was smiling about something now, in that ironic way he did, making some smart remark, but I studied his face, his eyes, their soft lashes, his nose, its smooth slope, and the fading bruise on his jaw. I'd lost everyone I'd ever cared about. I was cursed. I'd lose him too. It was inevitable.

"Alex, what's wrong?"

I slipped my fingers into his hair and tilted his head. His mouth opened, pupils expanding, so receptive. They'd beaten him, and I'd watched. I'd vowed never to watch someone I loved get hurt again. I'd failed.

My trick sparked through my hand, where I'd placed it on his bare chest. His trick bloomed under my touch, coming to me. Dom shuddered and exhaled. Goose bumps speckled his chest, lifting fine, dark hairs. His nipples hardened. To see him respond to me, so eager and hungry, triggered all my instincts to protect. These feelings were powerful, their own kind of surging trick. I was jealous of anyone who dared touch him. He was mine. He'd always be mine. And perhaps what I felt was wrong, too much, too overpowering, but I didn't care. I'd destroy anyone who dared try and take John Domenici from me.

I lowered my mouth, my hand on his chest holding him back, and licked over his left nipple, then gently puffed a little air over his cool skin.

He gripped my arm. "Fuck."

"So eloquent." I skimmed my lips over his, catching his breaths.

"Fuck eloquent." He grabbed my arse and yanked me

hard against him. His cock dug into my hip. To know he wanted me as fiercely as I wanted him, it thrilled me every time. We rocked as one, hands roaming, kiss deepening. We fit so perfectly—all of him was perfect.

Dom gasped from the kiss; eyes glassy, he fixed me in his gaze. "Would you ever... bottom? You don't have to. I mean, I—know it's not for everyone, I just—"

I nudged his mouth, teasing. "I'll do anything for you."

He bit his lip. I dropped my hand and cupped his erection. Even through his trousers, his heat burned. "I told you... What I like may surprise you."

"You're flexible?"

All the things I could do with him... I wanted him in every way. "Very."

His eyes widened, the possibilities endless. "Christ, Alex. You sly bastard."

I gave him a harsh squeeze. He bucked and grabbed both my arms. Abandoning his cock, I brushed my knuckles against his cheek. I hadn't believed anyone would look at me the way he did now, as though I was worthy. Like everything else John Domenici, I feared it. Feared him and what he could do to me, how he opened me up and saw inside. But I wanted more.

I dragged my hand down his naked chest. Trick left golden trails shimmering down his skin. "I'd do anything for you. I hope you understand what that means. I've never let anyone in the way I have you. But right now, I have to admit to desperately needing to bury my cock inside you," I whispered, almost losing my voice.

He thrust a hand into my hair. "That's a lot of words for *let's fuck*."

There were times when we were together that called for delicate touches and gentleness, for soft kisses and sweet murmurs. This wasn't one of those times. This was madness and insanity, desperation and a wildness only he brought out of me.

"Here." He produced a condom packet from his pocket.

"You're always so well prepared."

"That's because I plan on having you fuck me every chance we get." He tore the packet open with his teeth, his eyes sultry and fierce. "Let me."

Hands raised, I let him tug at my belt and trouser fasteners. His knuckles scuffed my dick, deliberately or by accident, and with each skim, my breath hitched. When we fucked, I wasn't going to last.

"There you are." His grin turned lopsided and he eased his hand into my underwear. His fingers folded around my cock and with his gaze on mine, I had to fight to keep from shoving him against the kitchen island.

"Alex..." He jostled closer and with deft, firm fingers slid the condom over me. "In that restaurant, when you were stroking me under the table, all I wanted was for you to take me out the back and fuck me in one of those shiny men's room stalls." He brushed a kiss over my lips, teasing and then taking away.

I grabbed him by the neck—not too hard, just enough—and his grin turned sly. "Next time, tell me." I'd have done it. I'd take him back there just to live his fantasy.

"You knew."

I had known. It had been all over his face—in his half-lidded eyes and his plump, bitable, parted lips. Lips I sucked on now and teased between my teeth while driving him backward against the island.

"Fuck, yes," he murmured as soon as I abandoned his mouth for one of his tiny pebble-hard nipples. "Suck me."

I flicked his nipple under my tongue and worked his cock from his trousers, then went to my knees and took his warm, veined length between my lips and over my tongue.

"Alex..." His fingers speared into my hair. "Yes, Alex. Oh God... Fuck me. Please. Now."

I caught his shoulder, flipped him around, and drove him down over the island. His trousers fell, revealing a pert arse I loved to get under my hands.

"Here..." He handed a little bottle back, retrieving it from somewhere.

"Is that... hand sanitizer?"

"The bottle *was*... now it's not. Don't ask. Just use it."

"You think of everything."

"I've been caught out with you before. Now fuck me, Alex, before I fuck you."

I spread the cool lube, and with no other preparation, lined myself up against his hole and pushed. Sweet tension rolled down my cock, tingling pleasure low. An inch, a little more, and I thrusted hard.

"Ah, fuck." Dom spluttered and gripped the countertop. He tried to writhe but I pinned him down with a hand, the other spreading his cheeks to get a look at myself embedded deep. A thrill trickled down my spine.

"That all you got?"

I laughed and thrust, slapping against his ass. He cried out, ordered me to fuck him harder, and then there was nothing but the tight thrum of rocking into him and the slap of skin on skin. His grunts and mine. Rough and hard and fast. I found the perfect angle to make him moan and pistoned into him, losing all sense of where I ended and he began, until it was just us, locked together, chasing the high.

"Yes, come in me."

He knew, could hear it in my breaths, feel it in my grip. And when he ordered I come, the thrill of it tipped me over the edge, dancing ecstasy up my spine as I shuddered and spilled, captured in the glorious high.

"Fuck," Dom panted, as soon as I eased myself free.

I ran my hands up his back, watching our tricks bloom and flow and mingle, then kissed him between the shoulder blades. "Turn around."

He twisted in my arms. I kissed him before he could say something smart, gave him a few sliding tugs, making him groan, then went back to my knees.

"Ugh... God... I won't... Shit..." His hands mussed my hair, then twisted. His hips thrust, driving himself deeper down my throat, and then I found that perfect motion under my hand and mouth, riding his pleasure with him, building it higher.

"Fuck-gonna-come."

Bitter cum clogged the back of my tongue. I swallowed, sucked, needing this and him, the way he gave himself freely, how he lost himself in the moment. John shuddered, swore, and slumped against the counter, sex-drunk. To know I could do that to him had my heart warming all over again. I rose from my knees and wiped my mouth under his intense gaze. He threw an arm around my neck and dragged me into a messy, savage kiss.

I propped up my feet on a low coffee table, seated in a chair positioned by the window that enabled me to see Dom sprawled on his back, snoring softly, half wrapped in sheets, while also allowing me to watch the early morning sun rise over the Hudson River.

I'd made the decision.

We were leaving.

After coffee, I'd arrange our return flight to England and leave Kage's disappearance to the authorities. Whatever had happened to him, it wasn't worth losing Dom over. Between the assassination attempt and the police beating, we'd already skirted close to losing our freedom. My main weapons, money and my name, were worthless here. If John went down, I wouldn't be able to save him. I had some tricks left up my sleeves, but not many.

And losing Dom was unacceptable.

I retrieved the coin from my pocket and rubbed it warm between my finger and thumb. It was still an artifact, of course, I could feel as much now my trick was returning. Being with Dom last night had helped coax more of my power back, like it always did with him. He'd given so much of himself already—brought me back to life in so many ways. I owed him everything and I would not lose him on some needless crusade to save a man who was not who Dom thought him to be.

Dom stirred, coming around. He shifted onto his side and propped his head on a hand. "That's a view," he said, voice rough as he trawled his gaze over me.

I dropped the coin back into my pocket. "We leave today. We'll be back in England by this evening, UK time."

"Wait—what?" He sat up. The sheet pooled in his lap. Mussed from sleep and naked, he was delicious. Like I could go back over there and, in a few strides, have him moaning beneath me.

I swept those thoughts away. "It's too dangerous."

"We can't leave," he said, more angry than upset. "We're obviously on to something."

"We're meddling in affairs we don't understand."

He threw the sheet off, stood—naked and half hard, his body a buffet I'd never leave—and stalked around the bed, searching for underwear. At the sight of his firm arse and thighs—both I'd had my hands clamped on, driving myself between them—I tore my gaze away, trying to will my own arousal away and failing. He knew what he was doing. Distract me and win the argument that way. A smile broke through my efforts to remain impassive. "Strut around naked and I can't be held responsible for my actions."

His dark chuckle made resisting him a hundred times harder—and the rest of me.

He leaned over, rested a hand on my shoulder, and murmured against my cheek, "We're not going anywhere."

He'd found trousers and put them on. Such a shame. "We are."

"Alex, we didn't come this far to give up." He poured coffee from the pot and padded back to my side.

"A sniper tried to execute you," I said.

"Or you." He sipped his coffee and stared through the windows over New York. "It doesn't look like somewhere latents get killed for daring to breathe."

"One more infraction and you might be one of those latents."

"I'll behave." He grinned.

He didn't know how to behave; it was one of the reasons I loved him so fiercely.

"Stop growling," he said. "Yesterday was a mess. We've got a handle on it now."

"I do not growl," I told him, certain it was true.

"Oh, you do," he purred, tone full of innuendo.

I couldn't lose him. Even now, panic mixed with lust and love and fear and anger and all the things he roused in me. "If you're hurt again, I'm afraid I won't be able to control myself," I admitted. "My trick has returned, and while it's not like it was, it feels different. There's too much I don't understand. Too much I can't control. That's when mistakes happen." Too much I still didn't know about Kage, about myself, and about Dom... Elements of our lives that somehow intersected like strings on a murder-wall, only I couldn't see the wall, just the strings.

His smile slipped. "I just want to see if we can shake something loose by being here. Someone thinks we're dangerous enough to have killed. Why? What are they afraid of? Who even are *they*?"

"And what if the sniper's round had been an inch to the right? What if you hadn't dropped your fork?"

His smile had died now and a soldier stood next to me. A colder, harder man trained to get the job done. No matter what. "I served in Syria. I've survived warzones. One sniper doesn't frighten me."

"It frightens me."

"That means we're on to something important."

"Kage doesn't deserve your sacrifice."

He pulled a face. "I'm not sacrificing anything for him. I'm trying to find him and find out what's going on."

"In his note, he said not to do the right thing. He wasn't often right, but in this I have to agree. You should listen." I needed to move and left the window for the kitchen area, where I rinsed my coffee cup. I didn't want to argue, but Dom and I did not see the same things in this mission.

"You keep talking in the past tense," he said.

I held his stare. It had been weeks. Bullet holes, blood, a turned-over apartment. Kage wasn't coming back. I didn't need to say it. Dom wasn't a fool. He knew it too.

He leaned on the island counter. "If you went missing," he said softly, "I wouldn't ever stop looking."

His words screeched my thoughts to a halt. Then I set the mug down with a clunk. "And I you."

"Then it's settled."

"If you care about Kage as much as you do me, then I suppose it is."

"That's not what I meant."

"You care deeply for him. So we should continue to put our lives at risk to find him, if that's what you want."

"Alex, you know I—" He cut himself off and his expression muddled. "You know how I feel about you. And it's not the same."

My phone vibrated on the counter.

The message on the screen read: Trent: *How are you this fine morning?*

I scooped it up. A: *Great. Thank you. I need your help with something. Lunch?*

Trent: ...

"I'll call Gina and see if I can set up a meeting with Annie's family," Dom was saying as I watched the ellipses ripple on screen. "Annie and Kage were close," he added. "Her family might know more about his life here."

"Fine."

Trent: ... *I'd like that. I'll pick you up. Just you?*

I locked my phone and looked up to find Dom frowning. "Are we good?" he asked. "You're not about to shove me on a plane back to England?"

"What? No. Yes. I mean, no, we're not going back. Yet. But one more infraction and I'll tie you up and throw you on a plane myself."

His eyebrows lifted and his sly smile made a valiant comeback. "You say that like it's a bad thing."

10

D^{om}

I called Gina near midday and brought her up to date on all things stateside, including how a sniper had interrupted our dinner and the unfriendly reception from the NY cops. She didn't tell us to come back, but I could hear it in her voice.

"You sure this is worth it?" she asked.

I glanced over at Kempthorne, with his fingers tapping on a laptop, the smallest of frowns pinching his forehead. With him, I had a chance of finding out what was really going on. Sawyer was dead. Kage was missing. This wasn't going to ever go away unless we dealt with it. "I have to know, G."

Kempthorne's phone pinged. He closed the laptop and grabbed his coat. "I'll be back in a few hours."

"Hold on a sec," I told Gina and covered the phone with a hand. "Where are you going?" I asked Alex.

"To lunch."

"On your own?"

"No." He pulled on a slim fitting pair of expensive leather gloves and glanced up, surprised at my glare. Christ, he stood there like a model right off the pages of a swanky fashion mag—all tailored and handsome, his hair smoothed and his face guarded, making him even more aloof. He'd have gotten away with all that before, and I'd have let him go, because he was Kempthorne and he kept his secrets close, but that was *before*. Now, he regularly fucked my arse and I'd become familiar with his cock between my lips. So I held his gaze, waiting for the explanation.

"I'm meeting Trent," he said. "He's outside."

"Oh..." I blinked. "Just you two, huh?"

He jabbed between his fingers, driving the gloves home. "Does it bother you?"

"No." I wasn't worried. Despite Trent being in the same top five percent wealthy bracket, the preppy golden boy wasn't Kempthorne's type.

"All right then." He hesitated at the door, hand on the handle. "It really doesn't bother you?" He half-glanced back.

"Have fun," I said with a smirk. "Tell Trent I said hi."

He left and I lifted the phone to my ear. "Sorry, just dealing with something."

"I heard... Who is Trent?"

"Good question. Some harmless family friend, according to Kempthorne. Which reminds me, can you dig up everything you can find on Trent Anderson?"

"I'll ask Cas, she has a knack for digging up dirt on people—that is what you want, right?"

"He's probably squeaky clean, but yeah."

"You asked about Annie's family? They're all in the UK, but Kage's father lives in Greenwich, Connecticut — you'd think the Americans would make up their own town names instead of stealing ours."

"The settlers probably had better things to do, like survive. How far is Greenwich from me?"

"Hold on... let me... do the map thing... So, how's things with Kempthorne?" She sang that last bit.

"Fine, G."

"You sorted out your issue yet?"

"He has some power back."

"That'll cheer him up."

"Yeah..."

"Okay, so Greenwich is like... under an hour, by car. Kage's dad, William Mitchell, is some financial hedge fund bigwig. Kage put his home address down as next of kin when he er... when he joined us."

"D'yah think Kage's dad knows his son is missing? You haven't heard anything from him?"

"Kage never mentioned he even had a dad."

"No, not a word to me either." That couldn't be a good sign. My gut was telling me Kage and William may not have gotten along, but I also had a shit relationship with my dad that could easily be clouding my judgement. "I'll check him out..."

"Maybe take Kempthorne?"

"What's wrong with me going on my own?"

"You can be a bit… rough."

I laughed. "Christ, I'll shave and wear a shirt." It would have to be a cheap shirt. My good one had blood on it from the dinner.

She laughed, but it soon ended. "Hey, Dom?"

"Yeah?"

"Be careful. It's different there. I don't like the way they treat latents."

"You and me both, G." I ended the call and quickly typed out a text to Kempthorne. If I vanished, he'd know where to look.

Dom: *Going to see Kage's dad in Greenwich. Did Trent buy you a croissant? Enjoy lunch.*

I'd thrown on a clean shirt and was halfway out of the door when Kempthorne texted back: *He bought bagels. I do not like bagels.*

I laughed and hurried downstairs to the foyer to meet the Uber.

11

Trent had chosen the location for lunch, a high-ceilinged 1930s-style bar that served tiny burger buns on slates. Dark green and gold wallpaper and low-slung lights gave the place an intimate evening feel, despite the time of day.

"I hope you approve. It's not fine dining but it's one of my favorite hangouts when I'm in the city."

We sat at the bar, slung our coats over the back of the high-legged chairs, and ordered food and drinks. Trent was an easy person to like; energetic and breezy, he'd skirted through life on the back of his family's fortune. He'd studied law and was exceedingly bright but hadn't settled either with a family or a career, preferring to sample life's pleasures, as he called it, with a charming glint in his eye.

I envied his freedom. His life could have been mine, had I not been born a latent and turned into an experiment.

"So, how are you really? I've been meaning to ask but we've not really been alone, and I didn't want to go into too much with your assistant listening."

"Associate."

Trent's warm hand settled over mine on the bar top. "I heard about... everything. You've had a difficult time of things, lately." His fingers squeezed mine.

Dom's smile, his teasing, his theory that Trent was gay. I heard it all again now and wondered. I was not as people-aware as Dom, and trusted his judgement. He could be right about Trent, which left me in the difficult position of dissuading him without offending him. If Dom insisted we stayed, we would need Trent's local knowledge, and we'd need his connections, especially if trouble was determined to find us.

I extracted my hand and reached for my water. "It has been a challenge, but we're through the worst of it."

"Shall we switch to wine?" He waved the barman over and ordered the house white, without waiting for my reply.

The wine came, and Trent lifted his glass. "To old friends and better times."

I chinked my glass with his.

"Your message said you needed my help, Alex." His hand fluttered over my arm, not quite a grip, more a friendly touch. "Anything, name it. It's been so long and I've always thought we had a connection."

Any kind of connection was news to me. "Well, yes…" I smiled politely. "You see, there's something that's been bothering me and I really must know."

"Oh?" His hand settled, fingers squeezing mine again. He leaned in and his freckles absorbed the golden glow from the bar's soft lighting.

My phone pinged in my pocket. "Excuse me."

Dom: *Kage's dad isn't home. Big house. Definitely compensating. Maid says he'll be back this evening. Gonna wait. How's lunch?*

I fear you may be right, I typed back.

Dom: *I'm always right.* He added a winking face.

I wasn't sure what to make of his casual reaction. If Dom had gone to lunch with Kage, as an example, I would not have been as blasé. I trusted him, absolutely, but wouldn't have trusted Kage. Yet Trent's presence hardly bothered Dom at all. Was it that he didn't care? I pushed that thought aside as unlikely, but it niggled all the same.

"Everything all right?" Trent asked.

"Yes, just my… just Dom, checking in."

"He's nice." He said *nice* like he'd chewed glass and had been forced to swallow it. "What kind of associate is he?"

"A highly valuable one."

"No, I meant… Never mind." Trent laughed at his own question and sipped his wine.

I should tell him we're partners, in the romantic sense. We were partners. Weren't we?

"You were about to ask my opinion on something, Alex?" Trent's hand brushed mine, fingers skimming.

"Trent." I plucked my hand away. "Dom and I are involved."

He blinked, face blank.

"Romantically."

"Oh." He laughed too loud. "Right. Sure. I see... Yeah, I get that... I guess. I mean, he's..." He winced. "I don't see, actually. He's not really your type." He said it through smiles, but the tone grated.

"I'm afraid you don't know me well enough to know my type." I wasn't sure I had a type. I had Dom. And that was all there had ever been. Every other encounter in my life had been out of passing need, nothing near what I had with him. John Domenici was my only type.

"I'd like to change that, Alex."

Oh dear. I cleared my throat. "I suggested we meet because I'm having some trouble with clearing up some things surrounding the *event* during dinner."

"I'm so sorry—about the police, all of it." He reached for my face. "Your jaw? There's a slight bruise—"

I jerked back. He really was exceptionally *hands on*. It hadn't bothered me quite as much before but now I knew where that energy was coming from, the touches felt like an invasion. "Yes, again, thank you... But that's not what I'm interested in. You see, the sniper—"

"There was a sniper? Really? God. I just thought it was some kind of shooter who didn't like latents. It happens all the time—Did you know more latents are shot in America than are born? Soon there won't be any left."

Good lord. "Dom and I were targeted, specifically, Trent." The sound of his name seemed to slow him down.

"How awful. Why?"

"That's not important. What is important is who knew we were going to be at Per Se at that time, besides the three of us. Who did you tell?"

"Oh?" He frowned. "Oh, I see! You think someone I told arranged it?! Oh my god. Really?"

"It stands to reason, as Dom and I didn't tell anyone."

He downed his wine and waved the barman over for a refill. "Damn, let me think... My assistant knew, she made the reservation for us, of course. My er... my sister knew. I mentioned you were in New York and she asked if we were available for dinner, that's when I told her we were having dinner together. Daddy knew." He snorted. "He knows everything. I can't sneeze without him knowing."

"Why did your father know?"

His blue eyes narrowed, and his jittery motions slowed. "It's as though... I don't know, you don't have parents—I don't mean it like that, just that... I'm not as free as you think. Sometimes I wonder if the Andersons ever left the nineteen-twenties? I'm supposed to be the eldest boy—man." He cleared his throat. "Daddy fears I'm... being difficult, when it comes to life in general. He thinks me incapable. It's suffocating, honestly."

"I'm sorry to hear that." So he'd told several people, who in turn could have told others, without realizing the information could be sensitive.

Trent had worked himself up and his smooth, charming persona had broken down into a man trapped between nerves and probably anger. He swirled the wine in his glass.

His shoulders folded in. "Did you... did you ever..." He glanced around. "*Come out...* to your parents?"

"They were rather more concerned with me being a latent. Anything else didn't feature in their thoughts."

His jittery nerves softened with concern. For me.

"Please don't pity me. It was all a very long time ago." Not all of it. Much of it I'd learned in the past few months and none of it sat well with me. But we weren't here to discuss me.

"When I was seventeen, I told Daddy I like men and he froze my bank accounts, my trust fund, everything. Unless I marry a woman, I'm in limbo. Financially. In life. All of it."

"Good lord. How archaic."

He laughed. "It was you, you know?"

"I'm sorry—what was?"

"At Chad's wedding, when we were boys. The last time I saw you. I couldn't take my eyes off you."

Goodness, Dom had been spectacularly right. "Trent—"

"No, I've held it in for so long, I must say it."

"I find some things are better kept inside—"

"You're so very English. I do love that about you."

He was getting rather heated, and loud, and this conversation was perhaps not for public consumption. I raised my hand and summoned the barman. "Can we get the bill?"

"The check," Trent corrected, finishing his second glass of wine in one gulp.

We gathered our coats and left, walking into bright winter sunshine and the endless buzz of New York's streets. A delivery van unloaded boxes ahead, scaffolding blocked some of the pavement, and a queue had formed outside a hotel for some reason. We maneuvered around it all and came to a small, grassy area, tucked between multiple high-rises. A viciously cold wind whipped between the buildings.

"I'd fooled around before the wedding, but I saw you there, looking stunning. You were chatting with another boy, I think, a cousin of mine. I was fiercely jealous."

Would it be impolite to text Dom and have him return to the city and extract me from a situation I had no idea how to handle? Trent talked some more about that wedding from so long ago I barely remembered any of it, or much of him, at the time.

"Alex?"

"Hm."

He stepped in—his mouth met mine. I froze. His tongue slid between my lips, his body pressed close, hard, warm, smelling of spicy cologne. The cold wind whipped around us. I pushed at his chest, making a conscious effort to stop my trick from blasting him ten feet back into a pile of snow.

"I'm sorry, I had to," he said. "I've wanted that for so long." Color flushed his cheeks, making his freckles glow.

A distant memory tugged at my emotions. Straps holding me down, instruments forced into my veins. Helpless. Used. This wasn't that, but it triggered some of the same fear. "Trent, you're... lovely, but I'm with Dom."

"Your assistant." He laughed and thrust his hands into his coat pockets.

"Associate," I corrected, again, and then added, "My partner."

"But he's not like us!"

"I don't know what this *us* is, but it's not what I want."

"He's a common latent," he snarled.

I smiled. "It's time I went back to the apartment. I'll get a cab." I turned on my heel.

"Alex. Don't go. Alex, wait."

Multiple yellow cabs drifted through traffic. I'd heard catching one was a skill but needed to put some distance between Trent and I before my trick did it for us. Stepping off the sidewalk, I lifted a hand and hooked a cab, then hastily climbed inside. "Hudson Yard." A sign blinked for my thumbprint. I tugged off a glove and jabbed at it, ignoring Trent standing outside the car like an abandoned puppy.

"Twice the cost for latents," the cab driver snarled.

"Fine."

The cab pulled into slow-moving traffic.

My phone pinged:

D: I'm bored. Has Trent hit on you yet?

K: I don't knw how but I belivce I may hav encuraged him. I noticed the typos after I'd sent it.

The ellipses started, then stopped, then started again. It seemed like forever until he replied.

D: want me to rescue you?

I exhaled, some fragmented part of me sliding back into place. How did he know the right thing to say or do when even I didn't know what that right thing was? I knocked on the plastic screen between me and the driver. "Change of plan, please take me to Greenwich."

"Which Greenwich?"

"What?"

"Greenwich Village? Greenwich Avenue?"

"No, Greenwich outside the city."

"I can but it'll cost you. A lot."

"Please..." I dropped back in the seat and messaged Dom: *I'm coming to you.*

D: Great. I haz donuts.

I smiled. Strange, how so few words on a screen could change one's mood for the better, in an instant. But it wasn't the words, not really, it was Dom.

12

D^{om}

Kempthorne leaped from the cab. The wind circled around him, whipping back his coat, as though he starred in a men's Christmas cologne ad, all windswept and sexy. His face wasn't happy though. He regarded the enormous house set back from the street, then cast his glance around. I threw a wave from inside my rental car—hired while I'd been twiddling my thumbs in Greenwich. His eyes brightened and a smile flashed across his lips.

"You all right?" I asked the second he climbed into the car, bringing a blast of cold air with him.

"Yes, I..." He stalled in the middle of taking off his gloves. "May I kiss you?"

I almost laughed. "You've never asked be—"

He lunged across the center armrest and smacked a

kiss on my lips that began as wooden and awkward, then heated my bones as his gloved hand slipped behind my back and the frantic rush eased into a smooth, silken kiss. It ended just as I was beginning to get into it, and he shifted back into the passenger seat, licking his lips. "Sorry. I've been thinking about that the entire drive out here."

He'd tasted of sweet wine. What had happened during the lunch to rattle him? "You okay?"

"Hm? Yes. Better. Now."

I almost asked if Trent had done something, but I had to trust Kempthorne would tell me, if it was important. "I've been watching the Mitchell's house. Donut?" I reached into the back seat and produced a box of donuts. "Americans have screwed up donuts, too, but they're a sugar rush."

He grabbed one and finished it in three bites. "Terrible." He grabbed a second.

"William Mitchell is a financial manager," I said, watching him thumb sugar from his chin. "One of those jobs nobody really knows what they do but they rake in a shit-ton every year."

"Kage's family is wealthy?"

"Looks that way. I mean, Kage does have that smooth confidence that comes from money." Kempthorne threw me a questioning look. Of course he'd have no idea what that confidence was. I couldn't explain it either, not without offending him. It was the confidence people had when they walked into shops or restaurants and didn't have to worry over the price tag on anything. They didn't have to check their wallets twice or rummage around for change.

"And he never mentioned any of this to you?"

"Nope. He didn't talk about his family, at all."

"Familial friction?" he asked, appraising the house.

"Probably. For everything he screwed up, Kage was trying to do good. He has that cop mentality. He told me he joined the FBI to try and help latents—which makes a whole lot more sense after what we've seen here."

"He's driven to right wrongs," Kempthorne said. "Wrongs that started at home?"

"A latent kid got killed at his school. Nobody did a bloody thing. Kage said he knew he had to do more. Maybe there's more to that story."

Kempthorne looked at me askance and was about to speak when a sleek black Tesla pulled into the driveway. Automatic garage doors opened, then rumbled closed behind it.

"Daddy's home." I smiled.

We climbed from the car and crossed the street. The wind rushed through the spindly, naked trees lining the wide sidewalk, kicking up fallen, brittle leaves. Old snow had been piled along the cleared sidewalks and driveways.

I flicked my jacket collar up. "You know what I don't get? The link between Sawyer and Kage. How are they connected?"

"We'll find it."

We stopped on the porch at the door. Kempthorne raised an eyebrow, waiting for my lead.

"How do you want to play this?" I blew into my

cupped hands. If we stayed on the front porch any longer my balls would freeze. "Good cop, bad cop?"

"You're dressed for bad cop. Is that a new shirt?"

I rolled my eyes. "C'mon, we both know *I'm* the good cop. All Americans think posh Brits are villains. And yeah. I picked it up today. You like it?"

He tilted his head, studying my shirt so intensely his gaze began to sizzle my skin. "It will look much better on our bedroom floor." He knocked at the Mitchell's door, lips quirked, knowing I couldn't think up a sassy comeback quickly enough.

The maid answered. "Oh." The mousey haired rotund woman had the kind of mean face that suggested she beat rugs for fun, and had the muscles for it too. We'd already met, when she'd told me to get off the porch or she'd get a gun. "You again," she said.

"Hi." I grinned. "Is Mister Mitchell home now?"

"I assume you saw him arrive?" Her beady-eyed gaze tried to make me smaller.

"Good afternoon, I'm Alexander Kempthorne." Alex stepped forward and offered his hand.

Fuck me, the maid might as well have swooned in his arms. She smiled, cracking her icy mask, and shook his hand.

"What a lovely ring," he said. "Platinum?"

"Oh no," she giggled. "Just steel."

"Oh well, it is lovely, all the same."

Color rushed up her wrinkled neck and flushed her cheeks. "Oh, you think so? You're too kind."

Gina was right. Alex could wear devil horns and a tail

and still sweet-talk his way into a nunnery with just a hello, and he had no idea he had such a superpower.

"Wait here, Mister Kempthorne and *you*." She gave me the side-eye, then shut the door.

Alex arched his eyebrow. "You're definitely the bad cop."

"Just because I can't Hugh Grant it up."

"*Who* is Hugh Grant?"

I snorted. "We can argue about good cop bad cop tonight... in bed. Do you own cuffs?"

Something dangerous and hungry flicked across Kempthorne's face and lit me up like a sparkler. Trick sprang to my fingers, thinking the sudden lurching heartbeat was a sign of attack. I quickly clenched my hands behind my back and chuckled. "Dayam, Kempthorne. You *do* own cuffs."

"Mostly for their intended purpose—"

"Who the hell have you handcuffed? Did a board meeting get out of hand?"

"Do you remember I was once Tasered at the theater?"

"Yeah, which you still haven't explained—"

"Oh, well, that same night I was forced to get rather creative with a pair of handcuffs." He smiled at the memory, making me wish I'd been there.

"You have to tell me *everything*."

The door opened and Mister William Mitchell filled its place. Big didn't cover it. The man was six-foot-plus, with a body that had been all muscle once. Middle age had loosened things, but he still carried enough lean weight that if he decided to pick up the weights again, it wouldn't take much for him to go from Dad-body to buff.

"Mister Mitchell?" Kempthorne asked.

"Obviously." He folded his arms, and it was like folding two trees. Kage was *nothing* like him, except maybe the eyes. Like burned caramel. In Kage the amber eye color was stunning, but in his dad the color reminded me of cold copper. And he wasn't as enamored with Kempthorne as the maid had been but seemed interested in me. The crawl of his gaze was clinical and thorough, tinged with knowing.

"Have you heard from Kage in the past few weeks?" I asked.

His eyes narrowed, then softened, as though he'd fought with something in his own mind and surrendered. "It's not every day two Brits come knocking. I guess you should come in."

The house was as sprawling inside as it was outside. High ceilings, white walls, cream carpet, and bunches of cream and orange flowers. There was no sign there had ever been kids, and although the house was spotless, it lacked a heart. Even its psychic resonance was eerily quiet.

"Want coffee?" Mister Mitchell asked. "Or tea, I guess? That is what you Brits drink, right?"

"No, thank you." Kempthorne and I followed him into a large open-plan lounge with a white piano in one corner. I hadn't known pianos came in white.

"Take a seat."

The sofa cushions tried to swallow me and while I

wriggled, trying to get comfortable, Kempthorne settled, immediately at ease.

"I'm guessing from the accents you're the English team who worked with my son recently?"

"Yes." Kempthorne angled himself toward me and William, who settled his bulk into the opposite sofa. "I'm not sure how much you're aware of your son's work, Mister Mitchell?"

"Not much. We er... we don't speak."

My heart sank a little. "Have you spoken to him at all recently?"

"Not for about six months. I knew he was in England from his Facebook status."

"Have the police been in contact with you?"

He sighed. "Yeah. I know he's missing. Not much I can do. I told them the same as I'll tell you. We don't really have... we're not very close. He left when I divorced his mother. He was old enough to do his own thing. I'd get a card during the holidays sometimes."

"You've had nothing from him in the past few weeks? Nothing at all? No texts, emails?"

"No, like I said, we go months without talking."

Shit. Kage's dad was a dead end.

Kempthorne got to his feet and picked up a framed photograph on the fireplace mantel. "Kage and his mother?"

Mister Mitchell nodded. "Er, yeah."

"Do you mind if Dom takes a look?" Kempthorne held the frame out for me.

"No, it's fine, I mean... you probably know him better than I do."

"Why'd you say that?" I asked, reaching for the photograph.

"He spoke about you, a while ago. Might have been the last time I talked with him."

"What did he say?" Kempthorne asked, intrigued.

I took the photo and lost myself in its image. It had to have been taken ten years ago, at least. Kage had his mother's lean figure and long-legged grace. Her smile too. She was gorgeous, and her son was well on the way to breaking hearts, although he had some filling out to do. The photo was one of those posed family arrangements, which always looked fake to me, although in this one the family appeared to be genuinely smiling.

"Who's the boy?" Seated in front of them on the floor, with his legs tucked under him, was a boy, younger than Kage. Pre-teen, skinny arms and legs, with eyes like saucers. He smiled, but there was something missing, like the something missing from this house. As though it was all for show, with no soul.

Mister Mitchell's entire body folded in, making himself smaller. "That's little Greyson. He er... we lost him not long after that photo was taken."

Lost him? A story simmered in my memory, a story about a boy Kage had known, the latent boy who had vanished. What had Kage said... something about a brother who had died?

The boy who had died hadn't been some random kid from school.

He'd been Kage's little brother. And his parents had been the people who'd done nothing. A lot of things about Kage Mitchell suddenly slotted into place.

'He had some issues...' Kage had told me. *'He got beat on.'*

I assessed William Mitchell again. A big man, lonely now, haunted in this big house.

Nobody wanted a latent kid. Especially a family with money and expectations.

'He'd vanished like I'd dreamed him up.'

Bile sizzled the back of my throat. "Did you own a firepit back then, Mister Mitchell?" I couldn't help it. Had to ask. Kage had left the second he'd been able to, not because of a divorce, but because he knew what had happened to Greyson, his little brother.

"I... I don't remember. Maybe. Sure, most everyone had them..." The man's eyes glazed over with memories. A twitch, a flicker, a knowing shimmered in that burned amber and was gone. The truth. He peered at me and he knew Kage had told me—he *knew,* and just blinked back, like shit happens. Then the fucker smiled.

Trick tingled down my fingers and bloomed across the silver photo frame.

As quick as a whip, Kempthorne snatched the frame from my fingers. He caught my wrist and pulled me into motion, snapping me out of my freefall into dangerous territory. I had to get out of that house or I was going to lose my shit.

"Well, I think it's time we left." He shoved me in the general direction of the front door and whirled around. "Oh, you were saying how you knew us, Mister Mitchell?" Kempthorne asked, like an afterthought.

"Kage said he... Well..." The big man swallowed so loudly it ticked like a clock. "He said he had a new family."

13

A lexander

Trick prickled my skin—not mine. Energy sizzled around Dom, lighting him up to my latent sight. Whatever had triggered the reaction, he wasn't going to be able to hold in his trick. I shoved the family photo into Mister Mitchell's hand, keeping hold of Dom's wrist in the other, absorbing as we moved toward the door.

"Thank you," I said, mind split between courtesy and getting Dom away as quickly as possible.

"Oh, okay... If he contacts me, should I call you?"

"He won't fucking contact you," Dom snarled. Something vicious and terrifying burned behind Dom's eyes— a ruthlessness I'd known was in him but hadn't seen. Mister Mitchell was saying something, but I had hold of Dom and ushered him out of the door. He resisted a little, his trick pulsing, surging, trying to snap free and spin out of control. But I had its threads, and him.

By the time we'd made it onto the street and reached the car, he breathed too hard and too fast. A horrible moan pealed from his lips, a sound of grief that made me want to pull him into my arms and hold him until the world went away. Instead, I pushed him against the side of the car, trapping him with my body. He slumped into me, mumbled something about bones and latents and firepits, then his arms folded around me, hauling me close, and his fingers dug in, all of him clutching on. He clung to me as though I was the only one keeping him afloat.

"I've got you." I didn't know what I was saying, didn't know if it meant anything, or if it helped.

He shuddered and his trick sparked like shorted circuits. "Get me out of here before I burn that whole fucking house down with him still in it."

I drove us north and kept on driving into the night, until sleep clawed at my mind. "I have to stop."

It had been hours since we'd left the Mitchell house, but Dom still ran hot, sizzling next to me as he stared out of the passenger window.

"Okay," he croaked. "There was a hotel or something a mile back. We can stop there for the night. If they rent to latents..."

The Salt Point Club was a mix of leisure facilities, golf, and swimming, with a sprawling hotel attached, surrounded by pine trees. Music thumped and laughter sailed through our room's broken window that wouldn't close. Some kind of party was happening in the main building. The grey sheets on the bed had once been white. Suspicious stains in the carpet added to the character. I had to wonder if we hadn't been latents, whether we'd have a more luxurious room.

I dropped the room key on the sideboard and poked at a dog-eared room service menu. *Dom should eat.* He sat on the end of the bed by the door, then braced his arms behind him and, with his eyes closed, lifted his chin.

"I need to go out," he said, springing to his feet.

"What?"

"I just..." He flicked sparkling trick from his hands. It fizzled in the air like glitter. "I need to be outside. Right now. I'm losing my fuckin' mind. Let's get a drink."

I'd have liked nothing more than to get out of the dingy room, but he was dangerously close to spiraling. "You can't use trick where you'll be seen."

All swagger and sass, he grinned and snatched the room key. "That's why I've got you to suck me off."

I swallowed. "Interesting choice of words."

His fingers locked with mine and he nudged close, muscling against me. The sharp glitter of his eyes darkened, and his smile switched to a grimace. "You know what that son of a bitch, William Mitchell, did? He killed his youngest son and burned his remains in a barrel. Kage found them. He told me... not all of it, but he told me about the bones. His father killed his little latent brother. That's why Kage is who he is, that's why he's fucked up, like the rest of us. So I need to go outside and I need to lose my shit for a while and forget everything before I blow. This is how I handle shit." His eyes softened. "Come with me, please. I need you to come with me. If I go alone I'll pick a fight with some American twat and end up with another mark on my card."

The horror of his words regarding Kage's brother slid off, unable to sink in, because I wouldn't let them. I couldn't feel all of *that* with everything else too. But I could feel Dom. I twisted my grip around his, locking his fingers with mine. He was hurting because he was good. I'd protect him. From himself. From everyone else. I'd been protecting him since we met. "All right."

Outside, we joined the flow of partygoers. Most of them were young, college-age, and either high or drunk. Nobody appeared to be interested in us, until we got to the main entrance door of the building where a doorman was checking IDs.

He crooked a fat finger at us and glanced at our cards. "No latents."

"This is bollocks." Dom started forward.

I flung out a hand and steered him away. The guard threw us a glare, and Dom threw back a middle finger salute, eager to start a fight with a man twice his size. Slipping his hand in mine, I led him around the back of a building, away from prying eyes.

"For fuck's sake," he grumbled, running a hand through his hair. "That guy's a tosser."

Power sizzled under my hand, where I held him. He slumped against the wall and sighed hard through his nose. "Fuck."

The Mitchell's revelation had hit him hard. He felt

things deeply, despite hiding his soft heart all the years I'd known him. I braced an arm over his shoulder, crowding close. His trick sizzled, threatening to spark between us. I'd never seen him like this. He'd always kept his calm in my presence, probably eager to show he was in control. But things had changed. We'd changed. "You need to calm down," I told him.

"I know." His throat moved. "But it's all so fucked up."

I forced a knee between his, smothering him, giving him something else to think about. His eyes glinted in the dark, widening and drinking me in. To have him look at me as though I was his everything—it cinched my heart, made me breathless, made my blood rush and my head spin. I brushed my knuckles down his bristly jaw, then skipped my fingers down his neck.

He shivered and his eyes rolled. "Yes."

"Hey..." a voice said from somewhere behind me. I peered over my shoulder, sending a scowl into the night. Someone had to interrupt us now? Really?

A hooded girl stood in the shadows, hands tucked into her pockets. She jerked her chin. "Follow me."

That was a terrible idea, but a glance at Dom's curious face and the sparkle of chaos in his eyes suggested he was going, and I had better join him if he was going to get through the night without finding trouble.

"Don't." But I said it with a smile.

"C'mon, hm?"

"You're latents, right?" the girl asked, after we hadn't moved. "You're gonna wanna see this."

Dom slid into motion, maneuvering out from under me, then caught my hand and tugged.

"I'm unconvinced following strangers into the woods is a good idea," I said.

He tossed a devil-may-care grin over his shoulder. "What's she gonna do?"

Good question. Dom couldn't see her latent glow, but I could, especially in the thick darkness. Her trick pulsed a confident gold. The petite, wily woman glanced over her shoulder, nodded, and pushed through the bushes onto a separate footpath lit by low pathway lights. We moved away from the thumping beat of the party, down a gravel path, deeper into the trees and toward new sounds of people and music. Another party?

The path opened into a clearing in front of a huge timber-clad red barn. Ancient equipment rusted outside, but inside, the double height barn sparkled with lights, as though the entire place had been filled with floodlights. I shielded my eyes, squinting into the glare, waiting for my eyes to adjust.

The woman chuckled. "Oh man, you're a seer?!" She grinned. "Nice. You'll get used to it. Come on in."

Dom raised an eyebrow. "What are you seeing?"

Music thumped, laughter bubbled. It wasn't any different from the party we'd been barred from, except trick flowed and sparked and bloomed, dancing around and through a crowd of perhaps a hundred latents. Some danced, some gathered in groups around a table, collecting drinks. "Latents..." I mumbled, unsure. "They're all latents."

Dom drifted forward, and in a few steps, we were among them. Nobody asked for our ID, nobody cared who we were. Trick simmered and flowed.

"What is this place?" Dom asked our guide.

She shrugged. "We always find ways to *shine*." Trick flashed in her eyes. She flicked a gesture toward the drinks table and trick sparked from her nails. "Have fun, huh? We don't turn friends away. Ever." She swaggered off, leaving Dom and I among latents freely displaying trick and some appearing to share it while dancing close, as he and I often did in our intimate moments.

"Bloody hell." Dom's gaze drank them in. The shifting light touched his face, sparking in his eyes. The sight of them, so many… and him, his eyes wide, his face alight— the words wouldn't come. He had no idea how he shone too. Brighter than all of them.

"This is insane," he muttered. His gaze settled on me and, without a thought, he took my hand again and poured trick into and under my skin, scorching my bones.

I hissed. His fingers tightened. Not letting go. He should let go, I'd take too much, I always did.

"Push it back," he said, grinning.

This was dangerously close to how we did things when we were intimate—the push and pull of trick through our bodies in a rhythm so like sex that it was the same in my mind. I pulled him close and hissed in his ear, "Not unless you want me to fuck you right here." My voice had turned slow and deep, shredded with need.

He laughed, golden sparks dancing through his eyes, then he dragged me toward the drinks table. "A drink then?"

His smile was worth the discomfort of trying to rein myself under control.

"A seer, huh?" a young man said from behind the makeshift bar. Dom nodded, smiling toward me, as though proud. He took a cup from him, but I barely saw, too dazzled by the crowd.

"Rare," the man said.

"He is."

They were discussing *me*. Dom placed a cup in my hand and chuckled. "We're a bit... surprised by all this. Alex?"

"Yes?"

The near laugh made his trick pulse, and it was all I could do not to grab him with both hands and kiss him.

"It's all right," the man said. "Seers see and feel it all more than the rest of us. Take some of this, it will tone things down."

For the first time, I blinked at the man, taking him in. Ginger-haired, same age as Dom and I, with a tattoo on the side of his neck. He held out a vial of dark liquid.

"Nah, mate." Dom dismissed him with a wave. "But thanks for the drinks."

Black liquid sloshed in the vial. "What is it?" I asked.

"Ink," the barman said.

It wasn't any ink I knew. I studied the man again, really studied. Stocky build, hard blue eyes, the eagle tattoo on his neck hinting at military.

He nodded, smile growing, and offered his hand to shake. "Name's Josh."

"Good evening." I gave his hand a shake and took the vial, drawn to its strange black shimmer. Dom shook Josh's hand and sipped his drink, eyeing me, watching for my reaction.

"Nice accent," Josh drawled. "A few drops of Ink on your wrist makes everything clearer, trust me."

"No offense, mate, but what's in it?" Dom pressed.

The man shrugged, told us again to give it a try, and then got drawn into another conversation.

Dom cocked his head, watching me seesaw the vial and slosh its smoky black contents. "Have you seen it before?" he asked.

"No." The Ink sloshed in slow motion, my senses buzzing, overstimulated, distorting my thoughts.

Dom and Josh talked again, with Dom trying to steer the man back toward the subject of what this *Ink* was made of. Josh only said it was made for latents, and that we'd like it. I wasn't bespelled enough by the American latents to go ahead and try what I assumed to be a drug without further investigation.

"LOA!"

"Shit!"

"Run!"

"NOBODY MOVE—STAY WHERE YOU ARE!"

People scattered in all directions. The table fell, drinks splashed. Dom hauled me between the barn stalls and out of a back door before I'd had a chance to get a look at who had burst into the gathering. Screams erupted behind us. Angry shouts. The sounds of countless feet thumping on dirt.

We swerved through bushes, over a manicured lawn, and down a bank, onto another meandering pathway that cut through a forest of bamboo. By the time we arrived at an ornate footbridge and a burbling stream, we'd left the barn, the raid, and the noise far behind.

"Christ." Dom doubled over, breathing hard. "I'm out of shape." He slumped against the little footbridge's rail and laughed. "I so needed that... What a rush."

"Hm, yes, fleeing the authorities, always at the top of my to-do list." I panted, breathing as hard as him. We hadn't been followed, but that didn't mean they wouldn't search the woods. We couldn't stop for long.

"You okay?" he asked, when I should have been asking him that.

I gripped the rail and breathed in the sweet smell of damp pine and the creek trickling below the little bridge. "Good." It had been a rush.

Dom's hand stroked down my back. "Because you look frazzled."

"The gathering was highly stimulating."

"Stimulating, huh?" Smiling, he took his hand from my lower back and folded his arms on the rail. I immediately grieved the loss of his touch and the trick that came with it.

"Do you have that vial?" he asked.

I took the Ink from my pocket and handed it over.

He examined it, swirling the smoky liquid inside. "Josh is ex-military, probably latent special forces, although he didn't say as much—we never do. He said Ink is widely available, if you know who to ask."

I waited, sensing Dom had more to add. He rarely spoke about his time in the military. I knew much of it, having bought the information from Sawyer, but even his CO didn't know everything Dom had been involved in. Sometimes, I wondered if even Dom knew the extent of it —and if he realized its significance.

He handed the vial back. "They use it to control latent soldiers."

"Control how?"

"They charge them up with artifacts, administer Ink, and they have themselves the perfect super-powerful puppets."

This wasn't news to him, even if it was the first time I'd heard about such a thing. It was possibly—highly likely even—he'd been subjected to trials of Ink. The British Military would have called it something else, but Dom knew what the smoky substance was.

The sounds of gunfire peppered the quiet.

I tucked the vial away in my pocket. "We need to leave."

"The car keys are in the hotel room."

"Then we'd better hurry."

14

D^{om}

People in blue jackets branded with the high-vis white letters *LOA* swarmed the front of the hotel. Latents they'd already caught had been rounded up in the parking lot. I didn't plan to be among them. The last thing I needed was another mark on my card. I just had to slip back into our room, grab our things, and we'd be out of there.

I left Kempthorne hidden in shadow at the corner of the building, keeping a lookout, and crept along the rear of the hotel, under the row of windows. Ours was easy to spot. With a bit of persuasion, the window frame popped open. We didn't have any bags, just our ID cards and car keys. I scooped up the keys and hustled with Kempthorne to the rental car, tucked at the far end of the parking lot.

The latent cops were more interested in the latents

they'd already caught and lined up outside than guests leaving the hotel.

We pulled out of there without being stopped. And as I watched the hotel's welcome sign shrink in our rearview mirror, I couldn't shake the feeling that our escape had been suspiciously easy.

It was true what they say, NYC never sleeps. But I needed to. There was still traffic at the crack of dawn. I rolled the rental into Hudson Yard, struggling to keep my eyes open. Kempthorne used his thumb to buzz us up to the swanky apartment. He looked as roughed-up as I felt, with his shirt untucked and his eyes bloodshot. We'd take a shower, fall into bed, and grab a few hours shut-eye. After that, we could regroup and figure out what happened next.

I'd learned a few things about Kage Mitchell, but not why he'd been taken or where he was. And with the latent cops breathing down our necks, maybe it was time to go back to Cecil Court.

My phone rang as the elevator pinged our floor and the doors rumbled open. "Gina, hey?"

"Hey, sorry it's late—"

I rubbed my eyes. "It's early here."

"Oh yeah, right, listen... You have a letter."

"A what?"

"A letter, you know, sent through the post."

"People still do that?" I clomped out of the elevator after Kempthorne. A warm bed was calling my name, and maybe a lazy hand job if Kempthorne would allow me to go down on him. He'd probably fall asleep during. It *had* happened before.

He pressed his thumb to the locked apartment door. "I could sleep for a week."

"I guess," Gina said. "It's stamped by the MOD, so I thought I'd call you..."

"Ugh... Does it look official?" I was too tired for their shit.

"It's handwritten."

Handwritten? Sawyer. It had to be. Nobody else would write me from the MOD. He could have sent it before he'd died. "Shit, open it."

Kempthorne glanced back at me at the same time as he opened the door. "What is it?"

"Mister Domenici, Mister Kempthorne," one of two suit-wearing men said. They flanked Trent on the sofa. But they didn't wear suits like Kempthorne wore suits—with class—they wore suits like the US government wore suits—packing heat. "Gina... I'll call you back."

"Wait, what's going on—?"

I ended the call and slowly closed the door behind us, thoughts racing. Government. That meant LOA. We'd just fled what amounted to an illegal gathering where latents had flaunted their tricks in the open. If they knew I'd been there, I'd get a third mark on my ID, and I was fucked. Had it been a setup? Had Trent fucking *known*? No, he couldn't have. We hadn't even known where we were going.

The skinny guy on the left got to his feet and flicked open his wallet, showing Kempthorne a very clear ID with LOA in large blue letters. He let me see as I approached Kempthorne's left and tucked my hands into my pockets. Trent sat very still.

"Agent Pierce," Kempthorne said, his smooth voice granular from lack of sleep.

"And this is my partner, Agent Palliser."

Agent Palliser chewed gum. He resembled the type of man who liked to color swastikas with crayons.

"What can we do for you?" Kempthorne asked, running a trembling hand through his hair.

"Well, it's what you can do for us." Pierce smiled, as though we were all friends. He planted a hand on his hip, revealing a hint of holstered gun. This wasn't London. And these people weren't the toothless IRL. The LOA didn't use Tasers. If we pissed them off, we'd get a bullet between the eyes, Kage Mitchell style. I almost missed Kage. At least he could be reasoned with.

If shit went south, and we had to go full-latent on their arses, could Kempthorne's money and name get us on a flight back to England before these guys locked us up and threw away the key?

"Where were you both last night?"

Fuck. Fuck. Fuck.

"I already told you," Trent squeaked. "They were with me."

Christ, he was a terrible liar.

"That's right," Kempthorne said.

Pierce frowned at Trent and then back at Kempthorne. He'd be an idiot to buy it. "Then how do you explain your IDs being used at a hotel upstate, at an illegal latent gathering?"

"Stolen," Trent blurted. "Tell them, Alex. They were both stolen at that place we went to."

"Yes." Kempthorne glided toward the kitchen area. "Last night—foolish really—Dom and I left our IDs in our coats, and when we left, they were missing. We didn't think much of it."

Palliser hadn't taken his eyes off me. He was either into guys or he didn't believe a word of the bullshit Trent and Kempthorne were shoveling his way, and he was one twitch away from going for his gun.

"What do you think of this, Mister Domenici?" Palliser asked. I couldn't be sure he'd blinked since we'd arrived.

"Yeah… right. That's what happened."

"You lost your IDs?"

"Yup."

"Coffee?" Kempthorne asked cheerily.

"You're aware that losing your ID will earn you an infraction, Mister Domenici?" Palliser got to his feet, which prompted Trent to stand as well and then rattle between them like the ball on a pinball table.

"I er… I'm new to all this." I shrugged, hoping I looked sweet and innocent, even though I'd never been sweet and innocent in my entire life.

"Your records indicate you're already at two infractions."

"A misunderstanding… during dinner," Trent beamed, trying to come to my rescue. "They're really both very sorry for any trouble caused."

Palliser got all up in my face. He had a tiny scar through his right eyebrow. Heavier than Pierce, Palliser could probably put me on my arse if we went toe-to-toe. "Are you sorry, Mister Domenici?"

Trent froze. Kempthorne side-eyed me. Pierce began to drift around the apartment, getting a good look at the maps we'd left on the table. If he studied them close enough, he'd see how I'd ringed Kage's apartment. An apartment an anonymous caller had recently reported as suspicious. An apartment belonging to one of their agents. Would they connect the dots?

I lifted my chin and swallowed the urge to punch Palliser's face. "Very sorry."

Palliser took a step back to check where his partner was.

Pierce flicked through the maps. "Do you know a Kage Mitchell, Mister Domenici?"

Fuck. These were Kage's people. If I lied, they'd know. They knew who I was. They knew who Kempthorne was, and they knew where we'd been last night. If they wanted to, they could haul us in, and we'd never see the light of day again. Kempthorne, they'd squirrel away somewhere, and I'd never be able to get to him.

Why the fuck had I insisted on coming to America?

"Yeah, we know Kage. He worked with us, in the UK, but you already know that."

Pierce left the table and approached his partner. They shared a nod, and Pierce turned to Trent. "Thank you for your time."

The pair strode by me and headed for the door.

"Oh, by the way..." Pierce turned. "You weren't anywhere near William Mitchell's house in Greenwich yesterday?"

Denials lodged in my throat. I wanted to glance at Kempthorne, but if I did that, they'd think me guilty as fuck.

Pierce flashed a fake smile. "Yah see, someone—likely a latent—torched the place. Nobody died, luckily. It's just so damn interesting, don't you think?"

Without waiting for an answer, Pierce and Palliser left.

I blinked at the closed door and, for a few seconds, wondered if I'd burned the Mitchell's house to ash—I'd thought about it. I probably would have if Kempthorne hadn't been there. "Jesus, those two are a double act."

Trent chewed on something, his pale face flushing. "You had better start talking or you can both leave this apartment and get out of New York. I won't help you again!"

"Because you've done such a fine job of helping us so far?" I snorted.

His blue eyes widened, and his nostrils flared. "If it weren't for me, John, you would already be in a latent jail, with no chance of seeing the light of day! I've covered for you both. And while you were both at some latent *party*, I had the Feds breathing down my neck all night! So it wouldn't kill you, *John*, to be thankful."

Shit. "Sorry, mate. I am... Thanks." Yeah, okay, I wasn't helping. Trent clearly didn't want to hear anything from me. "I'll just er... go take a shower." Kempthorne would talk him down. I trudged upstairs, catching Alex's eye from the staircase—he didn't look pleased—and dialed Gina's number as their voices started up.

"Hey, you all right?" Gina said.

"Not really. Why the fuck am I here, G? Why did I drag Kempthorne out here to save a guy none of us like?"

"Because you're a good guy, Dom. And Kage would maybe do the same for you."

"Would he though?" I dropped onto the end of the bed and flopped backward. "We should come back..."

"Maybe... I opened your letter."

"What does it say?"

"Not a lot. Hang on..." She rustled around and then came back. "It says, 'John P-O-Three-Eight-Four—'"

"That's my military unit number." The letter was definitely from Sawyer.

Raised voices bubbled up from downstairs. Kempthorne and Trent getting heated. Probably about me.

"And then a load of random words."

"Like?"

"Bluebell, sign, apple, razor, towel."

My heart stopped. "What?"

"Just what I said, like that, all in a line. And there's no signature. That's it. That's the whole letter."

I squeezed my eyes closed. Trent was ranting, something about owing him, but the words Gina had said, they stabbed into my memories, one by one. All I had to do was dig them up from where I'd buried them all those years ago. "Read them again?" She did. Bluebell. Sign. Apple. Razor. Towel.

"What does it mean?"

I sighed. "It means Sawyer was trying to protect me. But it's too little, too bloody late. The prick."

"You want me to come out there?"

The apartment door slammed.

"I'd like nothing more, but we need you there. Hey, did you find out any shit about Trent?"

"Nothing. He's as clean as a whistle."

"Of course he is." I sighed. "Keep looking. Nobody is that clean."

"Okay... and hey, you tried, yeah? If you gotta come back, that's okay too. Kage'll understand, wherever he is."

I thought about the bones in the burn barrel and how Kage had grown up knowing his own father had killed his little brother. He'd talked about me having a heroic streak, but he had one a mile wide. "Yeah, maybe."

Kempthorne climbed the stairs, still frayed at his edges, but now with added fury behind his eyes. "Stay awesome," I told Gina.

"You too."

I threw the phone onto the bedside table and watched Kempthorne prowl toward the bathroom. Heat and rage sizzled off him, and a moment later, the shower hissed. If I went in there, we'd fuck. It would be desperate and rough, like it had been in Cecil Court's basement. I hardened just thinking it, but I was also wrecked, inside and out, and so was he. I didn't want to be fucked. I just kinda wanted... to be held. But I didn't know how to say that without sounding like a tit.

The shower turned off and he padded out, towel wrapped around his waist, chest bare and hair damp. He still simmered, as though he was ready to burn the world.

"I'll just er..." I gestured toward the bathroom. Halfway there, I stripped off my jacket and shirt, tossing them onto a chair.

"Dom?"

"Yeah?"

He sat on the edge of the bed and rubbed his face. "Will you... sleep with me, in my bed? I mean... together. But not *together*—" He growled at himself and buried his face in his hands. "Never mind."

"Hey."

He looked up, his face full of soft, tired hope.

"Just don't hog the sheets, okay?"

"I don't hog the sheets," he spluttered.

I snorted with a smile and ducked into the bathroom. "Whatever, Alex."

15

D^{om}

Alex was asleep by the time I emerged from the shower. I climbed carefully into bed next to him and was out like a light in seconds. I dreamed of Sean Sawyer, of the bastard's smooth talk and how I'd been stupid and naïve, an eighteen-year-old recruit fresh off the streets and so desperate for somewhere to belong that I'd fallen for his swagger. It was obvious the guy had just wanted to get his rocks off, but when I'd been in the middle of it, he'd made me feel as though I was everything. As though I could *be* anything.

Kempthorne made me feel the same. But maxed out. Like the two of us together could take on gods—like Montgomery—and like we might... last. As though this was serious. And putting that much of myself in someone else's hands again scared me shitless.

I woke with my head full of Sawyer and an empty space beside me.

Alex was probably downstairs, but I didn't hear anyone moving around. I needed to talk with him about everything. About the military, about Ink—a latent drug I'd met before—and about Sawyer. And maybe about going back to England. Although, it wasn't much safer than the US.

I threw some fresh clothes on and padded downstairs to an empty apartment.

Kempthorne didn't have to tell me where he was going, or why, but a text would have been nice. I checked my phone, and nothing. I filled an hour by going over everything we knew about Kage's disappearance

Don't come for me.

Don't do the right thing.

It's what I deserve.

What did he deserve? What had he done that meant he got snatched and either locked up somewhere, or... killed? Was it because he hadn't handed Kempthorne over or was it more personal? The LOA had just muscled their way into our apartment. They could have carted Kempthorne off then and hadn't. So what was really going on?

Still no texts from Kempthorne. I texted him a *"Hey"* but the ticks showed he hadn't seen it. I rang. It went to voicemail.

I paced and sent a message to Trent, asking him if he'd seen Kempthorne.

Trippy Trent: He's with me.

His reply hit like a slap to the face. I typed out a *what-the-fuck*, and then deleted it and took a breath. I'd joked about Trent and his croissants. He wasn't a threat. I knew that. This was probably all innocent. I did not want to be the boyfriend who flipped tables for no reason.

Can you ask him to call me?

... the ellipses bounced for way too long.

My phone rang in my hand:

Unknown number.

"Hey?"

"Dom?"

My insides dropped. "Shit, Kage?"

"You have to stop. He won't let it go. Please—"

"Where are you?"

"Go home."

"You're in the US, right? Are you in New York? Can you tell me anything? Are you hurt?"

Breathing. Just tight, raspy breathing.

"Kage? Hey... you still there? Are you hurt?" I asked it softer this time, sensing he was. Why else wouldn't he answer? More breathing. He couldn't talk. Maybe someone was there, with him. But he could listen. "Who has you, Kage?"

"I can't tell you," he whispered.

"You know you're one of us, right?" I stared out of the huge windows overlooking a late afternoon Hudson River. "You've done some shitty things, but we all have."

He choked on what sounded a lot like a sob. "You have no idea."

"Hey, man. I killed my own dad. So yeah, I do."

Something scuffled in the background. Shouts. Voices.

"I gotta go."

"Kage, wait—"

"Dom, he'll kill you—"

The line cut off.

"Fuck!" I threw my phone at the sofa and thrust my hands into my hair. Okay, so he was alive. Which was better than the alternative. Someone had him. Some*one*. A he. Not a squad or unit. Someone who knew who I was. It wasn't much to go on. But it was progress.

Sawyer and Kage.

Military and LOA.

The LOA had made it clear they were on to us, but they hadn't hauled us in. The sniper had been military-trained. He definitely wanted me or Kempthorne out of the picture. Were there two separate forces at work?

Government agency and military. Two sides of the same coin.

Maybe if Kempthorne hadn't been lunching with his buddy, we could have made a murder wall and Kempthorne & Co'd the shit out of all this.

I grabbed my phone again and angrily thumbed a text to Kempthorne:

Need to talk. Where the fuck are you?

16

A lexander

I snuck a look at my phone—*Dom: Need to talk. Where the fuck are you?*—then slipped it back into my pocket.

Trent refilled my wine glass after I'd nursed the first one for an hour.

"Those are my terms," he said, inordinately pleased with himself.

"I see." I picked up my glass and cast Trent my society smile. He'd had me meet him at his characterful apartment on the Upper East Side, a high-ceilinged, open-plan affair with hints of old New York in its crown molding and pretty windows. Probably valued as much as Ravenscourt. The plush and sumptuous surroundings were somewhat lost on me, as Trent was trying to blackmail me into a—for want of a better word—relationship.

"Your assistant gets to go home and you get... well... *this*." He gestured at the apartment, and I assume he included himself in this proposal.

"You know, I might be more receptive of any terms if you accept that John is my partner, not my assistant."

He waved the words away and sat next to me on the white sofa. "Whatever he is, doesn't matter."

Almost every piece of furniture was a pastel shade of blue or white or green. Even the floorboards had been painted. I couldn't help but wonder what Dom would think of it. "Trent, I fear we've become tangled in a miscommunication."

"No miscommunication, Alex." He laid a hand on my thigh.

I stood, taking my wine with me. "You do understand you're blackmailing me?"

"No, not really. It's more like an agreement."

"You're threatening to hand Dom over to the authorities unless I agree to be your lover—that is what you're proposing?"

He leaned back and crossed his legs at the knee. "Well... I didn't put it quite as bluntly as that, but okay."

I laughed and knew the sound was harsh. I needed Trent to grease the wheels on this side of the Atlantic, as Dom would say, but I wasn't greasing anything else with him. And my patience was fast wearing thin. He was someone who, if they didn't get their own way, bribed or bought themselves the win. I had a small measure of respect for that tactic, having used it myself several times. But some things, one did not bribe. Relationships being one of them. "I fear you have grossly underestimated both Dom and I."

"No, I don't think so." He took his phone from his pocket. "One call from me, and the LOA will find John Domenici very interesting, and with a single strike left on his card, they won't have to dig very deeply to find something to throw him in jail for. I had them look the other way after that *latent* gathering. They can easily look at it again."

I gulped all the wine down in one swallow. "You should know, I do not respond well to threats."

Trent chuckled. "Then you had better start, or John will pay."

The fact remained, Dom and I were skirting close to the law. Dom especially. The LOA knew we were here and involved in various infractions. Kage, an LOA agent, was missing. And the visit from the LOA suggested they knew it was all connected and were feeling us out for information.

I set my empty glass down on a side table. "Then I'm sorry to say, we'll be on the next flight out of New York."

Trent smiled. "Unlikely."

I straightened and tugged on my shirt cuffs. "Why?"

"I sponsored you. Put my neck on the line to vouch for you. I can get you grounded."

Perhaps I'd underestimated Trent, and the hold he had over us. It had never occurred to me the man would turn out to be so... disappointing.

My phone trilled in my pocket, on silent but vibrating.

"That'll be John now," Trent said. "Perhaps you should tell him it's over."

I laughed and sent Trent a thin smirk, then answered the call. "Dom, I'm rather tied up—"

"Kage called."

"He did? That's... good news." It was good. For Dom. He'd needed to know the American was all right. Perhaps now we could go home.

"Someone has him. He talked about a he... Listen, you need to come back. Whatever the fuck you're doing with Trent, brush him off."

Trent smiled and tapped his foot. So confident in his *offer*. The fact remained, he could have Dom locked away. And there would be nothing I could do to stop him. Almost nothing.

"There's been something of a snag," I told Dom.

"A snag?"

"I'll be back later."

"Kempthorne—"

I hung up and turned my phone off, then turned to Trent. "And you'll make sure Dom is safe?"

"Of course. I'm a man of my word. Just like you." He leaned forward. "You and me, Alex. Two powerful families. God, it'll be perfect."

"And your father?"

Trent's face darkened. "I'll deal with Daddy."

I scooped up my empty wine glass and crossed to the ice bucket and bottle for a refill. "Go over, again, how this works. I want to be sure I know what I'm getting into, when we do this."

17

D^{om}

If Kempthorne was going to hang up on me, then he couldn't bitch later after I'd carried on with our investigation without him.

I was going back to Kage's apartment. Alone. It was that or rattle around Hudson Yard, thinking up all the ways Kempthorne and Trent had hit a *snag*. It shouldn't have bothered me. Kempthorne wasn't Sawyer. He wouldn't screw me over. I just had to keep telling myself that... on the way to Kage's apartment in the rental car.

I parked a block away and walked by Kage's brownstone a few times, checking to see if there were cops lingering from Trent's tip-off, then took a look around the back. A rickety old metal fire escape zig-zagged up the rear of the building. What the hell, I figured I may as well go all-in and venture up to the apartment window, especially as I didn't have Kempthorne's borrowed keys. After tugging on the pair of Kempthorne's skinny gloves I'd swiped off the kitchen island, I climbed onto a dumpster and grabbed the fire escape's ladder, gave it a tug, dislodging it with a noisy rattle, then scurried up and found Kage's apartment window.

His belongings were still strewn about all over the place. If the cops had been in, it didn't show. I jimmied the window open and climbed inside.

The quiet crawled over me, raising the fine hairs on the back of my neck. I could not get caught breaking and entering. I drifted from room to room, stepping carefully. *Nice an' quiet...* The gloom seemed thicker than I remembered. Or maybe it was the thick quiet of the building that was different from before, as though the place held its breath. Most of the buildings in NYC didn't have the same low-level psychic hum as those found in London, but this old brownstone had some stories to tell, if I cared to listen. But I wasn't here for that.

Maybe there wasn't anything here to find.

Maybe this whole trip was an epic waste of time.

Maybe I should have listened to Kage and left him alone.

In the bedroom, I gravitated toward the photograph on the chest of drawers. I'd glanced at it during my first visit and assumed the photo was of a boyfriend, or some part of Kage's life we didn't know about—which, as it turned out, was most of it.

I picked it up. The guy pictured had to be in his early twenties, not much younger than me. He crouched, one arm draped over his knee. He didn't smile. I'd noticed that the first time around. Maybe he was an ex. The one who got away?

I turned the frame over.

I forgive you, someone had written in free-flowing pen. And then in Kage's neat letters: Bluebell. Sign. Apple. Razor. Towel.

"Fuck…" There was the connection. Sawyer and Kage. The same code Sawyer had sent me in a letter, right before he died. A military code I knew well. The guy in the photo was military. But not any regiment. He was latent dark-elite. So fucking dark they didn't have a name. Just a few random words that didn't make sense to anyone, unless you'd been recruited.

Grit crunched in the hallway. I turned, saw a black-clad guy aim a gun, and lunged sideways. Silenced rounds *plinked* into plasterboard too close to my head. I sprawled, landing on my arm and shoulder, and flicked a card from the deck in my pocket. Charging it lit me up like a neon sign, but I figured the guy already knew where I was. Trick sizzled, burning through Kempthorne's gloves to reach the cards.

My phone rang.

"Christ, not now."

I peeked around the edge of the sofa. The gun dropped, zeroing in on my face. I ducked out of sight. Rounds splintered the floorboards. "Shit!" I flicked the card overhead without looking. Heard it blast and bolted out from behind the sofa. The guy's all-black had him blending into the gloom so only his eyes shone.

I knocked his gun arm up. Another round burst into

the ceiling. I landed a punch in his side. He buckled and tried to shove me back. We fought too closely, punches sliding off, and hit a sideboard, breaking one of its legs. It toppled, taking us with it. His fist slammed into my side as I hit the floor with the guy half-pinned under me. I had his gun arm wedged, pointing away from my head. But the bastard was strong and fighting back. A knife flashed in his suddenly free left hand.

Hell, no.

I surged trick through my hand and grabbed his shoulder. He barked a muffled cry behind his mask, and his eyes blazed. Trick surged out of him, into me. *Fuck.* I sprang backward, startled more than hurt. A latent. No time to make friends. I flicked a card through the air. He rolled. The card burst against the floor, raining sparks, and the ninja swung his gun around again. I kicked high, connecting with his wrist, dislodging the gun from his hand. It skidded across the floor. For a second, I thought I had him beat, then he came in hard, tackled me, brought a knee up, and slammed it into my jaw. I almost bit my own fucking tongue off and reeled, gasping. His hand locked in my hair.

I did the only thing I could think of and grabbed his balls. We both froze. He breathed hard, same as me. "A touch of trick, mate," I panted, "and you'll be singing soprano."

His glare was arctic cold. And familiar. Then he head-butted me.

The impact of his skull jarred my already fragile brain. Shit, he was strong, fast, and I wasn't winning this.

He slipped my grip. I raised a blazing card. "Back the fuck off."

He scanned the floor, couldn't see his gun, grunted, then thought better of trying to finish me off and vanished out of the bedroom door. I loped after him, my balance shot, slowing me down, and reached the window in time to see him leg it down the back alley and around a corner, out of sight.

"Bloody hell." I dabbed at my head, expecting blood, but my fingers came away clean.

Sirens wailed outside. Some helpful neighbor had heard the muffled shots and called it in.

"Shit." I climbed out of the window, hurried down the fire escape, and kept my head down as I jogged back to my car.

Inside, I slithered down in the driver's seat just in time as two cop cars roared by. Once I was sure they weren't spinning around to come after me, I started the rental car's engine and got the hell out of there.

Bluebell. Sign. Apple. Razor. Towel.

In that order, on the back of that photograph.

The same words Sawyer had written to me. A warning to run because I was so fucked. That sniper bullet had been meant for me and not Kempthorne.

"Son of a bitch!" I hit the steering wheel. I had to tell Kempthorne everything.

It was past eleven at night by the time I trudged into the Hudson Yard apartment. The punches the assassin had landed had begun to burn. "Kempthorne, hey."

He was sitting in the dark, illuminated by the soft hue of New York's light spilling in through the windows, his back to me, glass of wine in his hand, wristwatch glinting. He was a bloody sight for sore eyes. And probably pissed off I hadn't been home. Two could play that game.

I flicked on the lights, spoiling his brooding ambience, went straight to the freezer and grabbed a bag of ice, then stuck it on my jaw and slumped against the kitchen countertop. "We need to talk."

"Yes," he said stiffly. "We do." He got to his feet and noticed my more-disheveled-than-usual state and quickened his pace. "What happened?"

"Bad guy with a gun. I had him by the balls, but he gave me the slip."

Kempthorne leaned over the counter and removed the ice. He skimmed my jaw with his quick, fluttering touch, spilling trick, sending shivers down to my toes. "I ruined your gloves too," I grumbled. "They're in the car."

"Are you hurt anywhere else?"

His touch lingered on my now-healed chin. I tilted my head, studying his serious face. The cool, white kitchen lights made his eyes sparkle. Or maybe that was trick. How much persuasion would it take to have his hands on me elsewhere too? "I mean... Now that you mention it, kinda hurts all over?"

He arched an eyebrow. "Hm... Before we get to *that*, we have a problem."

"Yeah, we do… Listen, I need to explain some things about my time in the mili—"

He stepped around the counter and opened a tall kitchen cupboard. Tucked inside, bound and gagged with thick silver tape, was Trent Anderson. Trent blinked, squinting into the light, and mumbled.

"*Shit*… you really don't like bagels, huh."

Trent barely fit. His knees were up near his ears. I wasn't even sure how Kempthorne had squeezed him in there. With a whole lot of persuasion probably.

I raised my eyebrows. "Wait, is this some kinky sex thing?"

"Good lord, no," Kempthorne said, then arched an eyebrow. "Unless you want it to be?"

"What?"

"No?"

"No."

"All right." He cleared his throat. "So we're clear."

Trent mumbled behind the tape.

"You don't get a say in this," Kempthorne told him. Trent's mumbling became frantic. "Duct tape. Marvelous invention." He shut the door.

I'm not often lost for words, but this was one of those times. Trent Anderson was bound. And gagged. In a cupboard. In his own apartment.

"Coffee?" Kempthorne asked, flicking on the machine.

"So… I have a question. Why is Trent in the cupboard?"

"He attempted to blackmail me."

"Oh. Right… Okay."

Kempthorne sighed and braced both hands on the counter. "He threatened to have you arrested unless I... unless we..." He did that thing where he rolls his hand and expects everyone else to fill in the gaps.

"Unless you what?"

"It's ridiculous."

It had to be bad for Kempthorne to stuff the man into a cupboard. "What did he want?"

"Me." He sighed again. "Intimately."

"Oh, he fuckin' did, huh?" I yanked open the cupboard door. Trent blinked. "What the actual fuck? Jesus Christ, you're lucky Kempthorne got to you first or I'd have ripped your fucking balls off." I crouched and looked him in his wide eyes. He was scared, but mostly angry. He'd learn. "You're not worth it." I shut the door on him and turned to Kempthorne. "I'll take that coffee."

18

A lexander

"Latent assassins?" I was going to need more than coffee; preferably with a dram of whiskey.

We were seated at the kitchen island counter. Dom had told me how Kage had called, and how he'd taken it upon himself to visit Kage's apartment alone, and how he'd been attacked by a trained latent while there. *A latent assassin.*

"I was on the fast track for the same unit," he said, "I even made the cut, but I was pulled from selection a week later. Thank fuck, because they're machines."

I knew why he'd been pulled off that unit, although the pieces were only now falling into place. Sawyer had crippled Dom's career in the military. Dom believed it was because the man had an axe to grind against him, and from my limited number of dealings with Sawyer, Dom was right. But Sawyer's nose-diving of Dom's career might have stemmed from other reasons, too, reasons Dom probably hadn't considered. Such as Sawyer trying to protect him. It seemed as though Sawyer may have had a heart, after all. The letter had been his last attempt at trying to right the past.

"It's the Ink," Dom continued. "Or 'V' for venom, as we called it in Psy Ops. They tried it on a few of us to see who was receptive. The shit hollows you out. Turns you into... empty vessels. The MOD boost a latent full of artifact, dampen his will with V, and then they have themselves the perfect assassin. And those operatives don't fucking stop until their target is dead."

"The sniper? Was he the same person you ran into at Kage's apartment?"

"Yeah. I think so. It makes sense. I don't know why he was there though."

I sipped my coffee and considered this new information. Perhaps Kage had stumbled on some new information about Dom, but that didn't explain his links to Sawyer.

"What do the assassins have to do with Kage?"

"I don't know yet, but the picture I found in his place had the same code on the back. A code only a military-trained latent assassin would recognize."

Hm... So Kage was well-informed regarding such assassins. "Why now?" I asked, voicing my thoughts.

"Someone out there thinks we know something dangerous enough to kill for."

"So what is it they think we know?"

Dom sighed. "If the ninja had stopped trying to kill me for a second, I could have asked him." He shifted on the stool, stretching bruised muscles. I could, technically, heal all his bruises, but I suspected it would take some creative application of my trick, the personal kind. And we had a guest.

A thump sounded from the cupboard behind Dom.

Dom jerked a thumb. "What are we gonna do with daddy's boy?"

"I have a plan for that."

"Are you gonna share it?" His arched eyebrow suggested I should, and suggested something else too. I owed him the explanation.

"Are we going to discuss how you almost got killed and I had no idea where you were," I said, unable to keep the words in any longer. "If something had happened—"

Dom snorted. "Really?" His brow tightened. "You wanna do this now?"

"Do what?"

"All right, fine. You fuck off all the time and nobody has a clue where you are. You're off with Trent somewhere, dealing with a *snag*. Kage calls, there's a development you need to know about, and you're not answering your phone? What am I supposed to do with that?"

"I didn't think you'd react well to me visiting Trent—"

"Jesus Christ." He hopped off the stool. "You know what I don't react well to? Being kept in the dark. Again."

"I'm sorry."

He huffed and shook his head with a dry smile. "You say it, but you aren't."

I didn't understand. Why was he angry? That I'd gone

out without telling him, or that I'd met with Trent? And why were we arguing about this now? "It's not really pertinent—" He snorted again, cutting me off, and my irritation flared. "I wasn't the one who was attacked—*who could have died.*" My heart fluttered, panic a spark igniting my anger. Didn't he understand how much the very idea of losing him almost drove me out of my mind? "You have one infraction left. I can't protect you—"

"Don't twist this around on me, you clever bastard."

The apartment's intercom buzzed.

"Ah." I set my coffee down. "Will you get that?"

"Get what?" Dom didn't move.

"The door." I opened the cupboard, grabbed Trent, hauled him out and shoved him against the kitchen counter, then tore the tape from his mouth.

"Ow!" he screeched. "How dare you! This is assault—"

I slipped my hand around his neck and pushed in, meeting him eye-to-eye. Trent fell quiet but breathed hard. He didn't know me; he didn't know what I was capable of. That was probably for the best. "Listen very carefully. Your father is at the door." He paled. "I can explain how you tried to emotionally blackmail me into sexual favors, or we can keep this professional and you'll leave here with your pride and trust fund intact. Do you understand?"

Trent swallowed and nodded.

"Good." I tore the tape from his wrists and stepped back, giving the man room to collect himself.

"Ah," a deep voice boomed at the door. "You must be John Domenici, Alexander's associate. And there's the man himself—Alex! You look just the same. Thanks for the call! Happy to come by."

Mister Anderson, Trent's father, had silvering good looks and a brilliant smile. He breezed in, welcomed Dom and I with eager handshakes and a few slaps on the back, and mostly ignored Trent, who leaned against the counter as though without it, he'd have been on his knees. I'd summoned Trent's father under the pretense of a coffee while he was in the city. With the coffees poured, Mister Anderson made it clear we could stay in the apartment as long as we wished, and to mention his name should we need anything. The Kempthornes and Andersons were long-term family friends. We didn't discuss anything as sordid as blackmail, and Trent left with his father, rubbing his wrists and keeping his head down.

Hopefully, he'd learned a valuable lesson: not to fuck with me or Dom. He wouldn't get a second chance.

"Do you think that's the last we'll see of him?" Dom asked after they'd left.

"One can hope."

The apartment fell quiet again. New York hummed and sparkled outside the vast windows. "Was there anything else you wanted to tell me about today?" I asked.

Dom, beside me, cocked his head. "Kage is alive. I know you hate him, but Gina said he's one of us, and she's right. He did some awful shit, but he also tried to help. I'm not leaving until he's found."

"I agree."

"You what?"

"We aren't leaving. Kage must be found."

His half-smile made it all worth it. Even if my first instinct was to shove him on my plane back to England and squirrel him away at Ravenscourt forever. As hell would freeze over before Dom agreed to such a thing, the next course of action was to keep him safely at my side.

"Well then. What is our next move?" I asked.

Dom continued to study my face. His eyes had narrowed slightly, as they did when he was trying to peel back my layers. It usually preluded an interrogation, sometimes of the sexual nature.

Whatever conclusion his thought process came to, it seemed to please him, and he sauntered off toward the stairs. "Was it a threesome with Trent you were asking if I was interested in, or being tied up? Just so we're clear."

Oh. He hadn't forgotten my earlier question. I held his gaze. "As I said, I am flexible."

He climbed the stairs, smirking. "Good to know."

With him out of sight, I rummaged through the cupboards and found the bottle of wine Trent had left for us as a welcome gift, before his welcome had soured, and collected two glasses. I then searched the drawers for a bottle opener. The vial of Ink clunked against the side of the drawer, where I'd left it for safekeeping. The dark slosh of smoky liquid took on a more sinister feel, now I knew how it was used to subdue latents. Dom had come close to being one of those puppets, and despite hating Sawyer, I could only posthumously thank him for keeping Dom out of trouble. Even if he was likely the reason trouble had found us again now.

After leaving the Ink in the drawer, I climbed the stairs.

The sounds of the shower spilled from the bathroom. I poured two glasses of wine, downed one, refilled it, and rapped on the closed door.

"Yeah?"

I wanted him. I'd wanted him since I'd had my hands on him earlier, healing his wounds. I always wanted John Domenici, whether it was just to have him close or to have his muscular body moving under me. The hunger was insatiable.

I swallowed, my throat dry again, and pushed open the door. Steam wafted out of the room. And there was Dom, splendidly naked behind a glass shower door, drenched from head to toe. He had an arm braced on the tiles, his head bowed. Water poured over his shoulders and down his back, running in tiny rivulets over defined muscles and dappled bruises.

"You just gonna stare or join me?" He turned his head and smirked over his shoulder, and through the steamed glass, sly desire flashed in his eyes.

I set the glasses down on the bathroom counter, leaned against the doorframe, folded my arms, and tried to stop my heart from pounding out of my chest. "I was rather enjoying the view."

He laughed deeply, thickly, and the sound trembled through to my soul.

"Fuck that." He stepped around the glass door, splashing water all over the floor, and crossed the room in two strides. He grabbed my shirt in a fist and pulled me into a wet, stubble-sharpened, rough kiss. His hot, wet skin burned through my rapidly soaking shirt. He hauled me against the counter, cupped a thigh, and lifted me onto the countertop. The buttons on my shirt were gone, either undone or torn free, and Dom's hot tongue flicked over my chest, seeking a nipple.

None of this had mattered until Dom. Sex had been a release, little else, but with Dom, it was an adventure I hadn't known I'd been missing.

I cupped his face in my hands and forced him to look up. He smiled, then laughed and swooped in. "I'm not sharing you with anyone, ever," he growled against my mouth, then kissed me hard. His tongue swept in and I teased back, giving and taking.

Relief left me breathless. "Good."

His hands slid down my back to my arse. "Too many clothes," he mumbled.

I hopped down off the counter, shoved him in the chest, and walked him backward, into the shower. He breathed hard, chest heaving, and when the water hit him he shook his head, sending droplets flying. I crowded him under the jets, stepping into the stream with him. Hot water soaked through my jacket and into my shirt, weighing me down.

"Alex." He slipped his hands around my waist and hugged me close, his body so hot it burned through my wet clothes. I teased his mouth with mine, luring him into chasing a kiss, and made quick work of my belt and fly. His lips skimmed mine, then brushed my chin. I tilted my head back and his mouth branded my neck, scorching a path. I caught his hand and brought it around to my erection, moaning when his fingers clamped.

His trick sang, humming under his skin, tempting me to draw it out of him at the tips of my fingers. I'd meant to heal him, but he scuppered that plan the second he went to his knees and his warm, wet lips sealed around my cock.

He was everything. This was everything. Trent was lucky I hadn't done worse than tie him up because I would have. I'd have killed to protect this, protect us, protect John. I *had* killed for it.

I sank my fingers into his wet hair and hauled him off his knees. "Fuck me."

His groaning-growl strangled my breathing. He clamped both strong hands on my hips and maneuvered me face-first against the tiles. I leaned on my forearms as Dom yanked my sodden trousers down. Or tried to, but they clung to my thighs.

"Fuck..."

"If you don't want to..." I teased.

"Shut up, Alex," he hissed in my ear, then dropped. His lips touched my right buttock, then his teeth pinched. I gasped and then laughed until his hot breath fluttered on my wet neck, silencing me.

"Damn it," he growled, his hand firmly planted on my arse. "No condom."

"It's fine." I trusted him, more than he could know.

His fingers dug in. "You always wear one for me."

"Because we haven't had this conversation. Now we're having it."

"I haven't... been with anyone—not since... Kage—"

Now was not the time to mention the American. "Delay any longer and you'll hear me beg. Is that what you want?"

"Maybe I do fucking want that." His hands circled,

parting my cheeks, and I could feel the press of his hard cock tucked into the valley of my arse.

"Christ, Alex. I never thought I'd have you like this." His words burned my ear, his hands roamed up my back, under my wet shirt, and his erection stroked as Dom rutted against me.

I bowed my head against the cool tiles. I needed this, needed him. His trick tingled into me at every point he touched—hands, cock, mouth. More, I needed more of him. All of him. In me. "Please."

He shuddered, his breath coming fast now, racing like mine. "You beg so politely."

His left hand skimmed my hip, then dipped lower and encircled my erection, but despite my arousal, it wasn't just sex I needed. I needed John Domenici inside and all over me. Needed to drink him down and lose myself in him, his trick, all of it. "Fuck me, John."

"God, yes."

Heated, slick pressure pushed in, and his trick surged, scorching me through, bones and blood, body and mind. He said something about being tight, babbled soothing sounds at the back of my neck. I knew only John—how he felt inside, the soft rasp of his breathing against my ear, his warmth and strength holding me up. I knew I glowed, heard him gasp and moan and growl, felt his trick build, pushing into me with every mindless thrust— my body orgasmed, surrendering, but my trick and my mind soared free, brilliant and alive. So wonderfully consumed by the man I loved.

19

D^{om}

Was there such a thing as being dangerously in love with someone? Like... being so far out of your mind infatuated that it had to be an unhealthy obsession?

I had Alex tucked against my chest, either asleep or close to it. Warm and, right now, so stupidly soft—all of his stiff, upper-class persona had melted away, leaving a man so caring, so vulnerable, a man nobody knew existed. If anyone had asked me if I'd ever feel protective over Alexander Kempthorne, I'd have laughed. But I'd dragged him back from death, and I knew the man he pretended to be was a front for the stubborn, slightly neurotic, brilliant but vulnerable man he was. I loved him. There was no use dancing around it. I kinda hoped he loved me too. Because if he didn't, I was thoroughly fucked.

I had no idea what time it was, or which day. Too much had happened. And then last night, in the shower. I didn't even know how to begin to describe *that*. He'd been wet, and raw, and desperate, but still so bloody Kempthorne, in his drenched suit—shirt clinging to his wet skin—teasing me, giving orders. Our tricks had lit us both up like fireworks *in the shower*. It was a miracle we hadn't burned the building down.

I circled a finger on his shoulder and stared at the ceiling.

How could I tell him this was serious, without offering my heart to be crushed? We'd known each other for years. It shouldn't have been this difficult to say the words. But it was. It wasn't him holding me back, it was me. Christ, I needed Gina's input.

I extracted myself from Alex as he dozed, threw on a T-shirt, and plodded downstairs.

Hey, G. I texted. *I'm in trouble. Not the bad kind. Need advice.*

It was late in the UK, early in the US. She was probably still awake.

I flicked on the TV and let it play with the volume down, then rustled up some breakfast.

My phone buzzed.

G: Wassup.

I sat and agonized over what to say for so long that Kempthorne descended the stairs, impeccable in black trousers and a dark purple rib-knit sweater. If I was expecting any morning-after softness from him, the troubled expression on his face dashed all that. "Trent messaged me."

I rolled my eyes. "He doesn't take a hint, does he?"

"Well no, but look..." Kempthorne slid his phone across the counter for me to see and picked up a piece of toast from my plate.

I know who your sniper is.

I arched an eyebrow. "You think he's had more to do with all this the whole time?"

"Hm. Possibly, but not by choice. We should meet him."

"We have to. But we say where and give him twenty minutes' notice. I'm not making it easy for the sniper to pick us off."

My phone, by Kempthorne's elbow, buzzed again. He glanced down, then slid it over to me. The message on the lock screen read: G: *I think I know. If you love him, you gotta go get hi—* The rest was cut off. Shit, had Kempthorne seen? I slipped my phone into my pocket and stared hard at my coffee.

"How is Gina?" he asked, innocently. As though he hadn't read every word.

"Great. So, when are we meeting Trent?"

Kempthorne checked his watch and grabbed his phone. "Now. And I know just the place."

The New York Public Library off Bryan Park had the period appearance of a building that could have been lifted right out of Trafalgar Square, complete with flanking lions. As I climbed the steps, a pang of homesickness washed over me. London may not have been too welcoming of late, but I thought of Cecil Court as my home. I missed my messy bed, although I hadn't been using it so much. Missed the small, cluttered kitchen and its cupboard full of biscuits, and the way the stairs creaked every time I tried to sneak in late. I missed the little slice of London more than I could have imagined.

As we scanned our IDs at the library entrance, I silently vowed to get back home soon. We weren't welcome here. I just had to figure out who had killed Sawyer and why there was a sniper assassin after me.

Kempthorne's grin widened the moment he saw the walls of books. I sidled up next to him as he admired the hundreds of spines. "What's with you and books?"

"Books don't judge," he said, plucking one at random and flicking through it.

I scanned the shelves, the titles, trying to see what he saw. I'd never owned a book. Nobody had bought me any, and school had been more a lesson in staying alive than actual learning.

"You don't like books?" he asked, seeing what was probably bewilderment on my face.

"It's not I don't like them, we've just never had a chance to get along."

"Books were all the company I had during my... difficult years." He slotted the book back between its neighbors. Mention of his childhood summoned all the memories I'd inherited from a dirty artifact. They'd faded, mingled with my own, but at times like these they came roaring back, especially now I had new ones of Kempthorne out cold on a desk—dying in front of me.

I touched his arm. He smiled, his blue eyes haunted. Neither of us were very good at words. The touch was enough, especially as my trick reached out too.

The familiar bob of Trent's golden hair caught my eye. "Here comes Daddy's boy."

Trent glanced around him, jittery and nervous. He spotted us and headed over.

The library was quiet. No windows, other than some narrow ones a story up. Some of the desks were occupied, but everyone here appeared to be engrossed in their own worlds. I didn't sense anything out of place or suspicious. No assassins lurking in shady corners or government goons. Kempthorne had picked a good place to meet.

"I'm illegally parked by the park," Trent whispered. "I'd better not get towed. I shouldn't even be here." He glared at me, even though I wasn't the who had stuffed him into a cupboard.

"I've got to agree with you there."

He shot me scornful frown. He didn't like me because I was screwing the man he'd had a crush on for years. He spotted my hand on Kempthorne's arm and sneered harder, not even bothering to pretend to tolerate my presence.

"This man approached me a month ago in a... in a bar." He showed us a picture on his phone. The man in the image smiled, but the smile did nothing to thaw the piercing intensity of his eyes. I recognized him. This guy was the same one as the subject of Kage's photo.

Kempthorne glanced at me. I nodded. We'd discuss more after Trent left. "What did he want?" I asked.

"He asked if I knew you, Alex. I said I did but that you and I hadn't spoken in years."

"And?" I pushed, after he fell quiet.

"That was it." Trent shrugged. "He left. And I forgot all about it, but after you called," he said to Alex, "and I organized your visit, he er... he showed up again."

"Showed up, how?" I pressed.

Trent huffed and glanced over his shoulder. He couldn't have looked more shifty if he'd stuffed a load of books up his shirt.

"The same bar?" Kempthorne asked.

"Yes, I mean, I don't think he's... you know..."

"Gay?" I asked, smiling as he squirmed. He would have preferred I wasn't here at all, and he and Alex could have a nice chat together. As that wasn't happening because he'd tried to bribe my boyfriend into having sex with him, I was going to make him squirm every chance I got.

"Yes." He hissed it a bit too loud. A few people at the closest desks to us glanced up. "He wasn't there for *that*. He wanted information on you."

"And you gave it to him?"

"Not to start with. But he... he had pictures."

"Of you at this gay bar?" I suggested, raising my voice a little, just enough that others might hear.

"*Yes!*" Trent bristled. "I didn't want to, Alex. You have to understand, I would never do anything to jeopardize us."

Jeopardize us. This twat was angling for a knuckle sandwich. "And he threatened to tell Daddy unless you gave up information on our visit."

"How... how did you know?"

"Because, I hate to break it to you, you ain't complicated, mate. Did he give you a name?" I asked.

"Yes, although it could be fake. He said his name was Grey."

"Grey? That's a color." Didn't ring any bells.

"Grey*son*?" Kempthorne suggested.

Trent shrugged. "I suppose."

Wait. I knew the name Greyson... from somewhere. A photo... The boy in the Mitchell family photo. The boy who had died. *Oh fuck. Greyson Mitchell?* Kage Mitchell's little brother?!

Kempthorne shared a knowing glance, since I'd taken a few seconds to catch up with where his thoughts had already landed.

I forgive you. That was what it had said on the back of the photo. Kage's brother was alive. And he was a latent assassin from dark ops.

The dominos were falling, and my thoughts were tumbling with them. The words on the back of the photo. A photo of Kage's brother, now older. Kage had known his brother was alive. And he knew he was a latent assassin.

He won't let it go, Kage had said.

Greyson Mitchell, Kage's younger latent brother who was supposed to be dead. Instead, he'd been sent to kill me. And he had Kage. This was personal *and* business.

Kage's trashed apartment. That wasn't someone searching for something, that was someone pissed off. Someone who had come back and found me snooping through Kage's things.

"Does this Grey know you're here now?" Kempthorne asked.

"No, no! I mean… I don't think so. How could he?" Trent paled. "He only asked if we were going to meet. I told him about dinner. When the incident happened… That's when… That's when I knew he was bad news."

"You think?" Christ, Trent had almost gotten us killed. And still might. The quiet library no longer felt so cozy. "Did you tell anyone you were coming here?"

"No, why?"

I tightened my hold on Kempthorne's arm. "We need to get out of here. And you—" I pointed at Trent. "—are coming with us."

"What? Why? I can't. I have a business—"

"Because the second you stopped being useful to Greyson, you made yourself a target."

"What?"

"Dom is right," Kempthorne said. "It's safer if you stay with us."

And we could control the information. Trent stumbling about alone was a fucking liability.

"C'mon." I led them out of the main reading room, through the hall, and stopped at the library's rear doors, where the steps stretched down toward the park. Even in the cold, people milled about, walking dogs, chatting. Kids kicked at dirty piles of snow.

All right, so I'd known we were targets, but I hadn't

known Trent had been feeding the assassin information. "Does he know where we're staying?"

"No. I didn't tell him that. Why would I?"

"I don't fucking know, Trent. Maybe because he has pictures of you at a gay bar and you don't want Daddy to know."

He bristled. "Well, I didn't."

All we had to do was make it down the steps, across a section of park, and climb into Trent's SUV, parked against a curb a few hundred meters away. The space was open, but the majority of the buildings were beyond the tree line. Within sniper range, but difficult, especially with the gusting wind. "Okay, we're going to walk quickly down these steps and over to your car. We don't stop to fucking chat. Got it?"

Trent frowned, as though all of this was inconvenient. Kempthorne scanned the buildings, searching for our assassin.

"Grey, the guy you were giving information to—he's a fucking ghost. And he's not going to blink at shooting you," I told Trent. "Do as I say and you'll have a chance."

"M-maybe we should call the police?"

"They can't help with this," Kempthorne said, cool and calm.

More like *they won't.*

"Okay, let's go." I waved Trent on first, then tried to wave Kempthorne ahead, but he stubbornly hung back.

"You go. I'll follow," he said.

"It doesn't matter what order we're in, if he has a shot, he'll take it."

"Go, Dom," Kempthorne repeated, almost growling.

I started after Trent, checking that Kempthorne tailed behind. All this was hopefully for nothing, but it was better to plan for the worst and survive than to get a bullet between the eyes. People wandered around us, wrapped up in thick coats and scarves. Pigeons pecked at scraps fallen from a kid's bag of chips. I scanned the crowd, the tree line, the windows, looking for the glint of anything that shouldn't be there. My trick tingled, but my cards weren't any help here.

Trent opened the SUV's driver-side door.

I stepped back, holding the rear door open for Kempthorne to climb in first. He frowned. I glared back: *don't you argue with me on this.* A smile pulled at his lips, and then he glanced over his shoulder. I followed his gaze through the trees. Something in a distant window glinted.

Kempthorne grabbed my jacket, suddenly plastered closer. *Fuck, what—* I heard it then, the muffled thud of a high-caliber rifle shot. His body jerked. He exhaled hard near my ear. His shoving grip pulled, instead of pushed. "Get in the car," he gasped.

He'd been hit.

Everything slowed. My heart, the world, his breaths fluttering against my cheek. Warm wetness soaked into my shirt over my chest.

The passenger window shattered, raining glass.

I pulled Kempthorne down, into the back seat, over me. "Fucking drive!"

"What? Oh my god! He's bleeding!" Trent lurched the car forward. Another round plinked against metal somewhere. Trent screamed, swerved the car, and with another scream, our car jerked to a sudden halt accompanied by a screech of metal. The engine coughed and died.

"Kempthorne, fuck." I grabbed his face, lifting his head off my chest. His sleepy eyes blinked. Shit, this was bad.

I shoved and writhed out from under him, getting him on his back on the seat, under me. No, no, no... "You bastard... Hey, hey! Stay awake." His lashes fluttered. He mumbled something.

"I'm... fine."

"You're not fucking fine."

Blood made his sweater heavy. I scrunched it up under his chin and revealed a neat little hole in his chest pumping out dark blood. The heart. He was going to bleed out in seconds. I smothered the hole with both hands. Blood coated my hands and seeped between my fingers. "Listen... listen." I cupped his face, smearing blood across his chin. *Can't panic. Not yet.* "You've been shot—can you hear me?"

He mustered a nod but his eyes were soft and unfocused.

"Damnit, listen! You healed me, you can heal yourself. Focus, okay? You remember? Focus on my hand—on your chest."

Trent muttered something from the driver's seat.

"Call a fucking ambulance!" I snapped. "Kempthorne. Shit. Please." I'd healed him before, back in Wordsworth, but that had been different. I'd been charged up and buzzing, and the shadows had been there, and—God, I was fucking losing him.

The idiot had blocked the shot meant for me. He was dying *because of me*. "Why did you do that?"

His fingers skimmed my cheek. "Love... you." His breathing quickened, turning into ragged gasps. I'd held enough dying soldiers to know when death was the next gasp away.

"You stupid son of a bitch." I pressed my forehead to his. "I can't do this again. Alex, please. God, please..." I squeezed my eyes closed and focused on my hand, just my hand, over his heart. The screaming from nearby, Trent's stammering on a call, honking horns—none of that mattered. I shut it all out, listened for his heart, felt its beat. And poured my trick *in. C'mon... fix him.* "Alex... If you leave me, I swear, I will burn all your books." *C'mon, trick. Do your thing.* I caught his hand, the one that had touched my face, and slipped my blood-coated fingers into his, as though that alone could keep him alive. Blood still pumped through my fingers from the hole in his chest, but it had slowed, maybe. Or maybe he was dying. "Don't you fuckin' die on me... Please, Christ, please." Trick glowed between us, brilliant and golden and alive. A sudden pulse of it snapped from me into him. I gasped, disoriented, stunned.

"Get your hands up!"

Another voice, one that didn't matter.

Trent said something. I didn't care about him either. Just stemming the flow of Kempthorne's blood between my fingers. Another pulse tore from me and washed into him. His body jerked, mouth opening. C'mon... yes... bring him back to me. "You don't fuckin' leave me, remember? I didn't leave you, so you don't fucking leave me. It works both ways."

"Grab him!"

Hands grabbed my legs and pulled. I kicked out and flung undirected trick at whoever was trying to pull me from Alex. I'd light the whole city block up if they didn't fucking back off.

"Down—down! Get him down. Active latent!"

A small voice in my head warned me this was bad, that I should be the one backing off, but the roaring in my head drowned everything out. Armed men hauled me out of the car and dumped me on the road. I pulled on my trick, about to light the bastards on fire, when some dickhead jabbed me with a cattle prod. The electric jolt glitched my trick, cutting it off as well as my rage, stealing both for a second. I gasped and found my face meeting the sidewalk, hands yanked behind my back and cuffed.

"Your card says three strikes, asshole!"

I tried to lift my head, to see inside the car—was Alex alive?—but from the ground, I only saw flashing lights and thundering boots, and heard only shouts from the cops. This was bad. Really bad. I'd screwed up. I'd lashed out. He needed me.

"Is he okay?" I croaked.

Two cops hauled me to my feet and marched me from the car. I twisted, trying to see Kempthorne, or even Trent. "Just tell me he's okay?"

The cops—all geared up in body armor—weren't in the mood to chat with an unstable latent. They didn't acknowledge me, just continued to drag me from the scene.

"I got this," the guy on my right said as we approached a cop car. He opened the door and shoved me inside. A metal grate partitioned the back from the front. Metal grates protected the windows too. I was inside a metal cage, inside a cop car. Fucking great.

I peered out of the window, back to where a crowd had gathered around Trent's battered car. If Kempthorne was alive, awake, he'd tell them to back off. Why weren't they backing off? Why wasn't he barking orders at them? Why wasn't he coming for me?

My throat burned; my eyes blurred. *Shit, shit, shit.*

The cop climbed into the car behind the wheel and started the engine.

He wore a helmet, like the rest of them, hiding his face. I could take him. A flash of trick would stun him. But in the middle of a crowded park, I wouldn't get very far, especially cuffed. The cuffs would be heatproof too. They'd take some time to get off. If I ran, I'd get shot in the back.

I had to sit tight. "Hey. The guy in the back of that car. Is he all right?"

The cop stayed quiet and pulled the car into traffic. They probably weren't authorized to speak with latents. Christ, they hadn't even read me my rights. Did I have any?

I adjusted my hands trapped between my back and the seat. Couldn't use trick—had to stay calm. "Just... Is he alive? Tell me that. C'mon, mate. I was ... I was trying to fix him. I need to know."

Nothing.

Trent would tell them what had happened. He was an

idiot, but he'd tell them the truth... Unless he wanted me out of the picture altogether. He'd already proven we weren't friends. Having me locked up would solve a lot of his problems.

I couldn't think on that, or any of it. Kempthorne had to be alive. He just had to be. The alternative was unthinkable.

I chewed on my lip, drawing blood. New York's tall buildings blurred past as the cop built up speed, and nerves mixed with the bruises in my gut from the prod. This wasn't the IRL. New York cops and latents didn't get along. "Where are you taking me?"

"Processing," he grunted. He still had his helmet on, still hiding his face.

I was so screwed. Three infractions. I looked down. Dark smears of blood stained my jeans. Kempthorne's blood. He'd taken that round in the chest for me. He'd said he loved me. I dropped my head back and closed my eyes. He would be okay. He *had* to be okay. He was Kempthorne. We hadn't survived Wordsworth for him to die here. We were meant for more, him and me. It didn't end like this. It couldn't.

The car rumbled and my thoughts chased themselves around my head for miles. We'd joined a freeway, and New York's high-rises had fallen away. Where the hell was this processing center?

The cop's radio crackled with cop-speak, call signs, and alerts. The driver flicked it off.

"Hey?" I croaked.

He still wore his helmet, even now. Only his eyes showed through the slit.

"Hey?" I leaned forward. "Where are you taking me?"

"Sit back. Stay quiet. It will be over soon."

I held the man's gaze in the mirror. I'd seen those eyes before, behind a mask in Kage's apartment.

Greyson Mitchell.

lexander

A pair of paramedics insisted on examining me due to the alarming amount of blood I appeared to be covered in. But with no wound to mend, they relented, releasing me into police custody, who then demanded I tell them an account of the attack. I told them what they wanted to hear—that all of this was a misunderstanding and with no wound, there had been no crime. Trent had merely had an altercation in traffic.

Dom had been taken to processing, they told me.

I had to get to him.

The bullet had been meant for him. A bullet I'd taken to the chest, in and out. It should have been devastating. I should have been dead, not arguing with New York's finest police officers.

Finally released from the scene, with no charges being pressed, I climbed into the front of Trent's car and found Trent sitting behind the wheel, pale and wide-eyed. He'd hit a trashcan. His car appeared to be fine, the engine had likely stalled. But Trent's eyes were rimmed red, the man teetering on the edge of tears.

"Are you all right?" he asked.

"Yes. Fine." Apart from the throbbing headache due to blood loss, bone-aching tiredness, and a chill I couldn't shake. "We have to get Dom away from the authorities. He was the target. The shooter might try again."

Trent stared at me. Unblinking.

"Drive, man."

"Yeah, okay... sure. I just... you're sure you're okay?" He attempted to reach for my chest, finger out to poke the obvious hole in my sweater.

I slapped his hand away. "Drive."

The whole song and dance had taken too many hours. Dom had been out of my sight too long. I didn't like it. And wouldn't like any of this until I knew he was safe. While Trent drove, I pulled up the processing center's phone number and called ahead.

They didn't have a John Domenici. And no latents had been brought in matching his description.

I ended the call. "Did you see the police take Dom?"

"Yeah, they put him in a car."

"They aren't at the processing center."

"Oh, well... maybe they're caught in traffic?"

There was no more traffic than normal, and according to my phone's map, we were almost at the center. A quiver of panic fluttered my racing heart. Dom had been taken. I'd lost him. A tightness cinched my chest, squeezing my heart and lungs. I winced and slumped back in the seat. *Breathe. Just breathe.*

"Alex, what's wrong? You want me to pull over?"

"No..." The ghost of his trick ran through my veins, still healing. I could smell the faint scent of his after-shave, hear his voice in my ear, threatening to burn all my books. I'd have made sure to come back as a shadow and haunt him for that.

He'd saved me. Again.

There had to be a way to find him.

The assassin had him—had taken him right under my nose.

A stab struck at my heart. I gasped, fought to breathe, but the air had thinned. I clutched at the door and tried to fill my lungs.

"I'm pulling over."

My head spun, heart thudding in my ears. I'd lost him. I'd lost Dom.

The car rocked to a stop. Trent opened the passenger door. He said my name, but he seemed so far away. Then, suddenly, his face was in front of mine. "Breathe, Alex."

That was what I was trying to do! *Breathe.* My heart was on fire, trying to burn its way out of my chest. I'd lost John. I'd lost the one good thing in my life, like I'd known would happen. I'd lost him and I couldn't stand it.

"Slowly... count down from ten."

"*What?!*" I wheezed.

"You're having a panic attack. You need to roll it back, count down from ten backwards. Trust me."

I'd lost him.

It hurt. Everywhere.

Ten.

Couldn't breathe.

Nine.

He'd healed me, poured his trick in and brought me back from the darkness again. He was brilliant, and wonderful, and one of a kind, and I'd let him go.

Eight.

I loved him.

Seven.

Breathe.

I'd told him I loved him.

Six.

Couldn't lose him.

It would kill me.

Five.

"Alex... breathe..." Trent settled a hand on my shoulder. "We'll find him. I promise."

Four.

I could do this. *Breathe.*

My heart slowed, and an edge shaved off the pain.

Three.

Gina.

Two.

I fumbled my phone from my pocket and dialed her number. "Pick... up." It was either late or early in the UK, and I didn't care. The line rang, then her answerphone kicked in. I hung up and dialed again.

One.

"You good?" Trent asked.

"Yes." My hands trembled. "I will be. Thank you."

"It's all right." He took his hand back. "I just saw you die and by some miracle, you came back, so yeah... give yourself a minute. Okay?"

I didn't need a minute. I needed Dom beside me, saying something sarcastic and laughing about it.

"Kempthorne," Gina grouched. "This had better be important. It's like... four a.m."

"Gina. Do you have the app? The one where you find friends?"

"What?"

"When Dom bought his new phone, you connected on an app, didn't you? I heard you talking about it. You can find him, wherever he is. The app—"

"Slow down. Yeah, I think so. Why?"

"I lost him."

"Huh?"

"Gina, open the app on your phone and tell me where he is. Please."

She must have heard the panic in my voice because she didn't argue. "Okay, hold on..." She came back moments later. "I'm sending you a screenshot now."

My phone vibrated. I opened the picture to see a blue dot on roads I didn't recognize and had no idea where they were. "I don't know where that is."

"Wait... I got you on here too. Hold on. It's about twenty minutes north of where you are."

"Okay. Good."

"You should catch up... He's not moving."

Not moving. Not moving was not good.

"Oh god."

"What... what is it? What's going on?"

I thrust my phone into Trent's hand—"Directions."—and climbed over the center console and dropped behind the wheel. "Get in."

Trent climbed into the passenger seat. "You're not insured—"

I planted my foot to the floor and the big SUV lurched forward. "On the other end of that line is Gina, and she's going to tell you where we need to go."

Not moving.

No, no... He'd be fine. He was always fine. He was Dom. He'd survived war zones, and Renick, and a father who had despised him, and Wordsworth—all of it. He survived because that was what he was good at.

"Alex...?"

I blinked at Trent.

"Your hands."

Trick sparked from my fingers. I inhaled and drew it back under my skin. I knew the signs... Could feel my trick trying to snap free and devour everything within a five-mile radius. I was close to spiraling. Dom would be fine. I had to believe that. "Is his phone moving yet?"

Trent relayed the question and shook his head at Gina's answer. "Gina also says she's catching the next flight out."

"Don't," I snapped. "There's no use in her getting hurt too."

"Er... she er... she said something colorful that I'm not going to repeat."

I laughed a little. "I imagine she did."

He covered the phone and whispered, "These are your work associates?"

"They are my friends," I said, discovering how perfect the word was. Trent frowned, disappointed in my choice of friends, which was testament to how little he knew me.

"We're five minutes out." Trent played with the SUV's navigation, bringing up Dom's location for me to see.

I turned off the interstate onto a winding tree-lined back road. The next few miles crawled by too slowly. We rounded a final corner and came to a quiet stretch of clear road flanked by vast pine trees, and no sign of a car. Or anyone. If Dom were up ahead, there should have been a car, or some sign we weren't alone.

"He should be here," Trent said.

"Give me the phone." I grabbed it from his hand. "Gina, I'll call you back." Hitting end, I abruptly cut her off. If I was about to find Dom dead at the side of the road, it couldn't be with Gina on the phone. Not after Robin.

Skidding the car to a halt on the soft shoulder, I flung open the door and dropped to the asphalt. The road snaked away, toward a bend. Ditches lined its edges. I tracked along the left-most ditch, dreading every step.

The sniper had made it clear he wanted Dom dead. If the sniper had taken Dom and his location on the app wasn't moving, then logic suggested I was about to find his body.

My thoughts fell silent. Even my heart seemed to pause its beat.

I walked forward, one foot in front of the other, moving inexorably toward the answer. Fresh tire tracks left divots in mud. Where a driver had pulled over. To dump a body?

I dialed Dom's number on my phone and listened for its ring.

A tiny chirp sounded among the trees.

Trick tingled, eager to be free.

I skidded down the ditch and climbed a small bank, heart in my throat, and thrashed through the thorny brush. "John?" Time slowed. I wandered forward, through ferns and half dead saplings. And there, hidden among the grass, lay his phone. Intact. With no sign of Dom or a struggle.

He wasn't here.

"John?" I called, in the slim hope he'd answer from the trees. But the forest swallowed my voice.

In normal circumstances, Dom could handle himself. He didn't need my protection. But this was different.

The sniper was a latent assassin. Trained, ruthless, capable. Kage had said he would not stop. And Kage would know.

The sniper had pulled his vehicle over and tossed John's phone. But not his body.

So for now, it appeared as though he remained alive.

I climbed back out of the ditch with Dom's phone in my hand, and shook my head at the waiting Trent. Dom's phone had missed calls from both me and Gina on the screen, and one from an unknown number—perhaps Kage—but without the passcode or his thumb, I couldn't access it.

"Now what?" Trent asked.

My head was strangely calm, thoughts still, like the surface of a deep lake. All the nonsense and chatter had fallen away. Only one thing mattered now. Finding Dom. "Now we pay another visit to William Mitchell."

"That's great. Who's he?" Trent tried to climb into the car. I slammed a hand on the driver-side door, shoving it closed and making Trent yelp.

"Wha—?"

"I believe in clarity," I told him, stepping close. His soft eyes narrowed slightly, wary, but still hopeful I might come around to his way of thinking.

The forest surrounding us stretched for miles and we had yet to see a single car. People could get lost in these woods and they might never be seen again.

"We'll find him," Trent said, his voice quivering some. He'd noticed the isolation, the quiet, and how close we stood. He'd also noticed the cool determination in my eyes too. He lifted a hand, about to place it on my blood-soaked sweater. I caught his fingers and spilled trick into him, enough to make him gasp.

"Oh, I will find him. And if he's in any other condition than fit and well, it will be you who pays."

"What? But I didn't—"

"Do not make the mistake of believing you know me. You and I come from very different worlds." I pinned him against the side of his car. "John is all I care for. You barely feature in my thoughts at all. But the one thought that has crossed my mind is a rather unpleasant one regarding your usefulness and whether it outweighs my desire to leave your body at the roadside." He gulped. "I don't like to be unpleasant, Trent. Let's make sure I don't have to be."

His head bobbed in panicked agreement.

"Good." I let him go and straightened my sweater sleeves, ignoring the dried blood on my hands. "I'm driving."

21

A lexander

Gina, with the help of Cas, hunted down a second address for William Mitchell—a more modest single-story dwelling with a sprawling porch and pristine yard. By the time we arrived, the winter sun had set and the windows glowed. I kept my bloody sweater on, but buttoned my coat around it, and wasted no time in knocking on Mitchell's door.

Trent stayed in the car without the key—I had that in my pocket. He'd been quiet for much of the drive over. Perhaps he was only now beginning to understand what he'd become embroiled in and the kind of people he'd tried to cross. Charles Renick had learned that lesson the hard way.

William Mitchell opened the door, took one look at

me, and tried to slam it in my face. I wedged my foot in and bounced the door off my hand.

"The last time you showed up, my house burned down. Get off my porch."

"I hope you're not implying I had anything to do with that, when we both know it was likely caused by someone far closer to home, no?" It was a leap, but also too much of a coincidence that the family home was razed to the ground at the same time as Kage went missing and his not-dead military-trained latent younger brother was back in the neighborhood.

Mister Mitchell's eyes widened. He backed up as though I'd physically threatened him. "I'll call the cops."

"Hm." I pushed the door open and strode in. "Please do. I'll be happy to explain how you murdered your latent son."

The man's face flushed a bright scarlet. "Get out!"

"Let's talk about Greyson, shall we?"

He backed up some more, and I pushed on.

"I'm calling the cops *right now.*" He pulled a phone from his pocket.

"Whose remains did you burn in that firepit all those years go, Mister Mitchell? Because we both know Greyson is very much alive."

His mouth fell open, but the mock horror and surprise quicky hardened into cold fury. "I'm gettin' my gun."

I spilled trick into my left hand. "Please do try."

"You're a *latent,*" he snarled.

"And British. So, do not test me." I flicked a hand

toward the sofa. "Sit, and let's discuss this like gentlemen, shall we?"

He bristled, but he hadn't gone for his gun—wherever that might have been—and the phone rested unlocked in his hand. He could call the police, but if he did, I'd tell them all about his dirty family secret. What use was there in stirring up ghosts when all I wanted was to talk?

He glanced at the sofa, then back at me. I snuffed out the trick and nodded. We could both be reasonable.

Common sense prevailed and Mister Mitchell perched on the edge of his sofa cushions. "You know about Greyson?"

"I know enough." I clasped my hands in front of me and peered down at a man who, at the very least, had tried to hide his son's death but, in all likelihood, had thought he'd killed him. And being a latent, nobody had cared when Greyson vanished. Nobody but Kage.

"It's not what you think..." he said, wringing his hands. "The boys, they were playing. It got out of hand, as it does with boys and... Greyson lashed out with his trick. Kage is a good boy. He tries to be good, but he... He was defending himself. He didn't mean to hurt him."

"Kage hurt Greyson?" Elements I believed we already knew slid sideways, briefly dislodging themselves before sliding back into a new position, making up a different story to the one John thought he knew.

"It was better for everyone if Greyson disappeared."

It was always better for *everyone* if latents went away. I resisted the urge to sneer. "How so?"

"I made it go away. I had to protect them both. It sounds terrible but... it had to happen."

"What exactly had to happen?"

"Kage thought he'd killed Greyson, and I let him think it… I mean, I had a deer carcass from a shooting trip. It was just bones. Kage didn't know the difference. And it was done. Kage no longer had to deal with having a latent for a brother and Greyson was… sent away without anyone knowing."

Little surprised me these days, but this man's words did. He'd made the problem of having a latent son go away, and Kage had carried that guilt for most of his life —thinking he'd killed Greyson. I found myself in the startling position of knowing how Kage felt, having believed I'd killed my sister. Mister William Mitchell had managed to wash his hands of his latent son and his guilt, passing that off to Kage instead.

Unfortunately, the skeletons we keep in our closets often return to haunt us. Greyson was back. Trained to kill and working for the military, he had Dom in his sights, probably on orders from his commanding officers. But while carrying out those orders, he'd included some personal time on the side. He'd kidnapped Kage and burned his family home.

I forgive you. Words were cheap. Revenge was far more satisfying.

"Mister Mitchell, is there anywhere locally where Greyson would go, somewhere isolated and private? A cabin, perhaps? A lake house? You have multiple houses. Is there anywhere I might find him?"

"Do you think Greyson took Kage?" he asked.

"I do. As well as my partner."

"H-he's unstable. He was unstable then—"

"How did your house burn, Mister Mitchell?"

He rubbed his face. "I didn't... I thought... Faulty wiring... in the garage."

"Is that likely?"

A sob bubbled out of the big man. "My boys..."

My childhood had been a test of survival for multiple reasons, and I had no wish to inflict that on another soul by having children of my own, but it seemed to me that a parent's sole purpose was to love their offspring, no matter what. Such a thing wasn't complicated. In fact, it was rather simple. Yet a great number of parents appeared to fail at that one simple thing.

"Kage is missing, Mister Mitchell," I said, hoping to get some sense out of him before he succumbed to emotion. "As for Greyson, you discarded your latent son when he needed you the most. Believe me when I say the damage done to that boy is irrevocable. He likely has Kage and my partner, so I will ask again, is there a bolt-hole from his childhood he'd go to?"

He shook his head. "No..." Unshed tears made his eyes shine.

"Anything? Any place he was fond of visiting as a child?" There had to be somewhere. I needed a lead. Without one, I'd be helpless while Dom was at risk, and that was unacceptable. "A place he perhaps considers more welcoming than what should have been his home?"

"Oh wait... yeah," William said. "There is somewhere. North, near Franklin Lakes. There's a hinky amusement park, with crazy golf and climbing frames. We used to take him every Saturday. It closed down a few years ago, but he... well, he liked it there. More than anywhere else."

"Text me the address, Mister Mitchell." He did as I asked. He sniffed and wiped his eyes, but those unshed tears were lost on me. "The truth will come out," I told him. "It always does."

He sighed. "You don't know what it's like. I lost everything I loved. My wife, my boys. All of it. I paid for what I did. I'm still paying for it."

"You'd be surprised what I know."

I left Mitchell's house and climbed behind the wheel of Trent's car. The navigation system said the old theme park was forty minutes away—not far from where we'd found Dom's phone. I'd wasted hours chasing Greyson's tail, but I had him in my sights now.

"Can you drop me off somewhere?" Trent mumbled.

"No."

"I don't want anything to do with all this, Alex. This is my car. You can't make me get involved. If you don't drop me off, then this is kidnapping, plain and simple."

I started the car and pulled away from the curb. "'Kidnapping'? I could tie you up and lock you in the trunk—that is what you Americans call it? The trunk? *That* would be kidnapping."

"You know... you're not who I thought you were."

I smiled and sped the SUV out of the suburbs. "Finally, we agree."

22

D^{om}

Ink.

It was in my head, under my skin, slowing me down, making everything less... me. I walked through someone else's dream. Falling while standing still.

I knew I'd been drugged. Knew it was Ink. I knew Greyson and me were in a shack, in a derelict theme park, overgrown, abandoned, and spooky as shit, but none of it mattered because I couldn't feel a damn thing.

Ink did that, made everything so bloody hollow and far away.

Greyson sat in a spindly metal chair in the corner of the shack, hardly moving, apparently breathing, although I couldn't see it. He'd removed his helmet after we'd gotten into it at the roadside, when I'd tried to burn my way out of the car and he'd darted me with Ink—the bastard. I'd lost my phone then too. And any chance of being found.

Like Kage, Greyson had his mother's sharp eyes. His hair was short on the sides, longer on top. He carried more muscle than Kage and was nothing like the small kid he'd been in the Mitchell family photograph. He and I were pretty evenly matched in height and build. Both latents. Both military. We had a lot in common.

It was almost a shame one of us would probably have to kill the other.

I shifted my position on the chair, testing the ratcheted metal straps holding my wrists in place against the chair back. I could melt my way out, but if I used too much trick, Grey would notice and blast a hole in my chest. "You an' me, we could go for a beer? Talk this over." I had to go slow, so slow it was almost as though the trick wasn't there at all. Control. I'd had it trained into me. And with Ink, my control was *smooth as silk*. The military had gotten that right, even if they used it on latents for all the wrong reasons. "I feel like we'd figure it out." Just had to keep up the conversation while, drip by drip, my trick ate at the cuffs.

His eyes were the only part of him that moved—they flicked over to me and back to the shack wall where ivy had picked apart the boards over the years.

The Ink made my voice droll in my head. It wasn't important. None of this was important. Which was a lie, and I wasn't any latent. I'd had this shit in me before, knew how it worked, how it numbed the nerves, took away my will. Its whispers told me everything would be fine, if I sat back and let events unfold without me in them.

I slumped in the chair, adjusting my wrists, spreading the trick. "I get it... It's easy being their tool. You don't need to think. You follow orders. Get the job done. And the next day, you do it all again. It's seductive, right? Maybe not seductive... I dunno, it's... not your fault. None of it. You get shit done. Doesn't matter why. That's above your pay grade. I've been there."

"Stop talking."

"Okay..." But he hadn't gagged me so... "You had nowhere else to go, huh? Military seemed like the best place. Where else can a latent get a job? An' you guys have it way worse... The infractions, the ID cards. It's a shitty way to live."

"D'yah want me to Ink you again?"

"Why are you trying to kill me?"

He stared at the wall.

"They didn't tell you? Huh... okay. You execute people and call it done. Just like your brother."

He turned his head. "You don't know Kage—" He cut himself off, stretched a leg out, and leaned back, folding his arms.

"Kage is a good guy? Is that what you were going to say?"

Grey's smile was knifelike. "The opposite, actually."

"I saw him execute a latent." Grey twitched, almost snarled. That comment had hurt. There was a whole lot of bad blood between the Mitchells. "Where are you keeping him?"

He frowned, then chuckled. "You got it all wrong. If I had him, he'd be dead."

What? Ink made the words float. I swallowed and shook my head, clearing my thoughts. The floatiness wouldn't last. He'd shot me with a small amount, only enough to disorientate me. The longer I kept him talking, the more the Ink would slide off.

"You don't have Kage?"

He narrowed his eyes, but I already had my answer. If he didn't have Kage, who did?

"Kage has nothing to do with this." He pulled a phone from an inside pocket.

"He's late, huh? I mean, I guess we're waiting for someone. If we weren't, you'd have killed me. So, who are we waiting for?" Of course, he didn't reply.

I can't die here. That thought was a sharp one. It cut through the drug's fog. A few more of those thoughts, and the Ink would relent. "Your brother drugged me too. You have that in common." He didn't react. "I could have been you. Military grunt. A trigger robot," I told him. "I got out."

He leaned forward, fixing me under a cold stare. "We never *get out.*"

"I dunno." I shrugged. "I feel like I'm out."

"They *own* you, Domenici. The second you signed to join up, you sold your soul."

"Nobody owns me." Except maybe Kempthorne, but that was a whole other conversation.

He smirked. As though he knew something I didn't. Which was probably why I was the one cuffed to a chair and he was the one smiling.

Behind me, the cuffs slid away, snagging on my fingers so they didn't clatter against the floor.

Greyson's phone pinged. He checked it, then got to his feet, making the shack feel even smaller. "You should know, if it were up to me you'd be dead."

"Yeah, I kinda got that impression from the rounds you've been firing my way. But thanks for the clarity."

"You got a smart mouth on you, Domenici. It won't save you."

"I've heard that a few times, but I'm still kickin' around." Maybe not for much longer. Our chat was buying me time to figure out what the fuck was going on. Greyson wanted me dead, he'd been following orders, but... his bosses had put a stop to the kill order. What had changed?

And he didn't have Kage?

Greyson crossed the shack in one stride and crouched to my eye level. "For what it's worth, I reckon they've got the wrong guy."

"It happens."

His eyes scored through me, so like Kage's but without the warmth. He'd had any warmth stripped from him when his father had tried to kill him. That kinda shit would mess anyone up. I knew.

"You really talk to the source?" he asked.

The manic laugh just kinda slipped free. "What?" They really did have the wrong guy. Holy fuck, it was Kempthorne they wanted, not me.

"You'd better hope you can, or there's not much point in keeping you around."

That was what all this was about? The source?

Kempthorne could connect to the source, not me. Shit. At least he wasn't here. They could take me if it meant they kept their hands off him.

The shack's rickety door opened and a stocky guy in an all-black suit stepped inside, filling what was left of the space. Greyson backed off, tucking himself into his shady corner.

So this was The Man. I looked up. And up. Six feet and then some, with a neck like a tree trunk. Ex-marine or something equally badass. The suit screamed undertaker, but I figured it was the typical Men in Black uniform. Or mafia. "This is cozy. You got any more friends out there? Bring 'em in. Let's make a night of it. Did you bring snacks?"

"This him?" The Man grumbled in a deep, throaty voice.

"My mistake," I waffled. "You probably don't have friends."

"This is him, John Domenici," Greyson confirmed.

The Man gave an unimpressed sniff. "Thought he'd be bigger."

"Is that what your wife said on your wedding night?"

He snorted, and Greyson scowled. I wasn't making many friends.

The Man nodded once. "All this trouble for one ex-Psy-Ops Brit? All right, bag him. Let's go."

That wasn't happening. Once I was handed over to the military or whatever the fuck he was, the game changed. One assassin I could maybe take out, but not a unit of them. I'd learned all I was going to, the Ink had faded, and the cuffs hung from my fingers. Greyson's time was up.

The Man turned to leave, and Greyson came for me. And that was my cue to get the hell out of there. I dropped the cuffs, lifted a hand, and flung a chaotic blast of trick at Greyson—it should have hit him in the shoulder and thrown him back, but Greyson was fast. I only saw him twitch, and as quick as lightning his trick collided with mine in midair. Sparks flew. I dove for the door. On the way out, I slapped my hand down on the back of The Man's neck and sent a jolt of trick into him. He buckled, all his nerves on fire, and he had no choice but to go down.

Outside, rifles clattered.

A row of them.

All aimed at me.

In a blink, I swept up a bunch of cards from my pocket and let them fly in a dazzling arc. They lit up the clearing and the soldiers in a flash of heat and light, flooding their night vision equipment, rendering them blind.

I bolted deep into the theme park, passing under the rusted rails of a dragon rollercoaster and by some kind of log flume, now dry and full of weeds. The soldiers' guns would be useless in close proximity, but they'd give chase. I just had to find somewhere out of sight where I could pick them off, one by one.

My heart pounded, body lit up by adrenaline. I used to do this shit for a living, and I'd forgotten just how much I fucking *loved* it.

"C'mon then, bring it."

A teacup ride sat on a raised bank tucked against the forest behind it. The fence separating the two had collapsed. I had an exit, if I needed it, but what I really wanted was the soldiers to fan out and come looking.

I was ready to dance.

23

A lexander

The beams from multiple headlights glowed through the theme park's trees as we drove by the entrance. Rusted gates hung open. For a closed park, there was a great deal of activity happening inside.

I pulled Trent's car off the road and cut the engine.

"Wait here," I told him. He didn't have much choice. I had his keys and his phone. He could run, but he wouldn't get far in the dark.

"Alex?" he said. "Be careful."

I had no intention of being careful. I'd commit to doing what was necessary to get Dom back, no more or less. "I'll be back soon," I told him and left him in the vehicle.

Sneaking through the undergrowth was not how I

preferred to do things. The direct approach was more my style. But for that to work, I needed information on what I was walking in to.

Hunched low, I crept through the brush. Three black cars and a black van idled in the entrance to the theme park. They could have been LOA or military. None of the vehicles were marked. But considering the level of activity and the link with Greyson, Dom was likely here.

I needed a plan. And a closer look.

I left the undergrowth, straightened my coat, and walked down the middle of the entrance road, passing through the gates. I almost made it to the nearest car when the first operative saw me and veered away from his squad to intercept. The rifle cradled in his grip was alarming; hopefully he wouldn't feel the need to point it at me.

"Hello, I wonder if you can help me. My car has broken down and I—"

He held up a hand. "You can't be here, Mister."

I kept on walking toward him. "Oh, terribly sorry. But you see, my phone battery is dead and I saw your lights through the trees. I just need some help. Perhaps one of your friends has a phone?"

His 'friends' consisted of fifteen personnel in sight. Military, from the matte black rifles they all carried. Radios crackled and voices chirped, signaling more activity was happening *inside* the theme park. "Goodness, what's happening in there then?" I started forward again.

My new friend stepped in front of me. "Nothing to concern you. Turn around and leave, sir."

"I think I ran out of petrol. The gauge has been

broken for a while. I had planned to get it fixed, but you know how it is." I chuckled. "Always something better to do. I'm regretting it now."

"Sir." He jostled his rifle. "You need to leave. I ain't askin' nicely again."

Another soldier spotted our discussion and jogged over. "Robbs, what's goin' on?"

"Hi." I smiled. "My car has—"

"You need to get this civi out of here. The CO is pissed—target gave him the slip."

That sounded promising, just so long as the target was Dom.

"C'mon," Robbs, my soldier friend said, reaching out to guide me away. "You can't stay here."

"Wait. You're just going to turn me away? Aren't there bears in these woods?"

"A few miles south will bring you to a gas station, all right?"

I tugged my elbow free of his grip. "A few miles? In designer shoes? Are you insane, man?"

Robbs screwed up his face. "Look, mister. You can see we got an operation goin' down here. Now get lost."

I gave a dramatic huff, took a step, and buckled, making sure to lurch toward the rear of the parked van. "Oh dear."

Robbs and I were out of sight from the rest of his people. He attempted to reach for me. I caught his wrist, yanked, twisted, bent his arm behind his back, and shoved him face-first against the van's rear doors. "*Quiet*," I snapped, then spread my hand against his back. "A blast of trick to the heart will kill a man in seconds. The coroner will confirm you died from a heart attack. Neither of us wants that."

"*Sonofabitch.*"

"Yes, well, you're more accurate than you know. Tell me who the target is."

"I'm not telling you shit."

"Hm, I can see you're going to make this difficult." I sizzled trick through my hand. Robbs gasped, then made some strangled, choking sounds. I pulled the trick back, allowing him to breathe. "Trust me, the only way this ends is with me getting what I want."

"Go to hell."

"Give me a name." I leaned into him, poured more trick in, and the man trembled. Trick sank through his skin, and the more I drew, the smoother it came. The source was weak here, but it did exist—I could still feel it, summon it, have it burn for me.

"Shit-shit-shit, all right! It's a high value target. Wanted latent, ex-military or something."

"His name?"

"Domenici!"

The relief was so overwhelming it almost had me dropping to my knees. After breathing hard, I patted him on the back. "Very good. Now, where was the last sighting."

"I don't know!"

I clasped a hand around his clammy neck and squeezed. "I think you do."

"Please—I got a kid."

"We all have loved ones." *Mine is currently being hunted like a dog.* "Even latents." I settled my free hand on his back again. "Nobody needs to know you told me anything. Or your kid grows up thinking his father died of a heart attack." Trick sizzled and my friend whimpered. The sweet smell of burning clothes and skin laced my throat. "Where is John Domenici?"

24

D^{om}

I'd rendered three operatives out cold, moving location after each hit, but it was time to break cover and get the hell out of the freaky theme park before backup arrived.

Crouched low, I hugged the brush and scooted behind a weird clown structure with a huge mouth—for crazy golf, I figured.

Once out of the park, I'd have to keep moving, find a road, and hitch a ride. The bloody cold had numbed my fingers. I hadn't expected or prepared for a night in the woods.

A rustle sounded behind me. I ducked, more out of instinct than thought. A glowing, trick-infused hand swung for my head. Greyson missed, pivoted, and clashed against my raised forearm. The bastard was strong. I blocked, but his lunge threw my weight backward. We toppled, and the both of us plowed through the clown head, scattering bits of old wood in all directions. I fell under Greyson and clawed at the dirt to get away. His knee slammed into my back.

Pinned, I flicked a card free.

He punched my wrist—something twanged and heat flushed up my arm. I barked a cry and twisted, swinging a right fist across Greyson's jaw. He reeled, I shoved and almost bucked him off, but he dropped in, arm clamping down over my throat.

"Stay down," he growled.

"*Why are you doing this?*" I hissed, fighting for breath. My left wrist and hand throbbed. His weight on my chest crushed the air from my lungs.

"It's not personal. If they get the source, it's over for all of us."

Wait... he was trying to stop his bosses? "I can't do the things... you think I can..."

He almost laughed. "I saw it—the video."

What video? Fuck, I couldn't breathe. He was going to kill me over some stupid misunderstanding. My broken wrist screamed but I managed to pry it between us, teased a card free, and lit it up carelessly. Heat and pain sizzled across my chest, but it burned Greyson too. He flew backward but whirled just as fast, hand raised, trick ablaze. He threw a blast. I did the same. Our tricks clashed midair and exploded like a flash-bang grenade. He launched a second blast, firing it off in a blink. Mine skimmed his, and both bolts veered off course, into the trees. Trick flashed, fizzed, and set the trees ablaze.

A third time and my trick spluttered, or I did. Whatever the reason, I saw Greyson's ball of trick sail toward me, splitting the darkness and air, and knew I couldn't match it.

A vast surge of power rolled out of the dark, slamming into Greyson, knocking him and his blast to the ground.

Kempthorne approached, lit up with trick. It crackled and spat, sizzling the ground he walked on.

Greyson, on his back but readying to climb back to his feet, charged his trick.

Kempthorne would kill him. He whipped up a storm of golden trick, coiling it around his arm like a blazing python.

I got my feet under me and dashed between them. "Don't."

Kempthorne's dark eyes said he'd do it—he wanted to do it. And nobody could stop him. Except me. "Don't." I swayed, somehow still standing, now bathed in Kempthorne's light. Everything hurt. Everything was fucked up. But he couldn't do this. Not to Kage's brother.

Gunfire sounded and a round pinged off the dirt.

"Go!" I shoved at Kempthorne. His trick spluttered, cutting off, and we stumbled into the dark. A glance behind revealed Greyson wasn't on the ground and he wasn't pursuing. He'd fled, but he wouldn't give up. We'd underestimated him. The only orders he followed were his own.

25

D^{om}

We doubled back to the car and got the hell out of there. Trent sat shivering in the front passenger seat, while from the back seat, I brought Kempthorne up to speed on the military thinking I could connect to the source, and Kage having been kidnapped by someone other than his brother. He absorbed it all, asked me if I was all right, and said little else on the drive back.

Once we were inside the safety of the Hudson Yard apartment, Trent loitered in the lounge and kitchen, no longer radiating happy Labrador vibes. More a Labrador who had been caught chewing its master's slippers. He was less of a liability with us than on his own, but none of us were pleased about him hanging around.

Kempthorne immediately hustled me up the stairs, where his gentle hands cradled my wrist while his fingers stroked, massaging trick into my skin like warm oil.

But the silence between us gnawed on my jitters. Something was wrong.

"I'm er... glad you're okay," I told him. I was more than glad. I wanted to throw my arms around him, yell at him, shove him on a plane back to England. All of it. But he was so bloody quiet, I stayed quiet, too, sensing a storm approaching.

"It was just a scratch," he said, head down, concentrating on healing me.

"Yeah, no. I'm pretty sure the round missed your heart by half an inch." He didn't respond. "Hey..." His gaze lifted. "You are okay, right?"

He glanced toward the stairs, probably concerned Trent was listening. Worry pinched his brow.

"What's going on?"

His gaze found mine, and all at once, he was just Alex —just a guy in a bloodstained sweater caught up in things he had no control over. "I can't lose you." Soft eyes and the downward turn of his lips squeezed my heart.

I took his hand. "You're the one who nearly died." Even with his hand in mine, it felt as though he was slipping away.

"I don't think you understand what this is," he said, plucking his hand from my grasp. "What we are." He stood and turned his back, crossing the floor toward the windows. "What you mean to me. Which is partly my fault." He threw out a hand, then swept it through his messy hair. "I hardly know myself."

Alex stood with his back to me, admiring the twinkling early morning view of a cold New York. "I didn't expect..." He sucked in a breath and quietly tried again. "I didn't expect to encounter love. I rather thought it something that happens to everyone else."

This man.

How was he here, *with me?*

"Alex—" I moved to his side, a whole lot of emotions spiraling through me. Panic, mostly, that somehow all of this was about to slip through my fingers. I wanted to reach out to him. We could fuck like there was no tomorrow, but how to fix this... whatever it was, I didn't know.

"John, I would have killed Greyson," he said.

"Yeah, I know." I shrugged, standing next to him, hands thrust in my pockets. "But you didn't."

"Because *you* were there. You are the *only* reason I didn't kill him. And honestly, I'd have slaughtered every single person there to get to you."

I wet my lips, not sure where this was going but fearing it more with every word he said. "Okay."

"What I'm saying is... I think, when we get back to London, after... everything... you and I should no longer be in a relationship—"

"What?" I froze. My heart thumped.

"My life... The things I've done, been involved in, everything I'm capable of. It doesn't lend itself to happy endings. Eventually, it will all fall apart. It always does. Isn't it better if we stop this now, before somebody gets hurt?" He said all that with his soppy look and his stupid hair flopped over his forehead, vulnerable and so fucking

Alexander Kempthorne that I almost believed he was right.

A dry bark of a laugh shot out of me. Was I hearing this right? He was ending us? Oh, fuck no. "You've decided?"

"Yes, I believe so." He swallowed, held my gaze, and then turned back toward the cityscape. "It will hurt less now than in the long run."

Still so bloody high and mighty, even with dirt on his face and a bloody hole in his sweater where the fucking round had pierced his chest. And I didn't get a say in this? I was just supposed to swallow his bullshit because he was scared? I was fucking scared too. Wasn't that the point of relationships? Not that I'd ever had one that worked.

Maybe the problem was me? Who was I trying to impress? Alexander Kempthorne and me? We were from different worlds, different lives. It had been fun, amazing even, but I'd been dreaming if I'd thought we could last.

"Er, hello?" Trent's annoying American twang sounded up the stairs.

"Fuck off," I snapped, earning Kempthorne's raised eyebrow.

"But... there's someone at the door."

Alex stepped toward the stairs. If I let him go now, he'd think he'd won, he'd call it over. Fuck that.

I caught his arm, jolting him to a stop. "I'll get it. You wait here. We aren't done."

He frowned as I let him go. Hopefully, he assumed my voice trembled from anger and not the panic running like ice water through my veins. We weren't done. No way. He was everything—I loved the prick. He didn't get to brush us aside as though we were a weekend fuck and nothing more. I'd literally dragged him back to life with my own bare hands. I wasn't backing down, and I wasn't fucking walking away. Not from him. Not from *us*.

I jogged down the stairs. Trent tried to muster a fake smile, probably having heard every word of what had just happened.

The intercom trilled, someone leaning on the buzzer.

"Jesus…" I hit the view button, about to rage at the arsehole, when Kage's ridiculously handsome face, amber eyes, and half-smiling lips filled the screen.

He blinked, dark brows pinched in. "Dom? Buzz me up. *Now*."

Kage was here? I hit the unlock button, thoughts reeling. Kage was here… Christ, we'd spent weeks searching for him, and he just rocks up out of the blue? He'd looked all right. He was here, which meant he was free, which meant we could leave America? Was it all over? God, I hoped it was over.

"Who is it?" Trent asked.

"Someone with answers."

Sawyer, Kage's brother, the LOA, the military. Kage was the connection. And he was here. He'd give us the answers. In a few hours, we could be on Kempthorne's private jet and headed back to London.

I opened the apartment door and stepped out into the hallway. At the end of the hall, the elevator numbers counted up.

It was going to be all right, wasn't it?

My trick tingled. My fingers itched to grab my cards. Kage was here, which was good, so why did it feel *wrong*?

The elevator dinged.

I was about to find out.

A lexander

Panic fluttered inside my chest. I'd made a terrible mistake, but that was to be expected. It always hurt, letting go. But it was necessary. Easy, even. Everything would go back to the way it had been before. I could protect Dom from afar, without getting involved. It was safer that way, for everyone.

The fluttering in my chest squeezed my lungs. I leaned against the wall, willing my heart to calm and my head to clear.

Necessary.

Practical.

Better.

And nobody would get hurt.

I was capable of terrible things.

I'd burn the world for him. I'd raze cities for him. I'd kill without hesitating for him.

And that... that was dangerous.

The fear, anger, panic—all of it mingled together and stalked my every waking moment, like the shadows had.

The door opened and closed downstairs. Voices simmered. I had to get control of myself. Or at least appear to. I was a card castle inside, a swift breeze away from collapse. And all because I'd thought I'd lost him.

The voices lifted, their tone short and sharp. *Angry.*

I tore off my filthy clothes, washed off the dried blood from my miracle moment, and dressed hastily, then buttoned up my shirt as I walked down the stairs.

The sight that greeted me stopped me in my tracks.

Kage Mitchell stood between the kitchen and the door, flanked by the two LOA agents, Palliser and Pierce. Dom stood off to my right, eyes a little wider than they should have been if all had been well, and Trent was slowly, deliberately, backing away from my left.

I buttoned my cuffs. "How may I help you gentlemen?"

"Alexander Kempthorne and John Domenici," Palliser—the stockier of the two agents—began. "You are both hereby detained by the Latent Observation Agency for your own protection and the protection of the United States of America. You have the right to remain silent. Do we need to cuff you?"

Silence stretched between us.

Strange, how they'd arrived now, when we'd only been back in the apartment less than an hour. Almost as though someone had tipped them off.

And then there was the matter of Kage, standing pillar-still between his colleagues. I didn't trust the man as far as I could throw him, but he certainly didn't look pleased to be here, and even appeared somewhat ruffled around his edges. His long dark hair was loose, slick, and scruffy. Scratches marked the knuckles of both his hands. His lip sported a recent cut. These marks were fresh. Kage did not want to be here.

Trent cleared his throat and handed Palliser something.

The agent lifted the vial of Ink and tutted. "And who does this belong to?"

I sighed.

"Ink is a highly controlled substance," Palliser continued. "Possession by a latent carries a ten-year prison sentence."

"You little tosser," Dom hissed at Trent.

Trent visibly shrank and scurried toward the agents. "Agents, they are both extremely dangerous latents. Alexander threatened to kidnap and murder me. And John is... I saw him *do things*."

"We're aware, Mister Anderson." Pierce—the slim one—smirked. "You're safe now."

Trent had used the landline to call them here. I should have left his body in the woods.

"Yeah, I'm not doing this," Kage announced, out of the blue. He snatched Pierce's gun from its holster and aimed at the man's head with one swift, slick movement. Trent squeaked. Dom had a card in his hand and its burning edges under Palliser's chin in a blur.

Trent bolted for the door. I grabbed a vase off the

nearby table, charged it with trick, and flung it overarm. The vase shattered against the door in an array of dazzling sparks. Trent reeled, spilling straight into my arms.

"Oh god."

I turned to Dom, clamping a writhing Trent close. "It appears we've outstayed our welcome."

"Yeah." He grinned, eyes shining. "Nice throw."

Kage, however, was not amused and had the look of a man who might pull the trigger, having reached the end of his patience.

"Kage?" Dom asked. Kage didn't move. Didn't twitch. Beads of glistening sweat appeared at Pierce's hairline. "Hey, Hollywood? You're not going to kill an LOA agent. Grab his cuffs."

If Kage shot an LOA agent, there was little chance Dom and I would escape prosecution, even if Kage had pulled the trigger. We were latents. Everything was our fault. Even when it wasn't.

Kage shifted, blinking out of his murderous gaze, and worked the agent's cuffs free.

"You won't get away with this," Pierce growled as Kage cuffed him.

Dom dealt similarly with Palliser, keeping his charged card at the man's throat. "We haven't done anything wrong."

Palliser snorted. "The fact you're breathing is wrong." Dom tensed. Palliser smirked, thinking he'd won. "Whatever you do, we're coming for you, *English*."

That name, using it for Dom. Kage had called Dom

the same, and Dom glanced at Kage, the pair of them sharing some secret knowledge.

Palliser laughed. "You're all fucked. You just don't know it. The LOA has been closing in for weeks now. We have everything on you three. Your military records, Dom—Sean Sawyer was most helpful in handing those over, before he met with the business end of a Glock. Kempthorne, where to start with you… We've had our eye on you for a long time, but Agent Mitchell blocked us. And Kage, you stupid son of a bitch, you let them get into your head—"

Kage pistol-whipped Palliser across the back of the head, cutting off his tirade. Dom let the big man fall chin-first to the floor and left him there, out cold.

"You're never coming back from this, Kage," Pierce said.

"I'm done." He grabbed Pierce by his cuffs and yanked the man close, face-to-face. "It's over. All of it. It's wrong."

The kind of hurt brimming in Pierce's eyes said more than the man's words could. He cared for Kage either as a friend, or more. Perhaps they'd worked together for years.

Kage shoved Pierce to the floor beside his unconscious partner and opened the cupboard under the sink. After grabbing the duct tape, he went to work on Pierce's wrists, then taped his mouth.

"We have to get out of here—now," Kage said.

Dom snuffed out his glowing card and tucked it into his pocket with the others. "You need to tell us what the fuck is going on."

"I will, once we're on the road. Kempthorne?"

"Ah yes." I still had a hyperventilating Trent in my arms. "The tape?"

Kage taped Trent's wrists while the man blubbered and begged for me not to stuff him in the cupboard. Kage taped his mouth closed. Dom opened the cupboard, and in went Trent.

Pierce watched the whole thing with wide eyes and a great deal of mumbling.

"Grab what you need," Kage said, kneeling to steal Palliser's car key from the agent's pocket. "We can't come back here."

Twenty minutes later, we'd loaded our minimal bags into the LOA's black truck and, with Kage behind the wheel, left Hudson Yard in the rearview mirrors.

From the back seat, I resisted the urge to suggest Kage might like to drop us off at the airport, as tempting as it was to abandon this endeavor now he was back and appeared to be perfectly fine. There was still too much we didn't know. "On a scale of how dangerous this situation is, with ten being Dom and I are both about to die, and one, we can walk away unscathed, where are we?" I asked.

Kage considered it—amber eyes locking on to me via the mirror before sliding away again. "Nine. The LOA want you, Kempthorne, and the military want you, Dom."

"Alive or dead?" Dom asked. "Because I feel like something has gotten lost in translation somewhere. And why is your brother trying to kill me?"

Kage gave a weary sigh. "Where to start...?"

"Anywhere, frankly," I added from the back seat,

feeling like a third wheel, or Dom's conscience on his shoulder. The bad voice, naturally.

"Start with why the fuck you've had us running all over New York and here you are, perfectly fine," Dom said.

"I told you to stay away."

Dom laughed.

I wondered again, for the hundredth time, why I'd saved Kage Mitchell's life.

"Fuck you," Dom said. A sentiment I shared. "I thought you were dead."

They fell silent. Kage flicked the turn signal on and glided the big truck between lanes of traffic.

"Why don't you start at the beginning," I suggested, earning another sharp glance in the mirror.

"I was supposed to bring Kempthorne in," Kage said. "I bluffed, delayed, said it wasn't the right time, said I had leads on bigger things, but in the end, they'd heard enough and cut me out altogether."

"So the LOA had you this whole time?" Dom asked.

"Yeah, and they knew we were close, Dom. So they cold-extracted me, kept me locked up, tried to get the answers out of me. Before they took me in, though, I knew something was up... They'd been monitoring my every move anyway, but since Wordsworth, they switched their focus to you, Dom. Like they'd forgotten Kempthorne existed. Suddenly, they wanted all the intel on John Domenici."

"I'd gone from the latent you could fuck to get close to your answers, to the latent who had all the answers, huh?"

Kage didn't even flinch. "They asked about your military career, what unit you served in, who your squad mates were. Things I didn't know. I couldn't ask you, since you were on to me and I'd burned those bridges."

"So you went to Sean Sawyer?" Dom said.

"Yeah. But the LOA got to him first. He'd told them everything. And by the time I got in touch, he'd had second thoughts. Whatever he'd said to the agency, it scared him."

"Scared for his life?"

"I mean, yeah, I guess." Kage nodded. "I didn't realize how scared. I told him I knew you, that I'd try and help. He clammed up. Said he'd try and contact you. That was as far as I got before the agency came for me."

"Is that normal?" Dom asked. "For the LOA to kidnap their own agents and torture them?"

Kage cleared his throat. "I'd been compromised. I'm a traitor. I'm only out now because they needed me to get inside the apartment building after Trent Anderson tipped them off."

A few seconds passed in quiet. The truck droned. The city suburbs blurred by. The LOA—via Kage—had always had an interest in me, but not Dom. What changed?

"Why did they switch their focus to Dom?" I asked.

"Wordsworth. Dom... you... I dunno... The agency showed me the footage—Montgomery had a camera in the office. They showed me what you did to Montgomery, how you commanded latent forces and brought Kempthorne back. They had no idea you were so powerful."

"I didn't do anything. The shadows destroyed Montgomery and I just… I dunno… I kinda just didn't let Alex die. I'm not what they think."

"Aren't you?" Kage asked. "Because the LOA thinks you are, and the military does too. The LOA wants you off the streets, locked up and controlled, where they can keep an eye on you—or dead preferably—but the DOD wants you locked down in their research facility so they can turn their troops into boosted latent assassins, I guess."

"Speaking of assassins, you still haven't told me why Greyson is trying to kill me."

Kage swore under his breath. "Greyson is… The military is his life. They took him in when… after… I er… Shit, it's a long story."

"After your father fixed it so you thought you'd killed him and sent Greyson to boot camp?" I said.

Kage's gaze flicked to me in the mirror. "You know?"

"I had a talk with your father."

"I… I thought for the longest time that I'd killed my brother when we were kids. Greyson won't stop. He has orders to take you in, but… there's something else going on with him." From the back seat, I saw how Dom glared at Kage, not believing him. "I haven't been in touch with him. I swear," Kage said. "If I had he'd… he'd probably want me dead too."

"He torched your family home," Dom added.

"Yeah… I heard."

"He's not bringing me in, Kage. He's trying to kill me."

"Grey doesn't know you. And they have him spiked on Ink, so he hardly knows himself. My guess is he had the original kill order, knew we'd worked together, and the job turned personal. He and I... It's complicated. He's not bad, he's just... He's my brother."

"You need to tell him to back the fuck off."

"I can't. Dom, you don't get it. To everyone else outside this truck, you're a latent who controls shadows and brings people back to life—you're like a fuckin' latent messiah. The LOA killed your CO to get information on you. The Department of Defense wanted you dead but switched tack and now wants you brought in. I'm nothing in all of this. I just got in the way."

Another silence settled over us all. There was a great deal to unpack in Kage's information.

"They wouldn't think I'm the latent messiah if they'd seen me get my arse kicked in Soho."

Kage glanced over. "I've tried telling them you're just a guy, but they think I'm brainwashed by your latent voodoo."

Dom snorted. "I blow stuff up in fancy ways. That's all."

"But it's not all, Dom, is it?" Kage blurted. "You won't see it, but Kempthorne does. Why do you think he bought you from the British Military years ago or why he's kept you so close this whole time? He knows or has suspected what you're capable of. He probably saw it before anyone else." Those amber eyes flashed to me again. Entirely right, and we both knew it.

"It's not what you think," Dom denied. "I'm just a latent."

"Actually, no," I spoke up and cleared my throat when the words got stuck. "You're not. Kage is right. You've never been 'just a latent.'" His aura, for one, had always been brighter, and more tempting, than any other latent's I'd met. Olivia Barnes had seen it. Dom had always been different. I knew the source intimately, and I knew Dom's trick just as thoroughly. They were the same. He probably had controlled the shadows, and he'd brought me back from near death twice.

"You have got to be shitting me," Dom snarled. "All this because they think I'm special?"

He had no idea how special he was.

"Hold on." Kage gunned the truck's throaty engine and swerved across several lanes of traffic. "We've got company."

27

D^{om}

The truck carving through traffic in the rearview mirror looked a lot like the one we were riding in, suggesting we were being tailed by Kage's pals in the LOA.

"Should have ditched the truck," Kage muttered.

"I take it you are no longer considered an ally of theirs?" Kempthorne piped up from the back seat.

"No. I am firmly in rogue agent territory."

"How inconvenient," Kempthorne muttered, making no effort to hide the snark behind his words.

"File a complaint," Kage snapped.

"We have gone to great lengths to find you. You could at least be grateful."

"I told you not to come."

"That note?!" Kempthorne scoffed. "*Please.* Such an obvious cry for help."

What was happening? We were being tailed by LOA agents who'd proven they'd kill to get what they wanted, and Alex and Kage were bickering? "Stop arguing like a pair of old women. We need a plan."

"You have to leave the US," Kage said, checking the mirrors and then increasing the truck's speed. "Kempthorne, you have a private jet, right?"

"Yes."

I peered over my shoulder at Alex. His gaze snagged mine. He'd known I was something *special.* Not just suspected it, but *known* it. What else did he know about me that I didn't? What other info had he bought from Sawyer? Had he known I could heal, even when I hadn't? Just what the fuck was I meant to be?

"Call whoever you have to," Kage said, "and organize for the jet to be ready."

"These things take time. I can't snap my fingers and hop on a plane—"

"I'll get us to a safe house. Buy you a day, maybe. But I can't keep you from the LOA, Greyson, and the military. You have to get off US soil ASAP."

"What about you?" I asked.

He smiled his Hollywood smile. "I'll be all right."

"Come back to London?" Maybe it was a shit idea— his loyalties were all over the place—but something told me if we left Kage in the US, he'd be eating a Glock, same as Sawyer had.

"And what does Kempthorne think of that?" Kage asked, almost smirking.

"He hates you, but he doesn't want to see you dead."

Kage glanced in the mirror.

"My opinion is rendered moot by John's apparent inability to despise you," Kempthorne explained.

Kage chuckled. "Least you're honest."

"Look, mate, we've been through some shit together, but we're here, aren't we? You tried to prevent all of this. That's worth something."

Kage gave it some thought, still checking the mirrors and the road ahead. His heavy sigh shuddered. "I screwed up with my brother when we were kids. Did something bad. Hurt him in ways that are unforgivable. I can't abandon him. I have to help him. I can't come to London, Dom. Even if I want to."

What Greyson needed was an intervention and for Kage to take his sniper rifle away. But he was Kage's family, and *that* I understood. That didn't mean I was going to like Greyson anytime soon. "He shot Kempthorne through the chest."

Kage thought for a few seconds. "Not the head?"

"Wow."

"I'm just saying, if he'd wanted Kempthorne dead, he'd have taken the head shot."

"Jesus, are all the Mitchells stone-cold killers? Greyson did want him dead. Kempthorne literally bled out in my hands."

"All right, relax. It's just, he's fine. So…"

"He's fine because I fucking healed him."

"Tell me again how you're not some *special latent*?"

"Fuck you, Kage." I smiled though. "Greyson couldn't have known I'd save Kempthorne." Although, he'd mentioned seeing some footage of me, same as Kage had. And he could have taken a head shot. Chest shots were messy and inaccurate. Bloody hell, Kage was right.

"Remind me to thank your brother for missing, the next time we meet," Kempthorne said from the back seat, voice thick with irony.

"Everything still hurts from the last time I saw him," I said.

Kage winced. "He's my little brother. I screwed up before, so I gotta look out for him now."

"You were young," Alex said, "and your father orchestrated the lies to suit himself. Don't be too harsh on yourself."

Christ, Alex was offering Kage advice now? Even Kage frowned, either irritated or disturbed. His cut lip pulled downward and his gaze flicked to me. "I'm glad you're okay," he said.

"Yeah." I shrugged. "Likewise."

"For what it's worth, you coming over here means a lot." His smile was back, reminding me exactly why I'd fallen for him in the first place. Things were different now. We were all different. But after seeing his life and the world he'd grown up in, the man that was Kage Mitchell began to make a lot more sense. I couldn't hate him for being who he was.

"For a while there, I was sure we'd find your body."

"There's still time," Kempthorne said.

Wow. I twisted in the seat, about to remind Kempthorne who had just saved our arses from the LOA, when Kage anchored the truck's brakes and swerved toward an embankment. The truck pitched, its tires bit into the soft grass, and Kage sped us down the side of stationary traffic.

"They're closing," he said. "Strap in. It's about to get wild."

The black truck following loomed in the side mirrors, its front grille huge.

"Can you shake 'em?"

Kage half lifted a shoulder. "Not if they call in air support."

Oh fuck. "Is that likely?"

Kage jerked the wheel and the truck bounced off a curb, rejoining the road. Its engine roared and the rear end tried to snatch free, but Kage grappled with the wheel and plowed forward.

"Yeah, maybe. You're wanted latent *numero uno*."

The road was twice as wide as most streets in the UK and lined by squat little single-story homes, snow-covered yards, and spindly trees.

The truck's speed inched higher. Kage wove it between slower moving cars, but the grille of the second truck stayed glued to our arse. Kage jerked the wheel left and the truck veered sideways, tires screaming. I grabbed the Jesus handle, glimpsed an arm extending from our tail's passenger window, and saw the gun. "Oh shit."

Rounds punched into metal.

"I thought you said they want me alive?"

"Scare tactics." Kage grinned, the arsehole. "Fore-play." He did something with the truck, somehow demanding more power from the roaring engine, and threw me back into the passenger seat.

The LOA fell back, but not far enough. I glimpsed

Kempthorne's glare from the rear seat where he clung on, wedged against the door.

"Screw this." Flicking a card from my pocket, I hit the button for the window, charging the card in my right hand.

"I wouldn't…" Kage recommended.

"What are they gonna do, arrest me?"

"I think that ship has sailed," Kempthorne grumbled.

"Exactly."

Unlatching the seat belt, I twisted and wedged my back against the glovebox.

"Drive straight," I told Kage, then leaned out of the window. Ice-cold wind whipped against the back of my head and down my neck. My hair lashed in front of my eyes. Numbnuts with the gun leaned out, eager to get a shot at a latent.

Moving car. He wasn't even aiming down his gun sights. No chance he'd hit me. I flicked a glowing card into the air and watched it zip back and forth before slamming into the truck's front fender. Trick exploded and the truck bounced, swerving.

Numbnuts fired his gun.

I ducked back inside, grinning. "A few more of those and they'll think twice about chasing us."

"Hm," Kage grumbled. "We've got more company."

I stuck my head out again. The truck was still on us and gaining. Three black-and-white cop cars also screeched in, lights and sirens blazing.

"Hold on!"

I grabbed the door and center console. The truck bounced, throwing me up off the seat. My head hit the roof. My back scraped the glovebox. Then, with a jolt, we landed again. Kage fought with the wheel. The truck slid sideways. Grass and mounds of dirty snow flashed by outside. We hit the road and Kage fishtailed the truck back under control, gunning the engine.

"Shit. You drive just like Kempthorne."

"Dom, deal with our tails," Alex said, voice thin. He was done fucking around.

"Copy that." I fanned three cards between my fingers, leaned out, and let them *fly*. The cards fluttered into the air like fallings stars. One splashed into the LOA's front windshield, shattering it. Their truck veered suddenly. The two remaining cards blasted over the two following cop cars, exploding a hole in the front of one and punching out the tire of the second.

Two down, one to go.

The remaining cop car burst through the carnage, front bumper bearing down on our rear.

I'd seen all the cop shows. US cops didn't fuck around. They'd ram us off the road and then put two bullets in me and Kempthorne, citing reasonable force. Fuck that. The beefy cop car rammed our truck. We bounced, Kage swore, and Kempthorne growled.

Two cards.

I flooded them with trick, made them shine, and set them free. They spun and the wind caught them, dancing with them, but I'd planned for that. Those two cards splashed into the cop car's grille, blowing it wide open. Metal and trick rained and plinked, bringing that last car to an abrupt, smoking halt.

I slumped back into the seat and closed the window. "Get us out of here."

———

The safe house we pulled up outside of was an odd bunker-looking place, either built in the 70s to resemble some kind of futuristic concrete wedge with a huge wrap-around suspended deck and wall of windows, or the house was a cover for an actual bunker. The trees surrounding it stood leafless and bare, making the place feel isolated and cold. I'd been to more welcoming mausoleums.

We left the battered truck and climbed some steps. Moss had grown on the smooth concrete walls. A keypad blinked by a thick, grey metal door. Kage tapped in a code and pushed inside. We entered on the first floor. Stairs spiraled down to an open-plan lounge and library room with 70s furniture and a piano, of all things. The smooth concrete walls, varnished wood accents, and fabric sofas gave off 70s porn film vibes.

"It's old, but it all works," Kage explained. "We'll be safe for a few days."

I'd seen a perimeter fence on the way in. We'd passed through electric gates, unlocked by Kage's code; whoever this place belonged to, they were serious about keeping the neighbors out.

"Get settled." Kage flicked on all the lights as he breezed from room to room.

Kempthorne stood in the open-plan lounge, frowning at the piano. "Does Kage play?"

"I do, actually," Kage said, reappearing from the door at the back of the kitchen area. "There's no food. I'm gonna take a walk to the store and check the perimeter. It won't take long. You guys all right here?"

I tucked my thumbs into my pockets. "Sure."

"Great." He jogged up the stairs and was gone, leaving me alone with Kempthorne for the first time in what felt like days. In the last few hours, we'd hogtied an LOA agent, knocked another out, shoved Trent back in the cupboard, outrun more LOA agents, trashed three cop cars, and now we were here, in a 70s porn house in the woods. On the run from all the acronyms.

"The jet will be waiting tomorrow," Kempthorne said, breaking the silence. I'd heard him make the calls during the ride here. And afterward, we'd all fallen quiet in the truck. The quiet was too bloody thick here too, as though the building were hermetically sealed from the outside world. Despite the open-plan space, I struggled to relax.

I drifted around the sofa, drawn to the books. They were almost all fiction—a few thrillers, some fantasy, reference books on gardening. All old 70s covers, but no dust. The house hadn't been abandoned, but it had been preserved.

Kempthorne joined me at the shelves. "Not what I was expecting."

"No, it's weird, right?" I spread my hands at my sides, soaking up the low-level background psychic hum.

"Hm." He looked up at the suspended gallery, to the main entrance door. "As though we've walked into the past." He saw my spread hands and questioned me with a glance.

"I don't sense anything sinister lurking in the psychic resonance, it just feels... off."

"No gruesome murders? Bodies in the woods?" he asked.

I smiled, having had the same thought. "Nothing like that. The building is... I dunno... content. All good memories, I think. I could take a look outside but I don't fancy disturbing any woodland ghosts. They can stay out there."

Kempthorne plucked a book from the shelf and flipped through the pages. With his nose buried in a book, he looked like the old Kempthorne—the distant, untouchable man I'd worked with for two years, having no idea who he really was inside. I hadn't forgotten what he'd said about breaking up. We weren't done talking about that, but if I brought it up now we'd argue, and despite the weird house and being on the run, this little moment was soft and nice and what we both needed.

"Do you believe that stuff about me being a latent messiah?" I asked.

"I think anything is possible." He spotted something in the book, frowned, and showed me a name scrawled on the inside cover.

Isla Mitchell

"Kage's mum?"

"Likely."

"She died or left? I can't remember."

"Divorced," Kempthorne said, returning the book to the shelf. "Apparently." He tucked a hand into his trouser pocket and regarded the open-plan space again.

"Although, I'm beginning to wonder if the Mitchells are better liars than we've given them credit for."

"Meaning?"

"Greyson was dead, then wasn't. William made no mention of a house in the woods when I asked about bolt holes, but here we are." His gaze settled on the piano. "Kage is clearly hiding information regarding his brother and probably more."

"You think he's lying?" I asked, tracking his gaze and how it had fixed on the piano. Did Kempthorne play?

"I think it wouldn't be the first time he's lied to us."

I puffed out a breath. "I asked him to come back to London..."

"Because you keep trying to find the good in people."

I winced. "I don't think he's an enemy."

"You wouldn't."

"What does that mean?"

"When it comes to Kage Mitchell, you have a blind spot." He smiled a little, so the words were softened, but they still held a barb to them. He wasn't wrong, though. Kage and me, I couldn't hate him, even though I should.

"He has helped us, though. We're here, aren't we?"

"We are." He crossed the floor, passing between the brown 70s sofas, and opened the lid over the piano keys. He plinked a note. I had no idea which one, but it sounded good, I could tell that much. East End boys don't get music lessons.

He pressed another key, then a few together, making a short melody. He could play, all right.

I leaned my arse against the side of the piano. "You think I still have feelings for him?"

"Don't you?"

"No, Christ. Not like that."

He played a few more notes. "Dom, we didn't come halfway around the world to a country that despises our kind, putting our lives at risk, just to see if he was still breathing. You care for him. It's admirable, really. I'm not jealous." He smiled. "Much."

"Okay, fine, but only like I care for Gina, not... you know... like I care for my hot boss."

"Ah." He laughed and the sound flowed all the way through me, warming my soul.

"You play?"

"Not in a long time." He sat on the stool, pressed the pedals or whatever they were called, and immediately made music. His long, elegant fingers swept over the keys so fast I couldn't keep up. I lifted my gaze to his face instead, finding him already lost to the tune. I knew it too: *Wicked Game* by Chris Isaak.

He missed a note and cut himself off with a snarl. "I'm a little rusty."

I should have probably said something about how awesome he was, but my voice had wedged in my throat, and then he began playing again and the music was doing strange things to my insides. That daft cowlick flopped in front of his eyes.

That soft look in his unfocused eyes—the look I loved waking up next to—went straight to my heart. Right then, I decided: this man was mine, no matter what. Did I deserve him? Fuck no. Was he fucked up? Hell yeah, but I'd dragged him back from death with my bare fucking hands, and I'd do it again a hundred times over. He didn't get to end us. And if he thought I was just going to walk away because he said so, then he'd forgotten who he was dealing with. I never gave up.

The music dipped and rose, filled the house, my soul, ebbing and flowing, building to a crescendo. His whole body swayed—the notes flowing through all of him, not just his fingers. And then it ended, cut off. Silence rushed back in, broken only by his heavy breathing, and mine.

He looked up and smiled. "Do you play?"

"I'm from the East End," I croaked. "The only music lessons we had were to run from police sirens."

He laughed and everything I'd felt these past few days, all the fear and frustration, love and confusion, it broke me open and spilled out. I turned his face to me, slipping my fingers into his hair. The second he tipped his head back, I brushed my lips over his, falling into the kiss with everything I had. I kissed him like he was so fucking precious, as though I was scared he'd fall through my fingers. I kissed him like none of this was real, like we were in a dream and I'd wake up too soon. That was what it was like with him, in this crazy life. Cecil Court, Aston Martins, his body and memories in mine, his laugh when it was real and true, Ravenscourt, his ghosts, how he kept a whole world of power inside of him and somehow didn't fall apart around it. Christ... he was my impossible dream; he was everything people like me didn't get. He was the reason I was still breathing; he had to be. Why else had I survived a shit father, the godawful streets, a military desperate to screw me up, and a world that wanted to grind me to dust? It had to be for Alex. For us.

The kiss ended softly, and all I could see was the

honest openness in his eyes. He was scared too. I stroked my thumb over his cheek. "You don't get to throw us away, right? We're not done."

He swallowed.

"Cute," Kage said.

I dropped my hand and eased back. I hadn't heard the door open. Kage could have been on the galleried landing the whole time. I didn't bloody care what he'd seen or heard.

"You play well." Kage carried a grocery bag down the stairs and dumped its contents on the large kitchen island.

Kempthorne cleared his throat. "I should have asked for permission."

"It's fine... Was my mother's." Kage manhandled the groceries, every item landing hard on the countertop. "She played like you, like she was born with music in her veins."

"What happened to her?" I asked.

Kage's shoulders stiffened. "She left. She couldn't handle what happened to Greyson." He screwed up the bag, tossed it into a cupboard, and headed through the kitchen door, into the back corridor where I figured the bedrooms were. "Help yourself to food," he called. "I'm gonna get cleaned up." A door slammed.

It was pretty safe to assume he'd heard and seen everything—from Kempthorne's stunning music to the kiss.

"Perhaps we should refrain from angering him as our lives currently rest in his hands?" Kempthorne suggested, rising from the piano stool.

"He'll be all right." I hoped. He was tough. He knew I was *with* Kempthorne. None of this was a surprise. He didn't get to be pissed off after everything he'd done.

The rest of the evening passed awkwardly. Kage whipped up omelets and we made a painful effort at small talk.

The house had enough bedrooms for the three of us to bunk separately. I showered, shaved, and lay on the bed, too restless to sleep. I'd checked every window, every door, mapped several escape routes, and planned for an incursion, but my brain wasn't done. It had to turn over every new piece of information we'd learned, searching for angles we may have missed.

The door cracked open after midnight and Alex crept inside. A dangerous intensity burned in his eyes, or a touch of trick. He didn't say a word, just approached the bed, fingers working at his shirt buttons. I propped myself on an elbow, opened my mouth to tell him this might not be the best of ideas, considering Kage was a door down and we were rarely quiet, but he straddled my legs, pushed a hand on my chest, shoved me down, and pressed a finger to my lips.

"Hush."

I swallowed.

The finger stayed on my lips, sizzling with trick. Oh fuck, this was hot. He was always hot, but this was... something else. His shirt hung open, his chest golden under the slither of light filtering through the closed blinds. My heart already pounded and my cock was quickly getting in the game.

He straightened on his knees, reached behind him, and produced a length of thick rope from the back of his trousers ... with tassels on the end. Okay... Wait, what? I arched an eyebrow.

"Seventies curtain tieback," he whispered, snapping the rope taut.

Trick shimmered in his eyes.

Wait a second, was he going to—

He fell forward, hot mouth on mine, kissing me slowly, softly, tasting of mint. He twined his fingers with mine, and I knew... this was what we'd been missing. This was the distance that had yawned between us, open and aching, wanting to be filled. And now it was. It wasn't about the rope; this was about trust.

He caught my right wrist, lifted it above my head, then did the same with my left, bunched them together, and looped the tasseled tieback around them. I squirmed, grinning, cock aching for him to grind his hips against me. "Rope, huh?"

His eyes flashed in the dark, devilish and wicked. "If you want out," he whispered, "tell me it's raining."

"I... What?"

He reached up, jerked my twined arms higher, and looped the end around the bedpost. And now I was spread under him, starved of touch, body burning. Alex reared up, tore off his shirt, and started at his belt, his dark eyes fixed on my face. I already breathed as though I'd sprinted here. Christ, just when I thought he couldn't get any hotter… He tugged his belt open and made quick work of his trouser fly. My mouth watered for what came next. If he got himself off, I might fucking come from watching. But he stopped short of freeing himself and flicked off the sheet covering me, and there I lay, trussed up, naked except for the pants I'd left on, pinned under Kempthorne's thighs.

"There ain't no way I'm doin' this quietly."

His eyes flashed a warning. "Silence, or it ends."

I whimpered—fucking whimpered. I didn't do quiet. He was gonna have to gag me. But that was part of the fun, right?

He braced himself on an arm, hovering inches from me. "Have you done this before?"

I jerked an eyebrow and grinned, then lunged, trying to capture a kiss.

He jerked his head away and smirked. "You may speak."

"Not like this." Sawyer and I had fucked around, but it had been weird back then. He was into it, but I hadn't been sure. Maybe I hadn't fully trusted him because I was *definitely* into this.

Alex's hand swooped up my naked chest. "Remember, if you want to stop, tell me it's raining." He pinched my nipple.

I bucked. "Fuck."

He smothered my mouth with a hand. "*Silence.*"

Oh fuck… I nodded furiously, desperately, and his hand loosened, falling away, replaced by his tongue sweeping across my lips, then diving in and setting me on fire all over again. His touch skimmed my jaw and came to rest on my neck, then Alexander Kempthorne bowed his head and sealed his lips around a nipple. Shivers trilled through me and my cock jumped, eager and leaking.

"Wait..." He looked up. "I have an idea." He clambered off and in three strides was out of the door, leaving it ajar and me spread-eagled.

"What the fuck..." I panted. A wedge of light cut across the room and landed on me. I was tied up like a piñata, naked and hard as fuck, and he leaves? He'd better not be making a fucking midnight snack.

"*Kempthorne?*" I growled, quiet-like. Shit, if Kage woke up and found me like this... "*Alex!?*"

He stepped through the doorway, closed the door, and sauntered toward me with something in his hand that I didn't get a good look at before he left it on the floor beside the bed.

"Bastard."

He climbed over me again and the finger was back at my lips. "Shh."

I flicked my tongue out, lapped his fingertip, and almost laughed as his intense eyes widened with surprise. What I really wanted was his cock in my mouth, but a finger would do, seeing as I didn't get much choice in how this played out. He slid his finger between my lips. I looped my tongue around and sucked.

He breathed hard through his nose, then a growl rumbled out of him. He pulled his hand away, spoiling my fun, and shifted on my thighs, grabbing at the bulge in his loosened trousers, adjusting himself.

Aw, you hard, Alex? I stayed quiet but smiled, squirmed under him, and deliberately twitched my cock for attention. He glanced down, wet his lips, and all I wanted right then was for him to go down on me.

His lips quirked. "Close your eyes."

I exhaled and shuddered. He was killing me. I half-laughed, then closed my eyes. All at once, everything got louder. I could feel his solid weight on my legs, the thick curtain tieback burned my wrists, and the stupid tassels tickled. His weight leaned to the side, something rustled, he straightened, and a dash of bitter cold touched my chest, right over my heart. I hissed, not sure if it hurt or whether I liked it. Then the hard, cold nub slipped sideways across my skin and looped around my nipple. Ice, it was ice. The ice spiraled around my nipple, then Alex's warm, wet tongue swept the same path. A shudder ran through me, all the way to my toes. The ice skimmed a loop and slid south, its chill followed by Alex's warming tongue.

I wanted my fingers in his hair, wanted to touch and grip and dig my nails in. I twisted my hands and moaned.

"You're too much," Alex whispered, his tone weird.

I opened my eyes and gazed down the length of me, finding Alex poised on all fours, his head near my cock, as dappled light from my trick—apparently shifting beneath my skin—rippled over his face. There was some expression on his face I couldn't decipher, like a mix of admiration and wonder.

I wasn't used to anyone admiring me like that. Old voices said I wasn't worth it, that I was just some latent piece of arse that everyone used. My trick dulled. Alex saw, frowned, then slid his wicked ice cube down my cock from head to balls.

Pleasure lit me up like fire to a fuse, racing up my spine. I bit my lip to keep from growling. *"Fuck!"*

His body smothered me, his eyes all I could see, his hand on my cock. "Didn't I say to be quiet?"

"Fuck me," I demanded.

"Hm." His dark eyes turned sly. His hand—slick with pre-cum—quickened its pumping.

I bared my teeth in a snarl and tugged on the rope. *"I'm gonna come... ifyoudon'tstop."*

"Is it raining?"

"No, it's not fucking raining!"

He moved so damn fast I hardly saw him, or maybe my brain was too fried, because the next I knew, he had my leg over his shoulder, his hand spreading my arse, and an ice cube skimming my insanely sensitive hole.

I gasped, probably whimpered again. I was losing my fucking mind to him as well as my body. My trick danced under my skin, fizzing, and everywhere we touched, his trick sparked with mine, like nerve endings firing.

The ice cube vanished and his fingers slid in, right over my prostate. The intense pleasure flipped up a notch, turning less sharp, moving into mind-numbing waves that tugged on my cock, each stroke lifting me higher. How was he an expert at this? His fingers withdrew. I filled my lungs, trying to ground myself back in my body, and then the familiar push of hard heat opened me slowly. I made some kind of grunting, gargling noise and Alex thrust.

Christ, he was stunning, my leg hooked over his

shoulder, his cock in deep, his body aglow with writhing trick. Fuck, yes.

I couldn't pretend to know what we were doing, or what it all meant, or why our tricks painted the walls with light when we made love. I just knew it felt right, as though we'd always belonged together.

I'd been afraid love was a weakness. My dad had taught me that. To love was to be soft, to be pathetic, and to love another man was the worst thing a boy could do, next to being latent. My dad sure as hell hadn't loved me, and if I'd shown any hint of needing someone, of loving someone, he'd beaten it out of me. But he'd been wrong. I'd been wrong back then too. Love was fierce. It was furious. It was bright and powerful. You had to be brave to love. And I hadn't been. Until now, with Alex pulled close, his breath racing for me, his body hot, his skin sensitive, the taste of him—the feel of him—deep inside me.

He made all the agony and heartache worth it.

I writhed and panted, was lost, burning up, consumed. His thrusting turned frantic and, with his own stifled groan, he came, eyes rolling and his body shuddering into me. Christ, I loved to watch him come. His eyes fluttered open; he dropped my leg, braced forward, and swept up my cock in his confident fingers.

I lasted four strokes and came with a shout, muffled by his free hand.

He collapsed over me, hot and wet, panting in time with my ragged breaths, and then he reached up and tugged at the rope, finally freeing my arms. I winced, bringing them down, half numb and tingling, and flopped one around him, wrecked and spent in the best way.

"Well?" he mumbled, sex-drunk.

"I'm fucked," I croaked. "In all ways."

His rich, deep chuckle rumbled. "Good."

28

D^{om}

I woke with a jolt.

Kempthorne breathed softly beside me, deep asleep. The unfamiliar bunker house was silent. Maybe a dream had woken me? I rolled onto my side and let my eyelids close. We'd be back in England soon... Alex and me back at Cecil Court, with Gina and Cas, the way things were supposed to be. This whole bloody nightmare would be over.

A creak.

I opened my eyes.

The house was old, but not Ravenscourt-old, and it didn't creak. The stairs did, though. With weight on them. Or I was paranoid because I had a latent assassin on my arse.

I grabbed my cards from the bedside table, tugged on my jeans, and crept from the room, leaving Alex snoring lightly and out for the count. The bloody weird house was quiet. The fridge in the kitchen at the end of the back corridor hummed, then clicked off. I entered the open-plan area via the kitchen. Moonlight poured through the two-story wall of windows, illuminating the lounge and library and the piano's glossy black surface.

A silhouetted figure sat on the sofa. Smoky, like a shadow, but solid too. Or had I dreamed him up? I slid a card free and crept past the island counter.

A flicker of red danced in front of my eyes.

A second figure crouched on the landing, their laser-sighted gun trained on me. *Greyson*! I spilled trick through my card.

"I wouldn't do that, Mister Domenici. We're just here to talk," The Man said—the military guy I'd met in the theme park's shack.

I froze. Greyson's red dot danced on my chest.

The Man rose to his feet and approached, coming out of the shadows and into the moonlight. "We haven't been properly introduced. I'm Chief Warrant Officer Vergil Miller, Head of Special Projects."

"You've got about three seconds to get your arse—"

"You're in no position to make threats, John." His condescending tone dripped with the self-assured confidence borne from knowing you'd already won. I hated it, hated how he sounded just like my dad, like the commanding officers who had used my Psy-Ops squad like dogs.

"Call your dog off," I said. "You won't shoot me. You

need me alive, right?"

"This has gone on long enough, don't you think?" Vergil said, so fucking calm.

The downdraft *thwomp* of helicopter blades beat against the large windows.

I could toss a card at Vergil's chest and see how confident he was then, but despite my words, Greyson would pull the trigger—he wanted me dead, whereas his bosses wanted me caught. Accidents happened. A little to the right, a twitch, and oops, the East End latent gets a bullet between the eyes.

"Whatever you think I am," I said, "you're wrong. I'm just a latent. You have thousands of American latents to pick on. You don't need me."

"That's a nice story. It's also not true." Vergil stepped closer, bringing himself into the kitchen area and within a few feet of me. He filled the space he occupied, his suit crisp, boots polished. "Outside the public library, you healed the fatal shot to Alexander Kempthorne's chest."

Oh shit.

"That was a fluke." My heart began to pound.

"No, John. You did the same in the British prison, Wordsworth. Only there, you also controlled what you Brits call the shadows—those unfortunate byproducts of disturbing too much trick."

I laughed, trying to make light of the red dot dancing over my heart. Maybe if I could keep him talking, Kage or Alex would charge in, gun or trick blazing. They could already be listening. I just needed to buy some time. "Look, mate. This is all just some fucked-up misunderstanding. I just blow shit up. I'm a nobody."

"Denying the obvious doesn't change it. You're on American soil, and that makes you my property. Put the cards down."

My wooden smile died. I'd forgotten they didn't think me a person. I was an object, a tool. I gave a little, soft laugh. "I'm not leaving with you, so fuck off back to whatever government hole you crawled out of."

He sighed, as though I was the disappointment. "I had hoped it wouldn't come to this."

The chopper was close outside now, its downdraft whipping leaves against the windows and swaying the trees. If it was just him and Grey, maybe I could muscle my way out of this. Grey was the real danger here—

"Dom, don't do anything stupid," Kage said.

Thank fuck. Two-on-two was better odds. I stepped sideways, keeping Vergil in the corner of my eye, but any relief I felt at the sight of Kage quickly fell away as he guided a dull-eyed Kempthorne along beside him. Kage was fully dressed, coat an' all, as though he'd been prepared. Kempthorne, however, wore only a shirt and underwear, no trousers or shoes. His eyes were fogged. He didn't even look over, just gazed somewhere in front of him, drugged.

Ink.

Kage had given him Ink.

Kage drugged Alex!

Blinding rage surged through my veins, lighting me up. "You fucker!" I charged a card and aimed it right between Kage's pretty eyes.

A round hit the kitchen island a few inches in front of me, splintering wood, jolting my imminent attack to a halt before the card could leave my fingers. I froze. The red dot danced on my chest again. "You piece of shit."

Vergil smiled. "Nobody needs to get hurt."

Hurt? I drilled my glare into Kage. "I'll kill you for this."

He swallowed and continued marching the docile Kempthorne toward Vergil.

Fucking Kage. Kempthorne was right, he really was my blind spot. "How can you do this?"

"It's not about you," he said, keeping his eyes off me and on Vergil. "Are we good?" he asked Vergil.

Vergil raked his glare over Kempthorne, taking him apart under his gaze, turning him into an object to be weighed and measured. How much was his worth to the US military? How many billions of dollars could they bleed from him?

Trick sizzled through my fingers into my cards, leaking out of me.

"We'll get them to the safety of the compound," Vergil said. "Then you and your brother are free to go."

Kage nodded and swallowed again, still avoiding my glare. He had to be feeling it though, how it burned all the way into his soul. The son of a bitch. He was exchanging us for his brother's freedom. Fuck that. Fuck him. There was no way I was getting on a chopper with Vergil.

The red dot appeared on Kempthorne's cheek and my heart froze in my chest.

"Hey!" I stepped forward. "Don't—"

Vergil snapped his head up. "Hands at your sides, John. Put that card away. If you so much as ignite a single card, your lover will get a bullet through his brain matter."

I seethed, burning from the depths of my tattered soul. The card in my hand hissed. "If anyone so much as lays a fucking finger on him, I will rain trick down on all you arseholes—see how much damage I can really do, huh?"

Vergil smiled a friendly smile. "His welfare is in your hands. As I said, nobody has to get hurt."

Shit. They thought I was the powerful one, but it had never been me. Every time I'd performed some kind of latent miracle, I'd borrowed some of Kempthorne's link to the source. *He* was the special one—the boy who was made. I was nothing. But if they knew that, they'd take him, kill me, and lock him away somewhere—no fucking way was that happening.

"All right." I snuffed out my trick and tucked the card home among the deck. "Fine. I'll go with you. Just don't hurt him."

"That's good, John. I'm pleased to see you're a reasonable man. We have a promising future ahead of us."

I suspected his future looked very different to the one in my head where I lit him up like a firework.

Vergil climbed the stairs and opened the main door. The helicopter's engine whined overhead, probably from the bunker's flat roof.

Kage and Kempthorne went up the stairs next, Kage's hand on Kempthorne's shoulder.

"You're not even going to let him get dressed?"

Kage's shoulders twitched, but that was all. He guided Alex outside, toward the rooftop. I climbed the stairs, keeping Greyson in my line of sight. He still had his modified rifle trained on Kempthorne through the glass. He didn't care about any of this, or us. If Kage thought he was saving his brother, he was wrong. Grey had already told me there was no way out for the likes of us.

"You don't give a shit about any of this, do you?"

"Move."

He'd kill me eventually, whatever his orders were. Because, according to his bosses, I was the most dangerous thing on American soil. And Greyson had a hero complex a mile wide. Worse than Kage. Greyson had too much to prove. He'd been kicked to the curb as a boy, and he'd used that to make himself into who he was today. Fuck, it was like looking in the mirror.

"Move, Domenici," Grey said again.

I headed outside. The chopper's blades whipped up a storm of leaves and grit. Kempthorne and Kage were already on the roof, where the black, unmarked helicopter squatted. Kage helped Kempthorne inside the chopper, then climbed in behind him.

Grey prodded me in the back—*move*, he said, but the whirr of the blades drowned him out.

If I got in that chopper, I wasn't ever getting away again.

I climbed the outside-steps to the roof, keeping my head ducked from the vicious downdraft. The choppers engines roared, drowning out all other sound, except the thud of my heart. Lead weighed down my every step, as though I moved through water. This moment... If I didn't get free now, I never would. My instincts screamed to get away.

My dad had taught me a lot, mostly how to be chewed up and spit out and still come back swinging. He'd also taught me when to show my hand—when to lay it all on the table and make sure every fucker in the room knew you'd won the game.

Kage leaned forward and peered out of the helicopter's door. Kempthorne sat inside, staring dead-eyed at nothing. Kage had blocked Grey's line of sight to Kempthorne—just for a second, just one moment.

A moment was all I needed.

Sweat slicked my palms. The wind howled, blades whirring overhead. My heart raced. Trick flushed my veins. One shot. One way to end this. I flicked a card from my diminished deck, sliding it into my palm. Kage's pretty eyes met mine and widened.

One shot.

An impossible shot for most latents.

Couldn't miss.

Kage's hand started to lift.

There was only one person here more dangerous than me. In Psy-Ops, we were trained to take out the largest threat first.

Leaves and sticks whipped through the air.

Kage's lips moved, but the chopper's engines tore the sound away.

I smiled, just for him, so he knew the price for his actions.

Twisting, I dropped and flung the glowing card into the storm. It sparked alight, blinding. The shining card soared, whipped back on itself, and was tossed by the rotor blades—it danced, spiraled, and slammed straight into Greyson's neck. He stumbled sideways—a gaping hole in his neck—and collapsed, twitching on the ground.

Kage.

I whipped my head around, saw Kage's gun, so close now, I peered down its fucking barrel—and flung another card. It zipped through the maelstrom and struck his gun, blasting it clean out of his hand.

Another card sizzled in my hand. I let that one fly, hitting Kage in the shoulder as he jumped from the chopper. He fell to his knees, plastered his hand against the smoking wound.

Kempthorne was still in the chopper, staring ahead, drugged and oblivious. A prisoner in his own body.

Vergil screamed into his headset. The chopper's engines roared, blades whirring faster, taking to the air.

Fuck, no!

I fanned multiple cards between my fingers and flung them free.

The helicopter's skids lifted off. The cards fluttered, surging skyward like a flock of startled golden birds, and struck the blades. Heat and noise blasted me backward. Metal screamed and moaned; the chopper's engines whined, choking. Bent blades spun. The smell of burned oil coated my throat. The helicopter bounced down onto its skids, but the spinning blades rocked the chopper unevenly. It skipped sideways, tilting toward the edge of the roof.

I dashed through smoke toward the chopper's door. Its skids lifted. The chopper tilted. I jumped, caught the lifting skid, and launched myself inside. Vergil made a grab for me. I thrust an elbow under his chin, slamming his head back, knocking his headset flying and him out cold.

"Alex!"

He'd slumped against the opposite door, limp and tangled in a seat belt.

"Hey!"

The chopper shuddered. The cockpit door swung open. I glimpsed the pilot legging it.

"Alex." I clambered over him, tugged at the straps. "Hey, wake up." The chopper rocked, something metal groaned, and the cockpit tipped, gravity pulling me sideways. Shit. I flashed trick through the straps. Kempthorne jolted free. But the cockpit rolled. The engine's ungodly noises reached a deafening pitch. I grabbed at Alex and folded him inside my arms as the chopper tipped over the edge of the roof.

I'd save him.

He was all I had.

He had to live.

Trick roared through my veins, rising all around, making the world boil with golden light. So much trick, it tore free of my control, racing through me and out, like I'd opened a vast door and all the power at once came flooding out.

I was nothing.

He was everything.

If there was a way to make this shitty world better, he'd fucking find it.

As the world burned and the trick boiled and everything fell apart, I crushed him close. *I've got you.*

29

A lexander

I'd seen pictures in books of impact craters, blast radiuses, meteor impact sites. The hole in the ground I blinked awake in resembled one of those. Dom lay in the middle of the basin, legs bent, one arm flung behind his head, lips parted, and eyes closed.

Wheezing, I shifted onto an elbow and reached for Dom's neck—his pulse. Blood stained my fingers. Didn't know whose. Didn't know how I'd come to be here, wherever here was, didn't know what Dom had done or what had been done to him.

His pulse beat hot and heavy against my fingertips. Relief pushed air from my lungs, scratching over what felt like glass in my throat. A bout of coughing took hold, and I rode it out, then got my tingling legs under me and stumbled to my feet.

Good lord, I'd woken in the aftermath of a warzone.

"John...?"

His trick had made the crater. The sides arched up and away, glowing faintly, and where there should have been trees, there was only a cold, cloudless blue sky. He'd flattened everything for hundreds of yards in every direction. But not me.

This was significant. This was powerful and what I'd suspected all along.

I wiped my lips and spat a mouthful of blood to the side. "John...?"

Something metal stuck up from out of the ground near the top of the crater, narrow, bent, and buckled. It resembled a helicopter rotor blade... There *had* been a helicopter. I'd dreamed it, or thought I had. Dreamed of Kage putting something that had felt like ice on my wrists —it had spilled through me, numbing my thoughts, taking everything far away.

I scrabbled out of the crater, falling too many times. The majority of the bunker house had blasted away, like everything else around Dom.

The truck... Half of it was coated in grey concrete dust. Some of its windows had shattered. But it might still start. I raised my watch—the dial was shattered and the second hand was motionless. "Damn."

We had to get to the airport, somehow.

"John, John, wake up..." I stumbled back into the hole and knelt over him. "Hey. Wake up." There wasn't a scratch on him. No dust, no cuts. He looked as though he'd been gently laid in the middle of the blast zone.

I got hold of his shoulders and gently shook him. "John?" Why wasn't he coming around?

If he'd caused the crater, he might have overloaded himself. The same happened to me when I absorbed a nasty artifact or threw out too much trick at once. He'd be unconscious for hours.

Resting my arse on my heels, I grasped my *naked* thighs and sighed. "Where are my trousers? Wonderful."

What had happened? The meal… I'd gone to John's room—I vividly remembered how we'd both thoroughly enjoyed each other's company, and then… *nothing*. Just waking here, next to him in a hole in the ground. But there had been something, clearly. Fragments of memory drifted out of reach. Kage Mitchell was among them. He didn't appear to be here now.

Instincts suggested we had to get away from the crater. I'd think up the rest when we were on the move.

I got an arm under John's, scooped his limp, stocky body against my side, and dragged him out of the crater. Then I fought with his weight to get him through the debris-strewn blast zone and into the truck. I muttered things, silly things—told him he was safe, told him he was an idiot. Told him *I* was the idiot.

The truck started at the first push of the button— Kage had left the key inside for a quick escape.

I thrust it into gear and drove from the scattered debris of the bunker house. It didn't matter where we went, just *away*.

The forest rolled on and on, the tips of the trees lit by the rising sun. The more the road meandered, the more my mind wandered, trying to piece together all the broken bits of the last few hours. I'd been drugged. And now the drug was clearing, the memories bubbled to the surface.

Voices bargaining. John, in danger. I hadn't been able to move or get to him. Trapped in a waking dream, with no control. Other, older memories vied with the new ones: *Don't cry, Alex. You don't want to fail me, do you?* I hadn't been able to move then either. Trapped in my head. Trapped as they'd made me bleed power for them.

I pulled the truck over, clambered out, doubled over, and vomited the contents of my stomach.

Kage Mitchell.

He'd drugged me.

Ink.

At least the LOA agent was consistent.

He'd wanted this all along. To have me, control me. But he hadn't known about John, about the extent of his power. Nobody had known. They did now.

The truck door creaked.

"Alex?" John croaked, stumbling out.

He gasped, or sobbed, and tried to hide the sound behind a cough. "What... Are you... *Shit.*" He stumbled closer, threw his arms around me, and sighed in my ear. "Christ... I don't... Are you all right?" He thrust me away at arm's length and scowled. "You look like shit. Are you hurt?"

"Not really, no. I don't think so. Just..." I gestured at my head, lost for how to explain all the noise in my head.

He swiped something from my face, dirt or blood,

maybe vomit, and frowned harder. "That piece of shit Kage. But you're all right?"

"I er…" I cleared a horrible clog in my throat. "I don't know where we're going," I admitted. "We have to get to the airport. There's a plane—my plane. I organized it yesterday. It's waiting. We just… We have to…"

"Hey, it's okay." He smiled, and all at once, everything seemed just a little bit easier. He backed up, blinking too fast. "Yeah, the airport… Let's get the fuck out of here." Then his smile vanished. "Shit. I think I er… I think I killed Greyson. I couldn't… I couldn't let them take us. They were fucking taking *you*. I didn't have a choice. He would have shot you, shot me." Another step backward, this one unbalanced. "Vergil… shit." The memories flooded him fast now too. "I don't know if he's alive. Kage —*Fuck*!" He staggered and reached for the truck.

I caught his arm, reeled him in, breathed into his hair, and molded him close. He smelled of burned fuel and hot metal, and he sizzled with an abundance of trick. The steel-like feel of him softened. "Listen. Whatever happened, whatever you did, I know without any doubt that had they taken us, we never would have seen the light of day again. You did what you had to for our survival. It was necessary." He would always do what had to be done, and I loved him fiercely for it.

John's hands clutched at my back, fingers digging in. "I killed Kage's brother," he said quietly. "I know I did. I meant to. He saw it."

"John." I caught his face in both hands, made him look at me. His wide eyes brimmed with regret and hurt and all the things he'd never admit. He'd always tried to do the right thing, but sometimes the right thing wasn't enough. Sometimes the wrong thing was the only way. "It was you or him."

He nodded, but his eyes shone with too much emotion. "I don't know if Kage got out. I don't know what happened to me. There was trick, so much trick. And I... I wanted to *burn everything*. I didn't spiral. It was different." He broke from my grip and peered at his hands. Trick shimmered beneath his skin. "I feel it. It's different even now. Kempthorne, what have I done?"

I felt the change too. The trick had become ever present, as though he was plugged into the source and switched on. Permanently.

"Whatever it is, we will get to the bottom of it." I tried to smile.

He sighed hard and nodded, rebuilding his barriers while shutting away the emotion. "We need to get the fuck out of America."

"I agree—"

"And you need pants," he said with a smirk.

"Indeed."

In the city suburbs, John stole some trousers and shoes from a parking lot recycling bin and I tried not to think too long on the previous owner's choice of one hundred percent polyester mix. As I hadn't been wearing any trousers, I could hardly complain. We made a stop at a gas station and rinsed the concrete dust off the truck so it didn't look as though it had been driven through a warzone. We couldn't use our IDs, even if we'd had them. Neither of us had our phones. Everything we'd brought with us to the US, we'd left back at the safe house—now under several layers of rubble.

I'd rarely felt so exposed.

Not far from the small local airfield where I'd organized to have my jet fueled and waiting, we entered a diner-style cafe and—under instructions from John to *flutter my lashes*—I was able to sweet talk us some free coffee and some toast.

John grabbed the toast, thanked the waitress, and grinned. "It's your superpower."

"Hm." I cradled my hot coffee mug, soaking up its warmth, still trying to shake off the lingering effects of Ink and the surge John had pulled from the source. "My supervillain power, you mean?"

He shrugged. "Villain. Hero. It's all perspective." And then he ate all his toast in a few bites.

Outside the steamed-up windows, across double lanes of traffic and through a high chain-link fence, the airfield's lights blinked. Freedom was close enough to see but not to reach.

"We can't just walk into the airport," he said, staring out of the window too. "We don't have our IDs, and even if we did, there's no way the military doesn't have us on a watch list."

I'd assumed the same. Getting here had been the easy part. Boarding the plane would be far harder. "Ideas?"

"We have to break in. Once we're on the plane, we're free, right?"

"Let's hope so."

We were so close, but with everything that had happened to date, resting would be premature. More trouble probably waited between us and the jet.

Vergil Miller's disappearance would have been noticed by now. Kage Mitchell had likely updated his agency on the events at the bunker. The LOA and the military would turn their gazes toward all the local airports. I'd picked an obscure airport, used for freight, and told my pilot to file the documents under a different name. But my jet was sitting on that runway like a huge neon sign pointing toward escaping latents.

We had no choice. We had to get out of the US. Enemies waited at our every turn. England was our only safe haven. And even that was in jeopardy should the IRL and MOD discover the awakening of John's additional abilities.

I'd worry about that once we were in the air. Worry about *everything* then, like telling him the truth about what I'd always suspected—how the military had done more than turned him into a soldier, how he was the most powerful of us all.

His foot tapped under the table. He chewed on a nail. And to my latent sight, he overflowed with trick. It danced around him, golden and hypnotic. He should be spent, but he'd never blazed brighter.

"Are you all right?"

"Yeah." He folded his arms and leaned back. "Yeah. Fine." I stared—he was not all right—and he sighed. "No, I'm crawling out of my skin. I'm fucking buzzed, Alex. Like I'm high or something. It's getting worse."

"I can see that, in more ways than one."

He filled his lungs and slowly breathed out, struggling to contain himself. This wasn't spiraling; this was something else.

I set my coffee down, having hardly touched it. "I could alleviate some of what you're feeling."

"You mean… suck me off?" His lips quirked.

"In the latent sense."

"Not the other sense?"

"This really isn't the time." And we were both exhausted. Once on the plane, we could indulge, but not yet.

"You don't fancy a quickie out the back?" His smile bloomed into a full grin. "You and me and a filthy bathroom stall? You owe me a bathroom fuck, remember?"

"Hm, you make it sound so appealing. But, no."

He'd gone very still. But his smile remained, and his eyes sparkled with a kind of playful lust that had my heart skipping out of sync.

I leaned back, breathed in, and said, "Bathroom. Now."

We crossed the diner to the one-room bathroom stall. I locked the door behind us, and in the narrow room, John lit up like a firework. He turned to face me, smirking because he knew I couldn't resist him. Despite wanting to grab him by the shirt and pin him to the wall, then drink him down, I took his hand and watched as his trick lapped over my hand and felt its tingle beneath my sleeve as it climbed my arm.

He stepped in and thrust his hand into my hair. "It'll be a miracle if we do this without gettin' off."

"One of us has impeccable self-control."

He shifted his hips and nudged his mouth against mine. "Well, it ain't me."

Despite his insistence, I was trying to contain whatever this exchange was that happened between us. If I drank him down too fast, I'd lose consciousness like I did when absorbing a dirty artifact. It had to be slow, controlled, or we'd both be useless.

He wet his lips and blinked through hooded lashes, desire written all over his face.

I had to keep my hands off the rest of him, which was easier said than done when he peered through me, as though wanting to devour my every inch. "You're not making this easy."

"No?" He marched me two steps back against the locked stall door, rattling it on its hinges. "The way you look right now, in secondhand clothes that don't fit, your hair a mess, your face all cut up..." His mouth hovered over mine. His trick spilled into my veins, throbbing in waves, beating in time with my heart. "Christ, Alex, I want to pick you apart with my teeth."

"John... please don't. I must maintain control or this could go terribly wrong."

"This is how we maintain control." He cupped the prominent evidence of my arousal inside the trousers that didn't fit, wrenching out the growl I'd tried to keep inside.

As much as I wanted to do this his way, I didn't trust myself. It had to happen *my* way. I wrapped a hand around his neck and pushed him back. He didn't resist. He never had, not like this. He *liked* it. Liked my control. Liked being under me. Liked surrendering. I pushed him against the wall, plastered him there, his smirk a permanent fixture, and drew on the power he so freely gave. It rushed like a flooded river, so familiar now it was as though his trick were mine, and together, we made something impossible, something powerful.

Together, we were unstoppable.

30

D om

Having sex with Alex in a filthy bathroom stall was the hardest thing I'd ever had to resist. But it didn't matter, because him taking my trick left me spent and breathless anyway. He drank my excess trick and all the cuts and scrapes on his face slowly smoothed over, and the tiredness in his eyes sharpened to his crystal-like intelligence. By the time he'd stripped me of my overspill, he simmered with energy and I buzzed, like the comedown from losing my load.

He smiled, and before I could demand I do something like get on my knees and suck him off, he thrust a kiss on me that set my body ablaze. All he'd have had to do was touch my cock with his firm fingers, and I'd have come. Then he pulled back, arm braced over my shoulder, and peered into my eyes, while I tried not to appear as dazed and incoherent as I was.

"Better?" he purred, eyes shining like two blue gems.

"I mean, I dunno... I feel like I'd be better if we fucked on top of whatever that was you just did to me."

"Hm." More purring. "Don't worry. When we get on that plane and in the air, I'm going to make you beg for more."

He kissed me again, hard and rough, drawing a tell-tale moan from deep inside. "Yeah, okay," I croaked. "That'll work."

"Have I taken the edge off?"

"Uhhuh." I swallowed and adjusted my hard cock to alleviate some of its bloody awful pressure. "You're a fucking tease, Kempthorne."

He chuckled and that made my aching cock worse.

"Stop," I said, laughing. "You're killing me."

A hammering rattled the door. "C'mon, man. Open up!"

Kempthorne arched an eyebrow and ran a hand through his floppy, mussed hair—doing nothing to control it. He checked me, I nodded, and he unlocked the door.

The guy waiting shot us a frown that suggested he had no idea why two men would be locked in one tiny bathroom stall. And then his eyes widened as realization sunk in.

He muttered something derogatory, and the prick was lucky I had a plane to catch and that Alex, a few steps ahead, hadn't heard.

As soon as we stepped outside the diner, traffic

blasted by in both directions. We tracked along a wide sidewalk, keeping the airport fence and runways to our left. Bitter air had me shivering in seconds. With no coats and no bags, we were down to just our wits and Kempthorne's plummy accent. "Do you know which gate it's at?" I asked.

"No, but it's not a large airport. Once we get closer, I should be able to spot the jet."

"Can we just get on? No security checks?" I asked, scanning the fence that seemed to stretch so bloody far it might as well have wrapped around all of upstate New York.

"I've lubricated the way, somewhat."

"You what?" I burst out laughing and Alex frowned, oblivious to his wording.

"Bribed the necessary officials," he explained, then cleared his throat.

"I fuckin' love you, Alex." It had slipped out before I could think it might not have been the time to drop that bombshell, and then it was out, between us suddenly, and I couldn't laugh it off or take it back—I didn't *want* to take it back. He had to know I loved him, didn't he? I was almost afraid to look over and thrust my hands into my pockets, focusing on the fence in the hope of finding a weakness.

I probably should have said something as important as that over the dinner we still hadn't had, or the movie night we still hadn't committed to, or when we were supposed to spend that week at Ravenscourt that never happened. But if I kept putting it off, it might never happen, and that'd be a crime. I wanted him to know.

I snuck a glance back and caught him smiling.

Okay, so we were good.

After stopping where the sidewalk ended and the road turned to cracked asphalt, I nodded at the fence. "There, you see it? Service gate. Deliveries, utilities, it all goes through there. It's got one camera. And right over there is a catering truck that's heading this way. We can slip in while it leaves, using the truck as cover."

Alex studied the fence and the distant truck heading toward us. "You're good at this."

"I figure you bought me for other reasons, not just for my trick." I expected him to laugh or at least smile, but he glared at the truck and a muscle in his cheek twitched.

He caught me staring and flashed a smile. "Of course."

Too late.

What wasn't he saying? What *did* he know about me that I didn't?

"Okay, let's go," I urged. There would be time for questions on the plane.

At a break in the traffic, we jogged across the road and hurried toward the gate as the truck trundled closer. The gate opened, the truck rumbled through, and in seconds, we were on the other side—almost too easy. We took cover behind an articulated bus with grass growing under its wheels.

"All right, you see the jet?" I asked.

"Hm... I think so. Over there."

All the planes at their gates twinkled under the winter sun. Most were cargo carriers, but a few were small passenger jets. "Which one?"

"With the green tail."

I squinted through the heat haze rising off the runways and spotted two sleek jets, one farther down the terminal building. "There's two?"

"The one on the right."

How could he know that? They both looked identical.

"I think it's that one," he added.

It had better be, or we'd be crashing some other rich guy's ride. "All right, so we just have to get across the wide-open runways without being seen. Stay low. Move slowly. Keep your eyes up. Hope for the best."

"You make it sound simple," he said.

"Well, at least we don't have to worry about buried artifacts, waiting like IEDs." I'd seen latents lose their shit in warzones after stumbling over artifacts left for our squads. This wasn't that, but the jet was likely being observed.

I touched my deck, now missing quite a few cards. It didn't weigh the same without them, but I'd fix that as soon as we landed back in London. The deck's presence was still a comfort.

Alex noticed my hesitation. "All right?"

"Yeah. Do you have your coin?" I asked.

"No. It was left behind at the safehouse with everything else."

"Sorry." I knew how much that coin meant to him, despite the nightmares it contained.

"It was perhaps time to let her go."

I gave him a nod, not entirely convinced he believed his own words, but there was nothing to be done about it now. "Ready?"

"Not in the least."

"Follow me." I broke cover, stayed low, and moved between high patches of grass to a narrow taxi lane, then scooted across to an opposite section of tall grass. Even though the winter sun was weak, a haze did rise off the asphalt. Its ripple would hide us until we got close to the terminal building and the mown grass.

A big-arse refueling truck thundered nearby. I gave Kempthorne another nod, checking he was on board, and dashed out to jog alongside the tanker's huge wheels. Alex stayed close. As the truck turned, we broke off and made a dash for the terminal building, not far from the green-tailed jet. A truck parked next to the jet was loading up snacks or caviar or whatever the fuck these jets offered their passengers.

The stair truck was in place. Unmanned, and the door was wide open.

I dashed up the metal stairs, Alex behind me, and entered the cabin. I should have known it was too fucking easy.

A polite young woman yelped. "Er, sir, you can't—"

But it was the guy sitting in one of the leather chairs who stopped me dead. Alex stumbled into me and *growled*.

Trent Anderson reclined in that chair, wearing his grey pinstripe suit, legs crossed at the knee. He had a flashy watch on his wrist and his hair immaculately gelled. He looked like Kempthorne's evil blond Wall Street twin.

Trick danced between my fingertips. "You have three

seconds to leave or I'm gonna light you up like a Roman candle."

Trent's smile curdled my stomach. "Did you truly think it was going to be that easy to leave?" He chuckled. "Just get on a plane and whoosh." He made a flying plane motion and I added that to the reasons why I wanted to break his fingers. "You've made some powerful enemies, Alex."

"Get off my jet." Alex turned to the hostess. "Please, young lady, you need to leave, immediately."

"I er... Who are you?" the hostess asked.

"The owner."

She raked her gaze over his borrowed sneakers, ill-fitting trousers, torn shirt, and messy hair. Admittedly, he looked nothing like Alexander Kempthorne the billion-aire turned supervillain. "I'm calling security."

"No." He flicked a ball of trick alight in his palm and made sure she couldn't miss its sparkling glow. "You're not going anywhere. If you can't be trusted to stay quiet, you should sit down."

"That's an infraction—" she began.

"As you can see, I've not had the best of days and my patience is wearing spectacularly thin. Do not test me, madam."

"He won't hurt you," I added, and kept the *unless necessary* part to myself.

The hostess sat on the edge of one of the seats and Kempthorne turned back to Trent. "What do you want?"

"You don't have much time. The military will by now have confirmed a witness sighting of you both at this airport, and the LOA has already been informed." He touched his chest. "By me, of course. I'm your sponsor on US soil. You signed the forms when you arrived. You can't take off without my permission."

This man was a worm that just wouldn't fucking die no matter how many pieces it was chopped into. "You epic tosser."

"Yes, thank you for your input, *John*. But I couldn't care less about your opinion."

"You'll care when I shove my bloody opinion up your arse."

Alex's hand settled on my shoulder and he moved ahead, taking the seat in front of Trent. "Let's be reasonable. You clearly have a solution, Trent. So let's hear it."

The preppy man's eyes lit up now that Kempthorne's attention was all on him. "Alex, you will leave with me now. We'll retreat to the West Coast, where your kind are tolerated."

Your kind. I snorted and kept all the words I wanted to say deep inside. My trick sizzled, though, getting hotter by the second.

"And what happens to John?" Alex asked.

"I can pull some strings, have him committed where the military won't be able to get to him."

"'Committed'?" Alex asked, a thin veil holding back his anger.

"To a psychiatric unit. He'll live out his years drugged and docile, with all his meals paid for and some lovely woman—or man—to bathe him whenever he wants."

"Let me kill him," I said. "Nobody will care. Daddy will probably thank us."

"Fuck you," Trent snapped. "Alex and I were perfectly fine before you got between us."

"Jesus Christ, do you hear yourself?" I was done. Done with him, done with talking, done with standing there and taking it. I marched by Kempthorne, grabbed Trent out of the fucking chair, ignoring his yelp, and hauled him ahead of me, toward the open door. "There is no *you and Alex*. There never was, you delusional fuck." I dangled him out of the door, his suit all skewed and hair windswept. "If you think Alex or I would ever be owned by some piece of shit like you, you're the insane one. Grow a pair, get yourself a man who'll eat your manipulative shit, and leave Alex and me the fuck alone." I let go, he teetered at the top of the metal stairs, his face riddled with shock, and then he tumbled down.

It had to fucking hurt. Those stairs were brutal.

He collapsed on the asphalt, whimpering, but still moved. He'd be hurting for a while, but by the time he recovered, we'd be half a world away.

Alex appeared at my side. "When diplomacy doesn't work—"

"—use brute force."

Sirens squealed and, through the shimmer rising off the runway, an array of blue lights flashed.

"And that's our cue." Alex rapped on the pilot's door. "Karl, time to leave. Sharpish, please."

"That you, Alex?" The pilot opened the cabin door, grinned, and thrust out his hand.

They shook like old friends. "It's good to see a friendly face, and if you wouldn't mind, we're in a spot of bother with the authorities. A misunderstanding I'd rather have sorted from England."

"Righto," Karl said, far too English and chipper to be anything but Kempthorne's pal. "Buckle up. And this is the *plan* we talked about, Alex?"

"This is the one," Alex confirmed.

Karl dropped back into the pilot's seat amongst a sea of dials and buttons and flashing lights.

"Miss?" Alex said to the hostess. "You'd best leave unless you want to visit London with two highly wanted latents."

She huffed and teetered down the metal steps in her heels.

The jet's engines fired up, whining, then roaring. The jet clunked from its chocks. I tugged the cabin door closed and locked it, then peered out of one of the windows. "Shit." They were almost on us. "Alex? What plan?"

He saw the same as me. Worry flashed across his face. "Hold on," he said. "This could get interesting."

31

D^{om}

Alex had been plotting without telling me. Again. With the latent cops chasing down the jet, now wasn't the time to argue, but I wasn't about to let it slide so easily. "Out with it. What aren't you telling me, Kempthorne?"

He winced, knowing he'd been caught scheming.

The engines whirred as the jet rumbled along the asphalt, heading toward the takeoff runway.

"It's occurred to me that it really doesn't matter who captures us, we're not going to be able to outrun them all indefinitely. The LOA, the various military agencies... They clearly suspect you're more powerful than you've realized."

He rocked with the motion of the plane as it bumped over the asphalt but kept his gaze trained on me. He had that sorry look about him that meant he was about to do something insane, something I'd yell at him for.

"You had better tell me what the bloody hell you're thinking—"

The plane slowed and jolted to a halt. Karl's voice came over the comms. "Sorry, Alex. They've blocked the runway. I can't take off."

Alex peered out of the window and huffed through his nose. "Hm, troublesome."

When he straightened, he had his don't-fuck-with-me face on, as though a whole lot of people were about to have a really bad day. "What?" I asked him. "What's going on? Tell me the fucking plan."

"When I say, take my hand."

"What?" The last time he'd gotten all secretive, he'd drained me of trick and sent me to Ravenscourt.

He lunged toward the door, grabbed the handle, and heaved it open.

"Hey—" I shot to his side, desperate to get to him before the doors could open and everything that was waiting for us outside spilled in. "You had better not screw me over, Alex."

"You know I would never knowingly—"

"GET YOUR HANDS UP!"

"HANDS UP!"

"DON'T MOVE!"

I lifted my hands and peered into a huge crowd of what appeared to be every LOA agent or military personnel on the East Coast. Lights flashed, guns rattled, pointed at us. More cars screeched in at the back. Everyone was here for the party. We'd been so fucking close to making it—right on the runway. If it wasn't for Trent, that prick, we'd have been in the air already.

The crowd bristled with weapons. My mouth dried. They weren't supposed to shoot, but all it would take was one twitchy guy and we were done for.

"Alexander Kempthorne, John Domenici, you are hereby detained by the Latent Observation Agency for your protection and the protection of the United States of America," Agent Pierce boomed, his face smug and gun cupped in his hands.

A ladder truck trundled across the grass. Behind that, the black military vans paraded down the runway.

"Well, fuck," I drawled. "We must be special for them to lay out the red carpet."

"DON'T TALK!" Palliser barked.

I dropped the fingers on my right hand, leaving one standing to salute.

The tension in the air surged so high it tingled my skin.

"Let's not make them angrier than necessary," Alex said out of the corner of his mouth.

"Gentlemen!" Vergil boomed, as though we could all relax now that the big guns were there to take over. He sauntered from his military guys toward the LOA agents, sporting a limp and a few bruises and scuffs from the helicopter blast. "Stand down. These two latents are military property. We'll take it from here."

"The fuck you will." Palliser's chest puffed up. "The LOA has had Kempthorne and Domenici under surveillance for months!"

"If we wait long enough," I said, "they'll get their cocks out to compare."

Alex was quiet for a little while. The wind whipped around us, stealing Palliser's and Vergil's voices away, and then washing them back toward us. The truck with the stairs on it carved through the personnel, coming to a stop in front of us.

"My money's on Vergil," Kempthorne said.

I snorted. "No way. Palliser's is bigger. He has longer fingers."

"And the length of fingers is an accurate indication?"

"Have you seen yours?"

"Hey, latents! SHUT THE FUCK UP! GET DOWN THOSE STAIRS! NOW!" Palliser boomed.

Vergil's face boiled, full of thunder. He wasn't leaving here without his two prizes. But neither was the LOA. If Kempthorne had a plan, now would be a good time to execute it.

He started down the stairs first. "John?"

"Uh huh."

"Don't be afraid."

"Of those pricks? Nah."

"No. Of this." He turned on the stairs and offered his hands. "Take my hands."

I didn't hesitate. I had no idea what he was doing, but if he said to do it, I was there, because I bloody trusted him with my life, and my heart. He'd taken a bullet for me. It didn't matter it was some stupid test to see if I could heal or not—what mattered was that Alexander Kempthorne looked up at me, his eyes soft, and he trusted me too.

The second my hands touched his, he hooked into my trick and pulled, whipping it right out of me and into him. I swayed, losing myself under the sudden rush, and then he *pushed it all back in.* Somewhere a voice told me it was all about balance, about the push and pull, and not fighting who we were inside—embracing it. That voice sounded a lot like Montgomery's voice, but I wasn't focusing on that. He was dead. I'd killed him. Sent the shadows after him, just like Vergil had said.

Maybe I had done that after all.

Alex's eyes blazed, and suddenly they were all I could see. His heart beat heavy alongside mine, filling me up. I knew he was powerful, as though he were some posh West End angel that could light up a London street like a star. But what I hadn't known, and what I should have realized by now, was that together, our tricks were un-fucking-stoppable.

The second he tapped into the source, power scorched up my spine and burned through every bone and blood vessel. I hadn't even known the source was here but felt it now, a river of power I'd been plugged into it, through Alex.

Power rolled off us in waves. If the LOA or the military fired, I didn't feel a damn thing. I was outside that, outside all the hurt and pain, the aches and worries. The airport, the steps beneath me, the people still pointing their guns at us—they were all so small.

I could kill them.

Click my fingers. Poof.

Alex's eyes narrowed a tiny amount and he gave his head the smallest of shakes.

No, don't do that.

Him and me. Christ it was glorious. And simple. I breathed in, drawing trick into me, and set it free. The shimmering wall of light swelled around us, slowly washing outward. The agents and military personnel hadn't moved. I didn't think them frozen—it felt more as though everything had happened in a blink. The trick touched them, washed over them, and with every new person it touched, it scorched a mark inside of them—touching their souls, leaving its trace. *Infecting* them.

Oh fuck, I was *making* latents.

This was probably a bad thing, but it didn't feel bad, it felt... normal. It felt as though I was supposed to do this, as though I'd been fighting it all along. Evolution, Montgomery had called it. Was this what I was made for?

More and more trick surged, bubbling up around us, turning the world golden. And then in a final, devastating blast, it washed outward and collapsed, leaving a shallow layer of sparks and a whole lot of silence behind.

The LOA, the military, they all lay on the ground, and for a horrible second I thought I'd killed them.

"They'll be fine." Kempthorne dragged me down the stairs and right through the middle of them.

The agents stumbled, dazed, mumbling. We had seconds before someone noticed we weren't standing at the top of the stairs with our hands up and surrendering.

"Run," Alex said.

"Where?"

He pointed back toward the terminal building. "The other jet. Go."

The other jet... right. There had been two jets, almost

identical. I bolted with Alex sprinting beside me. Behind us, Karl's jet engines fired up again.

I spotted a bendy bus making a maneuver up ahead to ferry new arrivals to the terminal and skidded in behind it, using it as cover. Alex dashed in behind me. We hugged the side of the bus as it cruised back toward the terminal building. A glance back revealed the jet we'd been on was taxiing toward the runway, making a break for it.

"Shouldn't we be on that?"

"No. Definitely not."

Two of the military vans were on the move, racing after it.

Its engines roared and the jet surged forward. Within seconds, it was airborne, lights blinking, on its way to freedom. It really seemed as though we should have been on that plane.

Alex took my hand, redirecting my focus toward the lone green-tailed jet sitting quietly at the end of the terminal building. We climbed aboard, into the dark and quiet of a cold cabin. Alex shut the door and slumped into one of the comfy chairs. The lights stayed off.

"Okay, so..." I panted, "can you fly this thing?"

"Not in the least."

I didn't understand. I dropped into the opposite leather chair and peered out one of the small windows. Chaos was unfolding half the airport away. Lights flashed, vehicles raced. But at least it was happening all the way over there and not next to us. "You wanna tell me why we aren't on that plane?"

"Because." He leaned forward. "That plane will have

an unfortunate accident. All lives aboard will be lost. A rather poetic ending for Alexander Kempthorne, considering his family history, don't you think?"

My mouth fell open. "Hang on. What?"

"We're about to die."

That other plane was going to ditch? "You've faked our deaths?"

"We just have to wait here until this evening, when a second pilot will take us to Boston. From there, I've organized onward travel documents and a connecting jet to Prague, where we'll collect some new personal documents, including new identities, then we fly to Scotland. We do still have to be careful though. There are a lot of connecting dots but hopefully I've covered our tracks."

I rocked back in the chair. Jesus Christ, if this worked, the military, the LOA, IRL—every bloody agency and enemy we had would back off. We'd be... free. "What about the pilot, Karl?"

"Oh, he'll survive. A chopper will pick him up. He's being paid exceedingly well to disappear."

"Holy shit." John Domenici was about to die in a plane crash. "Gina? You have to tell her."

"In three days, she'll receive an email directing her to a PO box, where there's a note inside explaining everything. She'll have to keep up the ruse. Cassie, unfortunately, can't know."

I swallowed and watched the flashing lights recede and the LOA and military crawl back into their holes. No one thought to check for a second plane. Why wouldn't John Domenici and Alexander Kempthorne be on the one that had taken off, bound for London?

When would those people sense something had changed inside of them? When would they realize *they'd* been changed? Did I feel bad about turning them into latents? No fucking way. Vergil and Palliser could see what it was like on the other side of the fence. Maybe it would change some things for the better.

I let my heart slow and stared at the man seated opposite me, half hidden in the shadows. The only light to touch him came in through the small oval windows. He didn't smile, but he thought about it. "When were you going to tell me about this Plan B?"

"I wasn't sure it would be needed."

"You still could have told me anyway."

"I have multiple strategies in the air at any given time, and to tell you them all would be pointless. Trusting me saves time."

I did trust him… The prick.

The airport had fallen quiet again. A few busses trundled back and forth. A light plane swooped in to land, but all of it happened far away. And with no signs of any agents or military, I exhaled the last of my nerves. "Did we just turn a bunch of normal people into latents—is that what happened?"

"That remains to be seen but I believe so."

"We just fucked up a few hundred lives. Palliser is going to lose his shit."

"By then, we'll be dead." He finally flashed his smart-arse grin. "Whiskey?" He walked to the bar at the back and set about fixing two drinks.

We just had to sit and wait for his second pilot, and we'd be free. Totally free. A new name. A new life. I could be anyone? My heart tripped over itself at the idea. I didn't have to be John Domenici, Marco Domenici's fucked-up son, anymore.

Alex handed me the whiskey and sat in the chair next to mine, then leaned closer. He lifted his glass and I chinked mine with his. "To a fresh start?"

"A fresh start."

I'd believe it when it happened. Until we were off American soil and had new passports with new names, anything could happen. It usually did.

32

A lexander

Hope for Survivors Fades. Billionaire Latent Alexander Kempthorne Dies in Plane Crash. This is what the headlines read on the newsstands we passed on our way out of Edinburgh airport. *John Domenici Among the Missing—Presumed Dead.*

John didn't say a word. And I didn't stop to grab a copy. There was nothing the papers could tell us we didn't already know.

We were dead.

And we had to stay that way.

The airport was our first test of anonymity. Bundled up in thick coats and scarves we'd picked up in Prague, we left separately, took separate cabs, and met up again an hour's drive north of the city, where I'd rented a car under my new name, Harvey Lloyd.

I handed John a new phone, preloaded with only one number—mine—and drove north into the night, along winding, isolated roads flanked by gorse bushes and the occasional spindly tree.

John dozed, slumped against the door, but a pothole in the road jolted the car and woke him. "Where *are* we going?" he grumbled, another hour into the drive.

"Harvey Lloyd has a cottage near Fort William."

"Hm... and does Harvey have a fat bank account to pay for our new lives or do we have to get jobs at Tesco?"

"As a matter of fact, Mister Lloyd does have a comfortable salary. He's employed by a technology company, one of countless companies owned and operated by the Kempthorne estate. He's a small, insignificant cog in a large investment machine."

"You've thought about this *a lot*." Dom smiled, but there was some regret in his eyes too.

"The fall of Alexander Kempthorne was inevitable. I planned to control that narrative."

"Of course you did." He snorted, then went back to staring at the darkness outside and eventually fell asleep again. He hadn't asked me the important question, not yet. But he would. *How much did I know about him?*

The cottage was tucked away in a forest, down a track with grass growing in the middle. The trees had grown since I'd last visited. Hopefully there would still be a view of Ben Nevis' peak from the top floor. I woke John gently. Once at the door, I keyed in the code for the lock and flicked on the cottage's lights. Scandinavian in style, the cottage was all pine and glass. Once the fire was roaring, it would soon be cozy. And it would make a good home until we decided how best to proceed.

"You've been here before?" John asked, noticing my familiarity with the space.

"Yes, this is where we would come to pretend to be someone else. Ironic, now."

"We?"

"My sister and I."

His eyes widened, drinking in the cottage and the new information. "Isn't it risky? Can it be linked back to you?"

"We weren't Kempthornes here. We would stay to get away from all that. Anonymously. Nobody knows about this place." Jordan knew, but he'd always kept the secret and my apparent death wouldn't change that.

John drifted around the dining area, then climbed the open-slatted spiral staircase to the lounge on the second floor until he was out of sight. He hadn't said much since we'd left America. A few questions, some idle small talk. He mourned his old life, and there would be some adjustment. Perhaps I should have told him my plan, but I had hoped the burn-it-all-down approach wouldn't be necessary.

While he familiarized himself with the cottage, I flicked on the kettle and set about making a fire in the wood-burner. By the time he returned and settled into a chair by the fireplace, the fire crackled and spat, already warming the cottage through.

We didn't have any bags. Just the clothes we wore, new passports, and new phones. We hadn't stopped traveling in days. This was the first time we'd been able to pause to breathe.

I handed him a mug of tea with the right amount of sugar, exactly how he liked it, and pulled my chair close to his. He thanked me for the drink and stared at the fire.

The fire warmed my legs and the familiar serenity slowed my heart. The quiet of the Scottish Highlands was different from that found anywhere else in the world—it went all the way to the soul. But few things unsettled me as much as a quiet John Domenici. I'd learned a silent John was a bad omen. "Are you all right?" I asked.

"I will be." Firelight danced in his sultry eyes. "It's a lot... that's all. My mum... I can't tell her I'm alive, obviously. An' I mean, there isn't anyone else in my life that'll care I'm dead so... " He ran a hand through his hair, dropped his head back, and closed his eyes. "And then there's what we did. Making latents. Jesus Christ." His eyes shone when he opened them again. "Did you know we could do that?"

"No," I lied. Guilt writhed inside me. "I'm sorry."

"You didn't do this. If anything, it's my fault. I should have left Kage alone, like you said. If I had, we'd still be in Cecil Court." He made a frustrated growling sound at the back of his throat. "We can't ever go back there, can we?"

"It's unlikely."

"Shit." Rubbing his face, he set his drink aside. "I'm gonna call it a night. Maybe it'll all look better in the morning?" He tried to smile and failed.

I reached out and caught his hand, relishing the feel of his warmth and the way our tricks mingled. He leaned down and hesitated, his eyes searching mine. But his smile had warmed, turning real. We hadn't been intimate since the bunker house. Traveling had been too fraught with danger. I'd been distracted by making sure all the pieces of the plan fell into place, while his thoughts had been consumed by what came next for us. But we were here, in the Highlands, alone and safe. And it was worth it.

I slipped a hand behind his neck and pulled him into a kiss.

"I've missed us," he whispered, stroking his thumb over the backs of my fingers, then let go. "Come to bed," he added with enough growl for it to be an order.

"I will."

He climbed the spiral staircase. This strong, brilliant man, whom I'd come to love and admire, to need, to crave—it was hard to believe he was mine. Hard to believe I might lose him when he learned how much I knew.

"John?" I called.

Stopping halfway, he peered through the stair rails. "Yeah?"

"We're free."

"Yeah. I think we are."

He climbed the rest of the way to the second floor. I listened to the creaking floorboards and watched the fire dance behind the wood-burner's glass. I should have been content—we'd escaped—but guilt still squirmed.

I took my new phone from my pocket and opened photos, then checked the stairs to make sure John wasn't about to reappear. It wasn't hard to find the image I wanted. The new phone only had one photo, a screenshot of a text message to an earlier phone I'd since discarded.

Kage, the American: I know what you're doing, the message began—how he'd gotten the number remained a mystery. *You always knew he could do this, didn't you? You've known since you "rescued" Dom from the military. What I don't know is if you're in it together. I wanted to believe he was good. But you got to him, or I was wrong about him and John Domenici was never good. He's killed more people than most mass murderers. Killed Annie. Killed my brother. Whatever happened to him in the military, it tore out some part of him. Or maybe his father did. Or you. He's powerful, and he'll kill again. Unless I stop him, stop you, Kempthorne. I'll find you. I'll end this. I won't let this go. I won't ever stop. I'm coming for you. You had better tell him the truth, because when I find him, I will. And then maybe John Domenici will kill you.*

He couldn't track this new phone back to me.

He couldn't track *us.* But if anyone suspected John and I of being alive, it would be him. Clever, committed, obsessed, determined, righteous... Kage, like his brother, would never give up.

I leaned forward, staring into the fire, and cradled the mug of hot tea.

There was one last loose end. One niggling knot on my murder wall that I had to unpick. And it was one Dom would never agree to.

Ironic, really, considering I'd saved the man's life multiple times, but to protect John Domenici, to have him become who and what he was destined to be, Kage Mitchell had to die. And I had to be the one to kill him.

33

D^{om}

We hiked for what felt like hours along a gravel path, through prickly gorse and around multiple *wee* lakes. Lochs? We'd been in Scotland a week. I was still getting used to the lingo and how this new life was going to work. We were in what Alex called Phase One, which meant we hunkered down and waited for the chaos surrounding our supposed deaths to blow over. That could take anywhere from three months to two years. After spending a week in the isolated cottage, I was hoping for the months option, not years. There was only so much staring at mountains and fixing fires I could do.

Phase Two would be settling into our new lives as different people. Alex was already sporting his new country look. He strode ahead, hands thrust into his wax jacket pockets, looking the part of a local lord. He just needed a few Labradors and a shotgun slung over his arm. Even if he did have a gun, there was nobody out here to shoot. I hadn't known there was anywhere left like this in the UK, places so isolated you could go for days without seeing another face. And even then, it was just the intrepid postman in his red van, delivering elastic band-wrapped junk mail.

"Are you all right?" Alex asked, stopping to sweep back his hair and check I hadn't fallen into a bog.

"Good," I puffed, then doubled up and gripped my thighs. "Is there an end to this torture?"

He smiled, so close to a chuckle I heard it anyway. "We're here."

I straightened, then frowned at the stone circle we'd wandered in to. The moss-covered stones were only a few feet tall and appeared to encircle us, like a clockface. I arched an eyebrow and glanced sideways at Alex. "Is this some *Outlander* shit?" His smile played with the idea of a frown and I waved his confusion away. He never got my TV references anyway.

"My sister and I would come here to test our abilities," he explained with an air of sorrow.

Now my heart had calmed from stomping around the Highlands, I spread my hands at my sides, closed my eyes, and stretched out my senses. The breeze, smelling of grass and gorse, teased through my hair and touched my face. Some kind of bird started from a bush. And there, below the obvious background noise, a psychic resonance simmered. Nothing terrible had happened here, but the site definitely had a voice.

"I've often wondered if you'd feel anything here," Alex said.

"Yeah, I do." I opened my eyes and found him closer. "But I could also be feeling you." Since we'd combined our tricks in the US—maybe before that, when I'd dragged him back from death—Alexander Kempthorne was a constant beacon to my body and mind. I knew where he was just by thinking about the man. The incredibly sexy man, who gazed at me now as though I was the most amazing thing on this mountainside.

"Let's try something." He took my right hand in his left and the thrill of his touch spilled through me, never getting old. The sun was out, if weak, but it wasn't cold. Would he be up for a tumble in the grass? Outside sex was right near the top of my To Do list. We'd ticked off most of the surfaces inside the cottage—the floor, the stairs—when we hadn't managed to make it to the bedroom, with one memorable time against the wall that had knocked an expensive oil painting to the floor. "You're going to have to stop looking at me like that or I won't be able to concentrate," Alex grumbled, keeping his smile.

"Like what?"

"Like you are."

"This is my face. I can't not look at you with my face."

"You know very well what I'm referring to." He took my other hand so we stood facing one another, like two guys in some kind of Celtic ceremony on a Scottish mountainside. His tone had been just the right side of biting, and only made the ideas in my head all the more appealing.

His smile wilted, turning serious, and any thoughts that we might be exploring each other alfresco faded away. "What's going on?"

"It's just..." He swallowed and averted his gaze.

My heart fluttered. What was this? He'd brought me halfway up the side of a mountain to a place he and his sister used to hang out, and now he was getting all serious while holding my hands?

Wait, he wasn't going to do something stupid like... propose, was he? "Alex?"

"I need to explain some things, but before I do that, do you trust me?"

I exhaled hard. Okay, so *not* a proposal. Because that was ridiculous. "You know I do. Although, if you don't tell me what's happening here, that might change."

"All right." He took a deep breath and met my gaze. Blue eyes, so full of intelligence, sparkled in the Scottish winter sun. "You remember how we united our tricks at the airport in the US?"

I snorted. "When we made a bunch of latents. How could I forget?"

"To do that, to summon that kind of power, we have to raise the source. We're going to do the same again now. Here."

Isolated. No witnesses for miles and miles. There wasn't anywhere better to try it. "Okay."

"I want you to reach down with your trick and pull on the source."

"Me? Aren't you the one with the key to the good stuff?"

"That remains to be seen."

"This is because of what the LOA said, right? You think I'm some kind of latent messiah? It's not me. Every time I've pulled some stunt, you were there. Healing you, the shadows, what happened at the airport—you were there every time." I squeezed his fingers because the words were stuck, and I didn't even know how to explain the swell of emotion trying to choke me. I wasn't the special one. He was.

His smile was a soft little tic of his lips. "Close your eyes."

I did.

"Trust me, John."

Every time he told me to, I trusted what was happening here a little less. "Let's just do this."

His trick surged in, rocking me backward. I clung to his hands and pulsed mine back through him, hearing his startled little gasp. Did other latents get turned on by sharing their tricks like this, or was it just because Alex's gasp went through me like a lightning bolt?

As soon as our resonance flowed, in tune with each other, flowing back and forth, I did what he'd asked and reached *down*. In theory, there shouldn't have been much of the source in such an isolated location, so far from London, but as happened at the US airport, the source was here, a simmering, powerful stream of psychic energy rushing under us, as though the earth beneath our feet was alive and I'd just tapped into a vein.

Trick swelled, filling me up, spilling over. Alex said something, but it was lost in the sizzling wonder. His hands were still in mine, still warm and firm, and that meant everything was going to be all right.

"Open your eyes."

I did. Trick haloed us, rising into the air in a great curtain of rippling, golden energy. It pulsed, *twomp-twomp,* in time with Alex's heart, with my heart. This was the same wall of trick we'd thrown at the LOA and US military, the same wave that had turned everyone there into latents. It was beautiful, but terrifying.

Alex glowed too. Trick shone in his eyes, dazzled in his hair like glitter, and touched his lips. He was so fucking amazing.

Alex let go of my hands. He stepped back. Then stepped back again. The waterfall of trick washed over him, and then it was just me, surrounded by power beating in time with *my* heart. I spread my hands. Trick snapped to my fingers, sizzling and sparking, *playing.* More, I could pull more. The wall pulsed outward, growing. Gorse bushes shimmered and glittered, lit by magic. The stones, now inside my circle, glowed golden.

I was doing this.

The source was here, all around, waiting *for me.*

I wasn't spiraling, this wasn't madness. It was perfect, absolute control.

Oh shit. I was standing in a stone circle, summoning the source, controlling it, exactly as Montgomery had tried to do, exactly as Olivia Barnes had wanted. I wasn't just some latent that ran to the military to escape his life. I had the source at my fingertips. I could pour it far and wide, like casting a net, and turn the world to latents.

I was the god Montgomery had been trying to make himself.

Oh no, no, no. I couldn't handle it, I couldn't do this.

Not me. Not John Domenici. I just blew shit up and tried to forget the terrible things I'd done.

The source spluttered, the curtain wobbling, and the golden trick snapped back, trying to writhe free. Oh, hell no. I planted my feet and pushed, driving the source back where it had come from, forcing it back down. It didn't want to go. It wanted to be free, to rush away and consume everything it could find. I grappled with it, pushing it down and down, and when the last sizzling spark snuffed out, I blinked back to myself on my hands and knees, with the wind cooling my face and Alex on a knee, peering at me, his face so full of worry and his blue eyes shining.

He mustered a little smile and nodded. "There are some things it's time you knew."

"Holy fuck," I panted. "I *am* the messiah."

The Shadows of London series reaches its climatic finale in *Without a Trace*, coming later in 2022! Subscribe to Ariana Nash's newsletter for all the news and release dates.

ABOUT THE AUTHOR

Born to wolves, Rainbow Award Winner Ariana Nash only ventures from the Cornish moors when the moon is fat and the night alive with myths and legends. She captures those myths in glass jars and returning home, weaves them into stories filled with forbidden desires, fantasy realms, and wicked delights.

Sign up to her newsletter and get a free ebook here: https://www.subscribepage.com/silk-steel

www.ingramcontent.com/pod-product-compliance
Lightning Source LLC
Chambersburg PA
CBHW061316190726
48288CB00002B/526